Phoenix

IRISH SHORT STORIES 1996

Phoenix IRISH
SHORT STORIES
1996

edited by David Marcus

PHŒNIX

First published in Great Britain in 1996
by Phoenix House, Orion House,
5 Upper St Martin's Lane
London WC2H 9EA

A CIP catalogue record for this book is available
from the British Litrary

ISBN 1 86159 000 8 (cased)
ISBN 1 85799 728 X (paperback)

Typeset at The Spartan Press Ltd
Lymington, Hants

Printed in Great Britain by
Clays Ltd, St Ives plc

Dedicated to the memory of
Augustine Martin

ACKNOWLEDGEMENTS

'Thatcher's Britain', Copyright © Clare Boylan, 1995, first appeared in *Good Housekeeping* and is reprinted by permission of the author, c/o Rogers, Coleridge & White Ltd.

'Hydrophobic', Copyright © Jennifer Cornell, 1995, first appeared in *Departures*, published by the University of Pittsburgh Press and in the paperback edition, *All There Is*, published by Brandon Book Publishers and reprinted with their permission.

'Politico', Copyright © Katy Hayes, 1995, first appeared in *Forecourt*, published by Poolbeg Press Ltd, and is reprinted by permission of the author.

'Street Magic', Copyright © Philip MacCann, 1995, first appeared in *The Miracle Shed*, published by Faber and Faber Ltd, and is reprinted by permission of the author, c/o Rogers, Coleridge & White Ltd.

'In the Garden', Copyright © John MacKenna, 1995, first appeared in *A Year of Our Lives*, published by Picador, and is reprinted with the permission of Curtis Brown Ltd, on behalf of the author.

'Lost Notes', Copyright © David Murphy, 1995, first appeared in *Broken Heroes*, published by albedo one publications, and is reprinted by permission of the author.

'The Sticky Carpet', Copyright © Frank Ronan, 1995, first broadcast by BBC Radio 4, appears in *Handsome Men are Slightly Sunburnt*, published by Sceptre and is reprinted by permission of the author, c/o Rogers, Coleridge & White Ltd.

The following stories have not previously been published: 'The White-Walled Men', Copyright © Vincent Banville, 1995; 'Beyond the Walls', Copyright © Miriam Burke, 1995; 'Photographs', Copyright © Kevin Casey, 1995; 'The Rembrandt Series', Copyright © Harry Clifton, 1995; 'A Migrant Bird', Copyright © John F. Deane, 1995; 'Life in a Cracked Cup', Copyright © Ursula de Brún, 1995; 'Fleadh', Copyright © Jane S. Flynn, 1995; 'Sambo', Copyright © Marie Hannigan, 1995; 'Pandora's Box', Copyright © Martin Healy, 1995; 'Bread, I Said', Copyright © Margaret Liston, 1995; 'Mythology', Copyright © Molly McCloskey, 1995; 'Rosa's Fat Jeans', Copyright © Clairr O'Connor, 1995; 'Rum and Coke', Copyright © Julia O'Faolain, 1995, is reprinted by permission of the author, c/o Rogers, Coleridge & White Ltd; 'Watling Street Bridge', Copyright © Keith Ridgway, 1995, is reprinted by permission of the author c/o Rogers, Coleridge & White Ltd; 'Sudden', Copyright © Eugene Stranney, 1995; 'Marrying Damian', Copyright © William Trevor, 1996.

CONTENTS

INTRODUCTION

Since Joyce, Ireland has produced a disproportionate number of the world's leading short story writers, and almost always their work has been brought to readers by the leading British publishers. In recent years Irish publishers have supported the genre by launching the careers of some of the country's new writers, but the trend has been for them to have their subsequent collections appear under the imprint of frontline London houses.

Never before, however, has any of the latter undertaken such an ambitious and far-sighted initiative as the Phoenix annual anthology of the year's best Irish short stories, the object of which is to provide a platform not only for the work of Ireland's internationally acclaimed short fiction writers, but also for the most striking and exciting stories of those who seek to join their ranks. Understandably, publication gives an incalculable boost to a new or fairly new writer's confidence and future, but the literary environment in which his or her work appears must be of equal importance. The inclusion of very recent stories by Ireland's most prestigious writers – represented here by William Trevor, Julia O'Faolain, John MacKenna and Clare Boylan – sets the highest standard, but it is one which I am confident readers will agree is fully met by the other contributors to this collection.

In recent decades two developments have animated the love affair between Irish writers and the short story. Firstly, Irish women writers have established a literary presence far more considerable and impressive than ever before. Secondly, the spread of short story competitions throughout the country has given aspiring writers, young and old, annual opportunities, targets and rewards. The vital part played by such competitions in maintaining the excellence of Ireland's short story tradition can be gleaned from the biographical notes of many of the writers represented in these pages.

In launching this annual *Irish Short Stories* anthology, Phoenix House, who already publish the leading Irish writers Colum McCann, Michael Collins and James Ryan, embark on a journey of discovery and promotion that I am confident will greatly enhance the reputation of contemporary Irish writing.

DAVID MARCUS

JOHN F. DEANE

A Migrant Bird

The door opened and a draft of sour air hit Fonsie on the chest. He coughed his sandpaper cough and looked up from his low stool. A young man had come in, carrying what looked suspiciously like a guitar case. He wore a green baseball cap, turned peak to nape, a chunk of hair waving through the gap in front – like a crested grebe, Fonsie thought. A migrant bird, please God, for there was never a guitar stood up naked in Frankie's Hill-top Inn before. Cowshite! Fonsie said to himself, and bugger it!

The young man looked around the bar as if he had a mission. He wore a grey sweat-shirt with UP YOURS printed in purple lettering across his chest. A big brass ring was dangling from one ear. He had a small, silver ring fixed in his nostril. Fonsie shuddered.

Someone had left another pint on the table in front of him, one of the Germans, probably, and he dived into its sweet black depths for consolation. He left the cream along his upper lip a while, then slowly drew his tongue through it, sighed deeply and left the glass down on the table. Fonsie, his face the grey-brown of old harness leather, wore a black felt hat tilted at a challenging angle back over his head. He took a handkerchief from his breast pocket, folded it, tucked it and the tail-piece of the fiddle under his chin until everything was snug as a rabbit in its burrow. He lifted the bow and poured a long golden-liquid chord across the floor of the bar. The customers were bathed in honey.

Fonsie closed his eyes and took a deep breath. He began to play, slow-waltz time, two sharps, 'Rich and Rare were the Gems She Wore'. He saw a large and generous bosom, rising and falling like a summer sea, he saw red and flowering lips, opening and closing on perfect teeth and a moist, welcoming tongue, he saw emeralds and diamonds and pearls and a tiara rich as the lake of night that is alive with stars. He laid his head between those wondrous breasts and when he finished the tune he was resting by the hearth of a grand lord's manor.

The drinkers in the Hill-top Inn applauded noisily. Fonsie retuned his top string, twanging it close to his ear so he could savour it. The young intruder had drawn up a stool and positioned himself beside Fonsie. The old man sniffled loudly, took a long sweep from his pint, settled his fiddle again and leaped off the very edge of a high cliff into 'Bonnie Katie's Irish Reel'. He closed his eyes and giggled with delight. Didn't he know Katie well! Well? Intimately! he would go so far as to say . . . well, didn't he chase her, round and round and round among the hay-cocks in Horan's lower meadows, over the bottoms, back across the lower stream, her laughter like the challenge of the skylark against a morning sky, her petticoats lifting about her till she fell, tittering and joysome, down among the shakings, and he fell beside her, his fingers skittering along the meairns of her backbone.

When he paused he was startled by the wild clamour of applause that brought him back to the pub. He opened his eyes and there were people around him clapping their hands and smiling at him. He grinned, clumsily, and took the fiddle from under his chin. It was like taking a wedge of his jaw away, his empty mouth gaped after it, and he filled that gap with a long and cooling drag from his pint after his dry-throated chase around the meadows. The baseball cap leaned in, suddenly:

'Old man, they kept talking while you played! How can you put up with that?'

Fonsie looked at him. He was very young, though big and handsome, in a sledge-hammer sort of way.

'They do come here, sir, to have a pint an' a chat . . .'

'But how can they pick up the words if they keep chattering?'

'There's no words comin' from me fiddle, sir, I just plays.'

Fonsie dived for refuge into his pint. He finished it but kept the glass up against his mouth and glanced at the young man. He was reaching a big hand towards Fonsie; a large silver bangle clattered against a wooden one on his wrist. It was a strong wrist, covered with soft, golden down, like a migrant bird's.

'Hi!' he said. 'My name is Brad Pinkleman. And yours?'

'Fonsie, Fonsie Conlon.'

'Can I get you a pint?'

Fonsie nodded. Anything to be agreeable, and he had journeys yet to make, across arid grounds. He closed his eyes again and set off, a fine ash-plant in his right hand, a satchel filled with boxty bread in the other, and a paper-stoppered bottle loaded with Irish whiskey. He was on 'The Connaught Man's Rambles', out of Ballina and into Enniscrone, down to Sligo and beyond, to Carrick; a pause, in Dromod, for 'Peggie's Wedding', and then a dash to Castlebar where he dallied a while with his 'Fair Gentle Maid'. He leaned forward, his lips pouting, her lips pouting too, the space between him and her not that great, and closing by the second. He put his tongue out from between his teeth and as he did so he turned the corner into the last few bars of the tune, remembered he had no teeth, shut his mouth sharply and opened his eyes.

'I see you don't move up in the positions, Fonsie.'

It was Brad Pinkleman shouting into his ear, trying to be heard over the fine applause. Fonsie began his pint. The young man was drinking straight from a foreign-looking, long-necked bottle.

'No then, sir, I do shtop on this wan shtool th'whole time.'

'No, no, no! I mean you don't ever move your left hand up along the neck of your instrument, kind of limits your potentialities, if you know what I mean. Second and third positions. That sort of thing. See?'

'I do jusht play, like, you know. Sir.' Fonsie thought he'd lay it on a bit thick for this young genius. 'Sure you do only want to be in the wan position for "Fanny Power".'

Fonsie chuckled and gave the migrant bird a playful dig with his knuckle-sharp elbow.

'I don't quite follow you,' and the young man lifted his bottle and took a long glug from the neck. Like a suckin' lamb, thought Fonsie. Brad began to unzip his bag and – to Fonsie's dismay – a great yellow guitar was lying across his knees.

'Frankie told me I could try out a song or two, if you don't mind, of course. Might help to bring some of the younger generation into the Inn, if you know what I mean?'

Fonsie was dismayed. He had played on Thursday nights, in this corner, on this stool, for over twenty years and had hardly ever missed a night. Holy Thursdays maybe, or when Christmas Day fell on a Thursday. But what could he say?

' "Let Erin Remember . . ." ' he muttered, through his pint, a sound like stones stuttering in a mountain stream.

There was a big man standing over Fonsie, another pint extended out of the battlefield of the bar.

'For you,' the man shouted down at Fonsie. 'Ein pound of Guinness. Und can man hear "Die Koolin"? If I please? I come from Germany, no? Zis music pleases me very. Danke. Danke schön. Und *Sláinte*!'

' "As a Beam o'er the Face of the Waters," ' Fonsie mumbled, grinning; Germans! they'd soon have every house in the townland bought up and converted; migrant birds, all of them, stretching the winter season into several years. However! and he stretched out his hand for the pint.

'How's the meadows, Fonsie?' someone called to him.

'They're lyin' down, Vinnie, lyin' down. Thank God for the man that invited the silage!'

Brad drew a chord from his guitar and it fell onto the cement floor of the bar in a million pieces of shattered glass. Fonsie took a great swipe out of his pint and felt the cool hands within him massage his troubled soul.

'Fonsie,' the young man was leaning towards him again, 'what kind of an odd-ball name is that?'

The old man looked up at him. He was a looker, mind you, the young women would leap on him, surely. The way they never leaped on Fonsie. Except in his head, of course, when the music was flying. Brad had big, candid eyes; the hands lying ready on the guitar were covered in fine light-brown hair and every second finger sported a ring.

'Alphonsus. It's short for Alphonsus. Fonsie. After the saint, you know. Saint Alphonsus.'

Brad, his brown hair down over one eye, knocked another row of bottles off a high shelf and began, in a strong, bass voice, to sing. His eyes remained open, following the reactions of his audience.

'*Green,*' went the words, as Fonsie heard them, '*Green me a crew for the long voyage out, oh baby green me, green me a crew; yeah, yeah, oh baby yeah; flag me a wave for the long voyage out, oh baby lean on me.*' Then he knocked several rows of bottles off several rows of shelves, his head lowered and beating up and down to his rhythms, his lower lip clenched in his fine, calf's teeth.

'*Green me a crew for the long voyage home, oh baby green me, green me a crew; yeah, yeah, oh baby yeah; wave me a flag for the long voyage home, oh baby lean on me.*'

He has a good voice, Fonsie thought, if only he could find a song to fit into it.

When he finished, Brad seemed a little disappointed with the bemused applause that came from the crowd. But word would spread. His thews! His baby cheeks! It was between times, yet, between times in this back-wash corner of the world.

'How's about you playin' "Danny Boy", Fonsie? And maybe I can strum along?'

Strum along! Cowshite! thought Fonsie, and bugger it! Yeah! but outside himself Fonsie smiled and tucked his fiddle back under his chin.

'What key's she in?' Brad asked.

Fonsie looked down at his bow as if the long, curved timber held the answer.

'Two sharps,' he mumbled.

'Key of D. Right, old man, let's you and me strike up a storm for these innocents!'

Fonsie lowered his fiddle, reached for his pint and took a long, relieving scoop from it. Then he began to play, his eyes closed, his body moving proudly along from glen to glen and down the mountainside. He stepped out slowly onto a late summer meadow and Danny, young and eager and foolish, preening himself in his uniform of war, marched past him and away into the future. Don't be in such a hurry away from those who know and love you, Fonsie whispered to the brightly-coloured back. But there was somebody at Fonsie's shoulder, moving with him as he flew into a valley all hushed and white with snow, there was a large presence, a bulked shadow keeping pace, offering to help him over stones, to open gates for him, to take his hand . . .

In sudden irritation Fonsie leaped away into the air like a black cat pounced on by a dog and came back down running towards the 'Humours of Ballymanus'. This was better, he was free again, racing and cavorting round a noisy market square, in and out like a frisky pup between the legs of the cattle, nipping at them, teasing the big slow beasts while he whooped and skittered with laughter. He was joined by 'Paddy Haggarthy' and 'Nora Creina', and together they raced and frolicked, down side-alleyways, over gurgling waterways, tripping lightly along rough tractorways, back up the slopes and into Frankie's Hill-top Inn.

A great thirst had risen again within Fonsie's chest and he finished his pint with gusto.

'Well, old man,' it was Brad again, 'you could give Yehudi a master-class any day!'

Fonsie presumed, because he was that kind of an old man, that this was intended as some sort of a compliment; he grinned his cave-mouth grin and licked the froth slowly from along his upper lip. He got up, stiffly, from his stool and made his way to the toilets, shouldering his way through the air thickened with gratulations.

Fonsie passed the new Gents toilet and went out into the yard where he had been going these past twenty years. He stood against the stable wall and sighed with satisfaction. The stars were beautiful overhead; there was scarcely a breath of wind.

He felt a little dizzy and his chest was rough as a harrow. The world turns heavily, he thought, like an old, unoiled cart wheel. He thought he might give Frankie's a skip next Thursday night; the thought made him feel heavy as a haycock after rain.

'"And if you come,"' he sang it quietly, '"and all the flowers are dying, And I am dead . . ."'

He turned back towards the door of the bar. As he crossed the familiar, old rutted yard, he heard the shrill high call of a curlew passing west over the mountain towards the sea. He knew it well, the curlew, he knew the lovely whirring sound its wings made through the night air, he knew the loneliness and the challenge both mixed into that local, endangered, cry. He raised his head towards the darkness and smiled. He could hear the young man scattering his broken bottles about the floor inside. He giggled as another air came to his mind out of the darkness: '"Go Where Glory Waits Thee". One sharp,' he said aloud, 'and up yours, too.'

He paused again, his hand on the latch of the back door of Frankie's Hill-top Inn. 'Brad!' he said to himself, 'Brad. What kind of an odd-ball name is that?'

JOHN MacKENNA

In the Garden

Isn't it strange, my dear wife, how you, who accused me of allowing my fascination with the past to become an obsession, are now my obsession. Because you are past, you'd tell me. But that is too trite an assertion. David arrived yesterday, unannounced, to stay with me for the Easter holiday. A year on, he said, to the week. I must need some company.

There, you're saying, the past again. An anniversary. That is the reason for my fascination. But that isn't so, either. All of this is by the way. Let me explain. And, before I do, let me say that all through the winter, when this dream cottage of mine was damp, when I sat here at night thinking that if I fell down dead no one would find me for a week, all through that winter of freedom my only concern was the here and now. I did not go running back to the past.

Let me explain.

I have spent the last five days digging the big wild garden outside. Dragging more than digging. Dragging bindweed out of the earth, pulling the tines of the fork through the sinewy weeds until my fingers blistered and the blisters bled. Six hours the first day, six hours the second, five hours the third. And at the end of the day everything I had pulled and gathered went up in a twenty-second blaze and I was left with a cigarette pile in the corner and a roughly dug patch that mocked the idea of a day's work. And fifteen feet of grass and weed untouched between me and the fence. On every side. And then yesterday I looked up and there was David, leaning over the gate, watching me dig and telling me that kind of thing was lethal for a man in his forties.

'You need to work yourself into that kind of thing,' he

grinned. 'When was the last time you dug a garden? When you were first married?'

'Fuck off,' I said.

'Exactly my point. This kind of thing is neither good for the body or the mind. You're stressed!'

Unannounced. Uninvited. And I was bloody glad to see him. Last night we went out for a drink and when we got back he went on drinking in the bare yellow kitchen.

'Easter never made it,' he said.

He gave me no time to answer.

'Easter is where the human and divine parted,' he said. 'Christmas, now that is a human time. Happy ever after. Presents. Little baby. Choirs of scrubbed children. Love. All very well. But Easter is beyond us. Even the early Christians let it go. It floated away from them like a balloon that's slipped its string. Death. Pain. Suffering. Too depressing.'

'There's the resurrection,' I said.

He shook his head, smiled that big deep smile. You know that smile.

'Too much of a leap of faith. Anyway, it's too little, too late. Torture, death, humiliation. Too much to recover from. Not in two days and then the balloon was gone. Up, up and away.'

He turned his hand over, the way he does. I said nothing.

'I'm probably depressing you.'

I shook my head.

'No, I am.' He was insistent. 'And I didn't come here to do that. I'll tell you what – tomorrow we will attack that garden and beat the shit out of the bindweed.'

He swung an imaginary spade over his shoulder, marched to the back door and flicked on the outside light. He stood looking through the glass.

'No problem. We'll come at it from two sides. Phwup. Done.'

'Right,' I said. 'Weapon parade at nine a.m.'

He came back and sat down at the fire. 'Do you remember the Easter your mother and father were in England and I came and stayed at your house. Speaking of parading weapons.'

Note, I was not the one who began this conversation but, yes,

I did respond.

'Sligo,' I said.

'Wherever. You were studying and I'd met that girl. Carol.
Jesus, what was her second name? Carol something. She
worked in a jewellers in Carlow. She came and stayed and
stayed and came.' He laughed at his own joke. 'Do you
remember her? Huge knockers, short skirts, high boots and
always a red blouse. Didn't she always wear red blouses? Or did
I imagine that?'

'She did,' I said. 'Short skirts, red blouses.'

'Best blow-job I ever got and she was only nineteen. Why
don't we ever marry these women? You tell me that.' His mouth
hung open. He shook his head and sprang to his feet and stood
there glowering. 'And here we are, forty years old, facing a day
pulling bindweed, fucking bindweed out of a garden. Ah,
bollocks.'

I tell you all of this because it may amuse you. You may sit there
smiling and thinking, He hasn't changed, still the same David.
Or you may dismiss it. You may sit there thinking, I haven't
changed. Still as infantile. It doesn't really matter, of course.
Not now. But I am determined to go on with this because there
is a point worth making.

After David had gone to bed I took out my Bible and read that
passage I always read on Holy Thursday. I always read it to
you. The one that begins:

> 'He went forth with his disciples over the brook, Cedron,
> where there was a garden, into the which he entered and his
> disciples. And Judas also which betrayed him knew the
> place.'

I thought you'd like that. The element of betrayal. Last year I
read that passage at our table but we knew what was coming, if
not how fast. It may have been like that for Jesus, huddled there
among the unreliables, not knowing how quickly the pillars

would collapse, not suspecting how painful it all would be. It wasn't always like this, was it? Childhood Easters were full of starched daffodils and crocuses in the sleet. One Easter I was recovering from a long illness and on Good Friday I walked across the fields and smelt the dung from the gardens and I felt good. Life was starting again. But that is the past, isn't it? Let me stick with last night.

I closed my Bible and I started humming that hymn you always hummed.

'All in the April evening, April airs were abroad,
the sheep with their little lambs passed me by on the road . . .'

You were surprised, the first time you hummed it, that I knew the words. I never told you where they came from but I will now. It's all part of proving a point. Last night, sitting in the yellow kitchen, it struck me that out there, just across the fence, there were sheep and lambs and I felt good. And out there, in the shelter of the shed, there were four dishevelled daffodils. And I walked out across the roughly dug soil and leaned over the fence and listened to the gentle night-time sounds from the end of the field. And I looked at those four daffodils, standing in the light from the kitchen window, and I thought if my father saw them he would turn in his grave. He who had been so proud of his garden, who had been so certain that his drills were straight, who had edged the lawns to a line. He who had sown so many daffodils that they tolled in the dark breezes along the garden path. How often had I listened to their gentle swishing from my bed?

You see, I hear you saying, obsession. Perhaps, if we had been obsessed with each other, this would never have happened. Or perhaps leaving had become the obsession. Gentle memory always slid into obsession, you said, and perhaps you were right. It isn't that I haven't carried guilt but the guilt has never been heavy enough to do anything more than slow me down. And partly it is because the past is a safe place. Safe in its distance and its loss. You said that once. You told me I was obsessed with all the people I had lost. Well, let me tell you one more story now. One well-kept secret. I stood in that bloody garden, last night, and thought of this. Of that Easter when David stayed and Carol stayed. Let me tell you one more story. A story that leaked back into my memory despite myself.

That was the Easter when I met Ellen Burgess, the rector's daughter. Of course, I already knew her. There wasn't anyone I didn't know in our village but I had never spoken to her before. We met at a dance in Carlow. She was drunk and I was bored. We sat in the bar of the dance-hall and she talked, incessantly. About her father, who frowned on drinking, she said; about her mother, who was in John of God's, drying out; about school and life behind the rectory walls – she hated both in equal measure.

She took a lift home with us. She sat in the back with me. David and Carol sat in the front. I remember how ruthlessly she discouraged David's attempts at humour. He dropped us on the Square and drove on up to my house, where he and Carol had taken over my parents' bedroom. I walked Ellen to the rectory gate.

'My father is in there,' she told me, pointing through the trees, 'sleeping the sleep of the just and self-satisfied. And my mother is sleeping elsewhere. She's bloated and baggy now. When I was a kid she was the most beautiful woman I'd ever seen. He wrecked her. He doesn't even see that.'

'I don't think you should be telling me this,' I said.

'Why not?' she asked. She jumped up and down, tearing a branch from a laburnum that hung out over the rectory wall and twirling it in my face. 'How long have you lived here?'

'All my life,' I said.

'I've been here since I was seven. Ten years. I've never spoken to you before. Time to make up. Anyway he is an arrogant bastard. I don't care who knows. And now I'll stop talking.' She slid her hands inside my open coat and pulled me towards her. Leaning back against the wall, she pulled me closer and then she kissed me, sliding her tongue into my mouth. It tasted of whiskey. The kiss went on a long time and then she pushed my head away. 'And how many times more will we talk?'

'As often as you like,' I said.

She smiled a sly smile. 'Don't you believe it.'

'I'd like to see you again,' I said.

'I bet you would. Protestant girls do it, is that what you've heard?'

I said nothing.

'I'll come and call on you tomorrow afternoon,' she said. 'My father will be away for a couple of hours. He might not approve. Purely on biological grounds. Will you be there?'

'Yes,' I said. 'I'll be studying.'

She kissed me again but this time quickly and then she was gone. I picked the broken, budding branch from the path and walked home. I put the branch in a glass and put it in my bedroom window. I tried not to listen to David and Carol in the room next door. And then I fell asleep and probably dreamed. Of a great seduction. But, in the end, it was she who seduced me.

She came and called the following afternoon and we walked down the river, past Joe Shea's bridge, across the Rocks, back by the Mill Pond and in by the Barrack Road.

You see, I've forgotten very little. Par for the course, you'll say. Standing in the garden, in the darkness I imagined I could pick out the light of the rectory last night. Four miles away across the fields now. Of course I was mistaken. But yes, we walked back arm in arm and we lay on my bed and I kissed her mouth and her tongue tasted strangely different. I remember that. And afterwards David came back and she was as dismissive as she had been the night before. And when she was leaving I asked if I could see her the following day. Holy Thursday.

'Wait for me in the churchyard. I have damn choir practice,' she said. 'I'll get away as early as I can. It won't be for long but I'll get away.'

I waited in the churchyard. It was a dry hot day and the sunshine split through the branches and splintered over the flat and crooked stones. I lay on one, watching the crows circling and soaring in and out of the opening in the bell-tower beside the church. The organ churned, the voices rang through the empty church, the words came cleanly across the newly mown grass, like scent in themselves.

'All in the April evening, April airs were abroad,
the sheep with their little lambs passed me by on the road.
Up in the blue, blue mountains, pastures are sweet,
rest for the little bodies, rest for the little feet.'

Such a desperately sad song. And the voices went on singing:

'I saw the sheep with their little lambs and thought on the
lamb of God.'

The music swirled and died. Voices through the open window. A shadow across my face. And there she was.

'I only have a few minutes,' she said.

'What about tomorrow?'

'Tomorrow is bad. I'm expected here for service. Saturday night is good. My father will be away. All night. You come down to the house. I'll be on my own. And I don't really want to have to spend the night with the other pair. I'll telephone you.'

And before I could sit up she was gone again, weaving through the tipsy stones. The organ moaned another tune. I lay back in the sunshine. Frightened. Exhilarated.

Am I doing justice to your expectations? Have I remembered sufficient detail? I know I've been weak on the senses but maybe that will be clarified by the rest of what I have to tell you. Don't be over critical. Not yet.

She did telephone on the Saturday evening, just after seven. I walked across the land drainage yard, cutting between the diggers and caterpillar tractors to the back of the rectory. She saw me scrambling through the garden and waved from the dining-room window.

We sat in that room and drank coffee. I admired a photograph of her parents.

'Do you know what he preached on yesterday?' she asked.

I shook my head.

'On the mote in your brother's eye and the beam in your own. I've heard him return to that so often. And he never sees the point of it, he never sees the bloody great log that's across our family, never. I keep waiting for him to make the connection.'

I thought she was going to cry, with anger or sadness. I asked if she was all right.

She smiled a blazing smile. 'You'll get used to me. I'm just glad you're here to talk to.' She held out her hand and I crossed to where she was sitting and knelt in front of her chair. She held my head in her hands and then pressed my face against her breasts. The sweet smell of her body and her clothes. 'I can be very gentle and very loving, you'll see,' she said. 'But I hate him so much.'

I wanted her to stop talking about her father. I pulled my face away and knelt up and kissed her.

'Just forget him for a while,' I said.

She went on smiling. 'This is silly,' she said, taking my hands and pulling me up with her. 'Let's go to bed.'

She led me up two flights of stairs. It was dark but she didn't turn on a light until we reached her bedroom. It was a dim bedside lamp. Immediately, she began to take off her clothes. She noticed my hesitation. 'Don't,' she said. 'Please don't.'

Something wakened me a long time later. I looked at my watch. It was twenty past one. A light shone from the landing across her bed. She was awake.

'Did I hear something?'

'Just a car.'

'Why is the landing light on?'

'Just for comfort,' she said. 'Go back to sleep.'

Suddenly there were steps on the stair.

'Jesus,' I froze.

The footsteps passed the half-open door of Ellen's room.

'Is that you, daddy?' she called.

The sound of the footsteps came back along the landing and the door was pushed open. The light starched everything. She sat up, her breasts uncovered as she turned to me and kissed me lightly on the head. I saw her father's face, the skin loose and haggard, in the instant before he turned away. I'm sure he never focused on my face. I was just a figure. And then the footsteps went heavily down the stairs.

Ellen said nothing. Stepping from the bed, she pulled on a dressing gown and followed him. I stumbled after her, cursing my clothes and shoes. By the time I'd dressed they were both downstairs. I followed, tentatively. She was leaning against the jamb of the dining room door. I stopped behind her, feeling I must say something but there was nothing to say. Her father was slumped in the armchair I'd sat in earlier. She was smiling at him. And then she became aware of my presence.

'You can go,' she said.

And I did. Scampering across their garden and into the street. Joining the stragglers going home from midnight Mass. In confusion. In pain.

It wasn't the events that came to me last night, out there, more the sense of pain again, the loss of self respect. I just stood there and felt that cold feeling again. I wanted it to go away, I wanted no part of that memory but there was nothing I could do to exorcize it. And then David broke the spell. I had assumed he was asleep but there he was, stumbling across the heavy sods.

'Are you all right?'

'I'm fine,' I said.

'What were you doing out here?'

'I was thinking,' I said.

'What the hell about?'

'About the night that's in it,' I half lied. 'About Gethsemane, that stuff. It sort of came alive out here.'

'About frigging betrayal,' he said. 'You didn't betray anyone. Neither of you did. It just happened. You got to a stage, it was time to go. That's all. Wasn't it you told me one time that marriage was invented for people who married at fourteen and died at twenty-six. You've done your time. Both of you. Let it go.'

'You're right,' I said.

'Now,' he said. 'I'm going back inside. I'm making tea. I'm not going to sleep at all. Crack of dawn I'll be out here digging. I'm going to dig the shit out of this place. We'll make a garden your father would have been proud of. Right?'

'Right,' I said.

He's sleeping now, my dear wife, in the armchair at the fire. It'll be dawn in a couple of minutes and I'll wake him then. But first I want you to know that not every memory is obsessive and not every obsession is an escape. Not everything comes at my bidding and not every escape is to happiness. It's the loss that takes the longest, the real loss, the real hurt, to leak back through the years but when it comes, like this, it comes to stay.

It's raining out there now but we'll go out and we'll dig and some time around nine or ten we'll start fooling around and one of us will push the other and we'll roll around in the mud like two kids and then we'll come inside and leave the job for the day. We'll shower and make something to eat and doze in the afternoon. And then the sun will come out and we'll talk about what we'll get done tomorrow.

Oh, and just one other thing. It won't get better. I just thought I'd warn you.

MARIE HANNIGAN

Sambo

The afternoon they came ashore to replace the television set, as he was stepping out of the motorboat, Sambo Ndluvu noticed the dilapidated state of the ship. It was a shock to see the vessel from the shoreward angle. Although he passed it when he made weekly trips to the post office to dispatch a letter to his wife, he had never before noticed that the rust was so bad. It occurred to him that this dingy rustbucket was a poor ambassador for his nation. The thought deepened the miasma of homesickness that hung over him.

He was not one to indulge himself in such feelings. One way and another a sailor was always in exile; from home when he was at sea; from the sea when he was home. This was different – eighteen months anchored in a foreign harbour – no knowing when they would get home; this was more than a vague wistfulness.

As they loaded the replacement television onto the ship's tender, a couple of Irish crewmen from a nearby trawler came to lend a hand. One of the fishermen drew their attention to the fact that the motorboat was listing badly. The Africans made gestures of helplessness. There had been an argument with the ship's captain earlier in the day when they had warned him about the seaworthiness of the motorboat. Sambo had spent the evening attempting to persuade him to provide alternative transport back to their vessel. The captain, a European, reacted with indifference. He was booked into the hotel for the weekend, and would return to the ship via the agent's launch.

Sambo and one of the others balanced the set between them on their knees to keep it clear of the water, while the other men baled out. The ship was no more than a shape against the darkness now, but as they drew nearer, Sambo glared at her outline, brooding about the great splashes of discolouration on her hull.

He noticed the big breaker from the wake of an incoming trawler, too late to take corrective action. Out of the corner of his eye he noted the location of an island of silt, heard himself shout instructions to the others.

The television set slipped from his grasp as he plunged into a black world, glacier cold. His nerve endings confused, reacted as if scalded, the shock sucking air from his body. His feet found the muddy bottom, and he thrashed forward, calling to the others, guiding them towards the sand-bank.

I was in bad shape that night, coming down – the time when the craving is at its worst. Any kind of craziness can surface. It isn't even necessary to see anything. The twitching of a curtain moved by the breeze can push vague uneasiness into rampant paranoia.

In the bedroom I heard Evie turn over in bed and sigh. 'You're on your last chance,' she'd said this evening when I came in. 'And I don't care if you take it or not.'

At this point I didn't really care either.

I searched in all the old places. Down the back of the washing machine. The toilet cistern. Nothing. And though I knew there would be nothing, I continued to search.

When he had managed to guide the other three from the water, Sambo urged them forward. It was vital to keep moving. He would not allow them to rest, fearful that they might submit to the cold, to be found in the morning, dead of exposure. He felt his responsibility keenly. When the State had sold the ship to a foreign company, the new owners kept him on – though they normally preferred to hire bachelors – not solely for his ability to render first aid to the crew: he was a lay preacher, reliable, a stabilising influence on the younger men.

He kept talking, focusing their minds on the square of light ahead – shelter, warmth, a sweet drink to restore their blood sugar. He repeated the phrases over and over to give them heart, automatically touching the Sanka's tooth at his throat for comfort and luck.

As they drew closer to the building, he got the sense that it was a sleeping house – only one lighted window. He rapped hard to awaken those inside.

When I heard the knock, I waited, distrusting my senses. It came again, more aggressive. As I opened the door I caught a movement – the sense of something looming at me. The darkness rearranged itself into a face, almost as black as the night – beyond that other faces. The only light in that gloom was the wild flash of their eyes. This is it, I thought, the big one. The daddy of all horrors.

The one closest was mouthing something. What it was I couldn't tell from the buzzing in my ears. I let out a howl and fell back from the door, too weak to slam it. He took a step inside, moving in on me, and I swear there was smoke rising off him. I found myself stumbling against the wall as I shouted some inane, half-remembered incantation. Then I was running down the hall, screaming for Evelyn.

By the time Evie had the four of them planted around a blazing fire, fed, showered, and wrapped in towels and blankets, the damage was done. My low-level edginess had exploded into full-blown, red alert.

They huddled in a steaming circle while she fussed over them, bringing them mugs of cocoa, stoking up a blaze. To a man, they shivered violently like they had all been plugged into the one pneumatic drill. Yer man, the little fat one, was yammering away, nineteen to the dozen, as if he couldn't get it all out fast enough. Evie shushed him, urging him to save his strength. Yer man kept going, his fingers worrying at the weird-looking object that hung about his neck.

We had to hear every detail: the trip across the harbour with the rented TV set, broken down for the umpteenth time; the attempted return to the ship with the doubtless equally dodgy replacement; the sinking of the launch, landing them all in the tide, by luck close to Rotten Island. Had they been in deep water, they would have died of exposure. The mud helped to insulate them.

Yer man chattered on, fretting that they had no way out to their ship now.

'But you must stay here tonight,' Evie was saying. 'No, I won't take any arguments. You'll not budge out of here till morning.'

I tried to catch her eye. There had to be somewhere else they could go. It wasn't that they were black. I'd defy any man to rest easy while an alien male force invades his territory. I would have felt equally enthusiastic about sharing my home with a pack of Dublin gurriers, a crowd of glic Kerrymen, much less be relegated to the coldest corner of the room, while a shower of half-drowned Africans got the ring-side seats around my hearth.

Evie and the girls were tripping over themselves offering food and hot water bottles. The two girls were having a good gawk to see what was under the towels, until Evie sent them away to hunt out some suitable clothes from the pile Manus has scattered about his room.

They would have their work cut out for them. The tallest of the Africans was about five eight. All were compact, bar the Sambo fellow, who was small and round. None of them had the bulk to wear the clothes of a six-three Irishman, built like a shithouse wall.

The Wall himself squeezed into the fire beside the Africans and, miracle of miracles, offered fags all round.

I had to sit by and watch these guys getting the four-star treatment and me in worse shape than any of them, shaking and sweating – ready to throw up my guts. The whole plant just walked by, not one of them paying me the slightest mind – until yer man spoke up. 'Your friend, I think he needs a little something.'

Everyone turned to look at me as if I was the one who had just dragged myself out of the mud. 'I know what he needs.' Evie was too polite to specify.

'Without wishing to offend ... a sudden deprivation of alcohol is dangerous. It must be done gradually.'

I found myself warming to the fellow.

'How gradual?' Evie was suspicious.

'A dessertspoon every half hour. Reducing to a teaspoon every other hour.'

A *teaspoon*?

A stubborn look came over Evie's face. It had been a long time since she permitted alcohol to pass the threshold of this house. Yer man was persistent.

'There is a danger of convulsions.'

Evie's eyes widened at this talk of fits. 'Are you a doctor or something?'

'Ship's first aid man. I have treated alcohol withdrawal before.'

I could see she was sceptical, but she sent Val next door for the drink. Little as it was, it got me through till the morning.

Come opening time, I had the ultimate excuse to escape the house. I had to sort out these infernal Africans, didn't I?

We found the captain in the lounge of the hotel, half way through his liquid breakfast. Even at this early hour, there were a couple of good-time girls hanging around on the periphery.

I ordered a whiskey, while yer man explained the situation. The captain addressed me directly, ignoring his own crewman. 'This man's supposed to be in charge. How am I to tell the company that their ship's tender is lost?'

The African desperately tried to catch his skipper's eye. 'Sir, could you ask the agent to take us back to the ship?'

Still the captain refused to meet his gaze. 'It's Easter. Who the hell is going to put themselves out for a crowd of stupid blacks.'

'But Captain, we have no money.'

The captain gave a shrug that said it wasn't his problem.

'Perhaps it would have been more convenient to let ourselves drown.'

'Show respect. boy. You're a long way from home.'

I waited for yer man to thump the son of a gun, but his mouth closed tight as a crab's rear end.

'You miserly hoor,' I blurted. 'The least you could do is throw the poor divils a couple of pound for Easter.'

Yer man went grey in the face, as the captain turned and stared at me over the top of his curly head. 'You people,' he sneered. 'How tolerant you are of our poor black brethren. Hypocrites. I don't see you queueing up to share your roast lamb with them tomorrow.'

I couldn't ignore this slur to the traditions of a harbour that has given succour to ships, and their crews, as far back as records show. 'As it happens,' I declared recklessly, 'Mister Ndluvu and his friends are spending Easter with my family.'

I was reaching for my whiskey when a hand snaked out and swiped the glass from under my nose. Before I could stop him, the captain spat in it.

My insides flipped over. I made for the Gents at a run, barely reaching it in time. When I raised my head from the depths of the washbasin, yer man was standing by with a paper towel. He was getting on my nerves. 'Why didn't you stand up for yourself? You don't have to take that shit. I'd have hit the louser myself if I was in better shape.'

'If we make trouble, we will be dismissed. They will not give us our passage home.'

'They couldn't leave you stranded here.'

'Captain says.'

'Bullology. All you have to do is walk into the Gárda barracks and ask for political asylum. The government would have you out of the country on the first plane.'

Yer man was still fretting, and I began to wonder why I was going to all this trouble, when all I really wanted was the cure. 'We'll get it sorted out, but I need a jar first.'

The look he gave me, you'd think I'd poisoned him. 'You don't need alcohol, your hands have stopped shaking.'

'Of course I don't need it. It just helps me get my head straight.'

As I turned back to the lounge bar, I caught the look on his face. For a fraction of a second it stopped me in my tracks. This guy had some nerve – dressed up like a plantation slave in my son's outsized clothes, not a tosser to his name and no way home – and he was sorry for me? Fuck him.

In the lounge, the ladies of the bar edged closer to the captain, courting him for a drink. He was getting to the stage of telling them what a fine fellow he was, and they were nodding with the most sincere expressions they could plaster across their hung-over faces. I caught my own expression in the bar mirror – an exact replica of the look yer man had given me a moment earlier. Sod this, I thought. No so-and-so African is going to look down his nose at me. He'd be out of my hair soon. Then I could drink my fill.

That evening the local stringer for Seaboard Radio got hold of the story. The broadcast went out on Saturday night – repeated on the Sunday-morning local news roundup. The parish priest heard the report as he was preparing for half-eleven mass, and took up the resurrection of the Africans from the slimy depths of the harbour as the theme for his Easter sermon. Had it been Christmas, it would have been a great 'No room at the inn' story, but that's showbiz.

People began calling after mass, with food, Easter eggs, bottles of wine and spirits. Mostly they came out of curiosity, and stayed when they saw that it was turning into a party.

Somebody put on the stereo and people began to dance. The Africans had flocks of young ones round them. Lassies that would have run a mile to avoid foreign sailors in the local disco were vying for their attention. Young fellas were threatening what they wouldn't do to the gobshite of a captain. Older people talked of bringing in the priest, the local politicians, the Legion of Mary.

The daughters were in the thick of it, orchestrating proceedings, like a pair of queen bees. One of the lads, growing cocky with all the attention, announced that he would bring both sisters home with him to be his wives. The younger doll pointed out that wherever she went, her child must go too. The lad was not to be discouraged. His family would be impressed, he declared. It would be an achievement indeed to return with, not alone two wives, but a half-grown son also.

My eldest tossed her head. 'Only two wives? You're not greedy, are you?'

The young fellow picked up the irony and ran with it. Only two *Irish* wives. Three maybe four African.

The other lads, not to be outdone, piped up that they would have five wives, six, a dozen.

Yer man's head shook through this interaction as if he'd just developed a nervous tic.

'These boys – who cannot afford even one wife!'

'What about yourself? Would you never be tempted to get a young one? Seeing as it's the done thing and all?'

His eyes popped like a couple of hard-boiled eggs. 'I am a Presbyterian, sir. Besides, I love my wife.' This guy – if he wasn't so black, he'd be mister lily-white perfect. 'Would you supplant your fine lady for some flighty young woman?' he enquired.

I made no comment, since the lady in question was approaching with a fresh load of visitors to introduce to our hero. It was Sam this – Sam that – Sam the other, like he was some kind of film star.

'Pardon me,' said yer man. 'My name is Sambo.'

'You don't mind if I call you Sam?'

'Sam – BO'. He spelled it out.

'I can't call you that.'

He gave her a stubborn look. 'But it is my name.'

Evie looked about her for assistance, too embarrassed to explain. Manus rescued her. 'It's like some foreigner calling me Paddy.'

'But your name is not Paddy.'

'Right. It's a term of endearment used towards people of the Irish persuasion.'

Yer man considered this. 'As wog is a term of endearment towards people of the coloured persuasion?'

Evie nodded, mortified.

'But Mrs Maguire, I am not asking you to call me a wog.' The room went silent, everybody listening. 'There is a saying, is there not, that one should call a spade a spade.' There was a glint of mischief in his eyes. 'This spade was christened Sambo.'

There was uproar. Evie hung on to yer man, breaking her sides laughing. The fellow could do no wrong.

I had never seen so much booze in the house. The table was covered with liquor of every variety. People came to have their glasses refilled. Evie was nowhere in sight. Manus and the girls were occupied entertaining the guests. It was the perfect opportunity to slip something into a glass for myself. As I lifted a bottle, a voice behind me, hissed. 'Go ahead. Drink your fill.' Evie banged a glass down in front of me. 'I'd be glad to see the back of you.'

I made for the hall and flicked through the phone book for the helpline. It rang once, twice. A switch clicked on the electronic sound of an answering machine. A voice informed me that they'd gone away for Easter and rhymed off a backup number. One day at a time, the message ended. This too shall pass. *Great.*

The stringer from Seaboard Radio arrived. For months she'd been promising to record my sea monster story for their local history slot. But it wasn't me she'd come to interview. The lads were prompted to recount their misadventure once again. When they got to the part about the mud and slime of Rotten Island insulating them against hypothermia she marvelled at their luck.

'It was the blessing of God, and perhaps a little luck.' Yer man reached inside his shirt and took out a leather thong. Hanging from it was the curved white object. The stringer described it to her listeners, and asked yer man its significance.

'When I was a young man there rose an alliance in my village, between fishermen and a strange sea mammal. We called this creature Sanka. When Sanka drove the fish inshore, the men held their nets across the inlet. It was a happy arrangement. An abundance of fish for man and Sanka.' He fingered the object. 'Many years later, when the time came for the creature to die, it threw itself upon the beach.' And wouldn't you know, yer man just happened to be there, on the spot, to lift the tooth out of its head.

The stringer switched off her recorder, well pleased. 'It's a bit like your sea beast story, Owen.' Too damn like it, I thought. Bang goes my moment of glory with Seaboard Radio.

'You have a story of a sea creature also? Please. I would like to hear it.' He smiled at me with his big round innocent face. I felt like hammering his noggin off every wall in the house.

I pushed my way into the kitchen for a bit of peace and quiet. There was a newly opened bottle of Black Bush sitting, forgotten, on the draining board. I lifted it to my nose and sniffed its bouquet.

The kitchen door opened behind me as I poured. I didn't have to turn to know who it was. 'Will you take a drink?'

'I do not drink. Thank you.'

'Aren't you the great man.'

'I am not that, sir.'

The edge in his voice took me by surprise.

My hackles rose with a chill of recognition as he detailed the restlessness of his son; his own frustration at his inability to impart hard and painfully won knowledge to his offspring.

He spoke of his daughter – and his granddaughter, the child of an artist who came from the city to study the native dyes of the village women. I heard his sadness and some pride as he described the man who deserted his daughter, his great height, over six-and-a-half feet, the blackness of his skin – much darker than Sambo's clan.

I swirled my whiskey round the mug. 'The wife blames all our kids' problems on this stuff. Where did *you* go wrong?'

'I have failed them, sir. I spend my life at sea. Never with my family. My children have no father.'

Evie came into the kitchen with a stack of empty plates. She regarded the mug of whiskey in my fist. Sambo observed her look of distaste. He took the mug from me and wet his lips with it. Evie's eyebrows lifted in surprise, but she made no comment, leaving us alone again. He poured the whiskey down the sink.

'Thanks.'

'It is I who owe you gratitude, sir. For your kindness, and the kindness of your wonderful family.' Removing his lucky charm, he regarded it, as if trying to make up his mind, then handed it to me. I was at a loss. The gift seemed to call for some reciprocal gesture. I took the brown scapular from about my own neck. I had worn this heirloom since my grandfather passed it on to me, on my first fishing trip.

'You'll never drown as long as you wear this.' Sambo looked at it, torn and ragged as it was by time, like it was some voodoo charm. 'It's alright. It's been blessed and all. By a priest.'

His Presbyterian face took on a look of real alarm then, but he took it from me, and hung it about his neck. I did likewise with the fish tooth. I would keep it on while he remained in the house, though there was something almost too intimate about wearing an artifact that had absorbed so much of this man's life – soaked in the sweat of years.

Sambo fingered the cord of the scapular. A rash had already begun to redden his neck where the cord chafed against his skin. I guessed that he would not wear the scapular for long either. A flicker of amusement crossed his face as if he, too, had read my thoughts. As he exploded into mirth, my own laughter ripped up from my belly – unstoppable.

Evie put her head around the door, alerted by the mad howls. She noted the empty mug and came to her own conclusions. 'God forgive you, Owen Maguire,' she complained. 'You've led this good man astray.'

FRANK RONAN

The Sticky Carpet

My genitals withered the day that I left him, and soon afterwards I discovered food. At first it had seemed that there was no pleasure left in life, and no escape from the pain. The company of others compounded misery, and isolation fragmented what shreds were left of my sanity. The consumption of alcohol or other drugs changed maudlin thinking into morbid imaginings. If Tom had not locked himself out of the flat things might have ended badly. As far as I was concerned I was dead already, and it was only through inertia that I hadn't made it official.

It was a divided house and Tom had the upper half. At a quarter past six on a Tuesday evening in early October he rang my bell. It was the first conversation of more than three words I had had with him. He seemed distressed, apologised for disturbing me and asked if he could use my phone to call a locksmith.

'That seems a little extreme,' I said, as I showed him in. 'Haven't you got a spare set somewhere?'

He said that he had keys at the office, but wouldn't be able to get them until the morning. He made his predicament sound unreasonably hopeless.

'That's hardly the end of the world,' I said.

He smiled, embarrassed: a good smile. I made my offer without thinking, in response to the smile.

'You're welcome to stay here for the night. There's only the sofa, but it's perfectly comfortable. Locksmiths cost a fortune these days.'

He made some token protestation out of politeness, and then offered to take me out to supper in return for my hospitality. The thought of going to a restaurant filled me with a dread that would be inexplicable to a stranger.

'Nonsense,' I said briskly. 'That won't be necessary.'

There was no food in the house, so I settled him in front of the television with a whiskey and said that I had to nip out for a minute, praying that the delicatessen in the next street might still be open.

It was nothing elaborate. I made him watercress soup and bacon sandwiches. Sometime between lighting the stove and watching him eat I realised that, for the first time in a long time, I had some sense of normality and a first stirring of sensual pleasure. The bacon was paper thin and smoked; the soup a clear deep green. The smell that filled the flat was enough to revive even my forgotten appetite.

'Sorry,' I said. 'It's nothing much.'

He attempted a look of scepticism, but failed on account of the effect the food was having on his features.

'Delicious,' he said.

The next day I made my own bread and the day after that it was chutney. Samples of both were sent upstairs to Tom. He accepted them with a refreshing greed, and an understandable awkwardness.

'Don't let it worry you,' I said. 'I spent a long time with someone who couldn't appreciate good things. We broke up not so long ago. If you take my food you are doing me a favour. Believe me.'

He asked me what my lover's name had been. It seemed an odd question.

'If I never say his name, someday I might forget it.'

I could see what Tom was thinking: that I was odd but harmless. That would have to do for the moment. After my previous experience, being thought harmless seemed like a compliment.

By the following week I was having friends round for supper. Some of them were people I hadn't seen for a long time. There is a limit to how much you can bore your friends with bruises and tears. Now, watching them eat my food left me nothing short of elated. I had made a perfect steak and kidney pudding. I was shaking with nerves as I cut it open and couldn't sit still until it had been tasted and its perfection declared. Tom was a guest also and I had been nervous about that, but my friends liked him. There was good conversation in the flat for the first time in ages.

Clarissa cornered me in the kitchen while I was fetching coffee and asked if Tom was my new man.

'Don't be such an old woman,' I said. 'He's just a neighbour. I don't even know if he's gay or straight.'

I took no notice of the knowing look she gave me. But she did say it was nice to see me being my old self again. Like someone risen from the dead she said. She was dipping her finger in the remains of the blackberry mousse.

'Delicious,' she said.

In time the two flats became a whole house again, by degrees, over the years. Tom and I were considered a couple. He ate my food and entertained my guests while I was in the kitchen. It was assumed, wrongly, that we shared a bed. He never made that demand and I was grateful for his forbearance. We had contentment and, looking about us, it seemed that our lives were better endowed than the lives of most others.

The name of that other person became dimmer, and thoughts of him less frequent. I had left him to save my life, or his, because it had come to a point where one of us would have killed the other. At first it had seemed that I hadn't a life worth saving, but in time I no longer thought about those things, only of the next meal. I worried about boudin blanc, not happiness. Food is very reliable. If something goes wrong it is entirely your own fault, and nothing is beyond salvation.

Inevitably, Tom sometimes suggested that we should go to a restaurant. That brought visions of all the restaurant meals in the past; of attempted conversation and long inebriated silences between a couple who were painfully in love and had nothing in common; of him being so drunk that he would vomit across the tablecloth and of me carrying him out under the pitying glare of the management. This was none of Tom's business.

I said, 'I have yet to eat at a restaurant where the food is as good as my own. It is a sinful waste of money. Don't you like what I cook for you?'

He would point out that I hadn't been to a restaurant for years; that things had improved.

'I read the papers. I know that the prices have gone up and the portions have got smaller and that the waiters now have ponytails. The food is still a matter of profit, not passion.'

If it had been anyone else but Tom we would have been fighting. He would have told me that it was a fat lot I knew about passion. He would have stormed out of the house and gone to a Burger King. But, being Tom, he put a forkful of gnocchetti into his mouth and said, 'Delicious.'

I did begin to wonder why he wasn't as hungry in the evenings as he used to be. Unbeknownst to me he was plotting; researching restaurants in his lunch breaks until he found one that would meet my standards. A week before his birthday I asked him what present he would like.

'The Sticky Carpet,' he said.

'The what?'

'I want you to let me take you to The Sticky Carpet.'

I thought it might be a play or a film or, perhaps, a particularly sordid nightclub.

'Fine,' I said. 'What time does it start? Should we have supper beforehand or should I make something for when we get home? I was going to do duck in red cabbage.'

'It is a restaurant,' he said. 'And you can't back out now. You've agreed. Birthdays are sacred.'

That week I cooked as I had never cooked before. My work was late and the editor complained, but some things are more important than reviewing obituaries for the *Telegraph*. If Tom was out to prove a point, then so could I. Whatever The Sticky Carpet might produce would pale in comparison to the meals which preceded it.

Tom was right. He had found the one restaurant in the country where the food was unimpeachable. Better than that, it was exciting. At first, I pretended not to be impressed.

'Anyone can buy good foie gras,' I said.

'Apparently,' Tom said, 'they make it themselves.'

For the second time in my life I had to admit defeat, but only to myself. And this defeat was full of pleasure. He had watched, amused, as I chose the most difficult and unlikely things (the foie gras was served on what the menu called 'Toasted Mango Brioche', which I was certain would be disgusting), and laughed when I had got to the stage of tasting things from his plate as well as my own.

When the bill was paid I had mellowed enough to say how nice it was not to have any washing-up to face. I was almost tempted to say something sentimental, but thought better of it.

By a quirk of architecture there was a door which connected the cloakroom with the kitchens, and this door had a window let into it, which I peered through as I put on my coat and waited for Tom to return from the lavatory. Chefs and cooks ran and shouted and stainless steel gleamed, and I was feeling pleased with myself that a ghost had been laid and that I had spent the entire evening without once thinking of him. There was something familiar about the man who was washing the saucepans and, as I took a second glance, he turned. It was him. Paunchier and at once more haggard, with that complexion like raw suet pastry that kitchen staff acquire, but him all the same.

I backed away from the door in case he saw me, afraid of what my mind would do next. I had lived for years with a terror of running into him again; of how the anger he had caused would manifest itself. Nothing happened. I felt nothing. I went and had another look. It was just a sad man, brought low by drink, in a demeaning job. There was a hand on my elbow. It was Tom.

'Are you ready?'

My hand brushed his as we left and it was like getting an electric shock. I began to shiver a little, knowing what was now inevitable. He asked me if I was all right, and I said it was just the cold.

When we got home he looked as though he was ready for

bed, but I poured a drink for us, and we were at opposite ends of
the sofa, and I was thinking that in all the things I had tasted
over the years I had forgotten the taste of skin.

'Tom,' I said. 'Take your clothes off.'

He did it without question, and I looked at him for what
seemed like a long time before anything happened, as though
there might still be some way out of it. He waited, as he had
always done, until I was ready. His body seemed extraordinary
to me, and I thought if I touched it it might break. I hadn't the
power to go any further on my own.

'Perhaps,' I said, 'you had better take mine off too. I don't
think I'm able.'

He put his lips to mine and said, 'How's this?'

I was tempted to say that it was delicious, but that was a
word for food, not lust.

Politico

Jeananne became a feminist when she turned eighteen. She went to UCD and met a fabulous lecturer who inspired her. Dr Oestes was a very beautiful authoritative woman who lectured in critical theory, a subject which drove Jeananne wild with excitement. Jeananne developed a sort of crush on Dr Oestes and wangled her way into her tutorial each year, where she became the star student. But she had a rival, Cormac.

From the first day that he walked into the class, he was her enemy. That very first day. They had been looking at one of Sylvia Plath's poems and Jeananne had rubbished it, saying that it was a typical whining defeated female voice. She exaggerated her views slightly for effect. Cormac had almost dived from his seat to throttle her in Sylvia Plath's defence. He seemed more than irate at the insult to the dead writer. Jeananne was appalled at his outburst, and thereafter dubbed him the 'fanatical literary critic'. Dr Oestes seemed to be somewhat impressed by his passion.

When their first term major essay results were due out, Jeananne went discreetly to the board every day to check. She didn't care where she came on the list, so long as she beat Cormac. When the list finally went up with her name at the top of it, she smiled coolly across the concourse at him, her smile loaded with malicious pride.

'Hi,' he called back, taking her smile for a greeting. They never spoke out of class.

Dr Oestes started a women's group, and Jeananne was the first to sign up. The group functioned quite well as a forum for personal and political discussion and as a general focusing aid on feminism. Cormac headed a deputation from a number of men who wanted to join the women's group. After democratic discussion amongst the group it was decided that certain sessions would admit men, and others would exclude them. At Cormac's first meeting, he made a beautiful speech about how honoured he was to have been admitted to this sanctum. It was like gaining access to the womb. He felt that if men and women worked together towards an egalitarian society, nothing would stop the tide of feminism. He was an impassioned and highly skilled speaker, the burden of strongly held unpopular beliefs through his adolescence having sharpened his tongue. This particular speech was more reserved and humble than normal, same cunning fox though, just a slightly different register. The other women all swallowed him. Jeananne didn't.

Not only did they tangle in class, they now started to spark off one another in the women's group. He would preface all his arguments with a humble acknowledgement of the inferiority of his views, owing to his not possessing ovaries, and then go on to contradict her on everything. You would scarcely believe that they both claimed to represent the same political creed. One day he annoyed her so much that she wanted to thump him. She started to completely ignore him on the campus and in the restaurant. The only intercourse between them was in class or in the women's group, where they sparred in clipped post-structuralist language. Jeananne hated him, but she came to look on him as a stone upon which to sharpen her developing intellectual powers. The others in the women's group couldn't understand Jeananne's antipathy to this boy. After all, male feminists weren't tuppence ha'penny. Those that existed should be cherished, or at least encouraged. They felt that Jeananne was being unreasonable about him.

One day, when she was drinking coffee in the restaurant, he came over to her and asked if he could join her.

'It's a free restaurant,' she went back to her newspaper. Cormac gathered his courage and gently took the folded newspaper from her hand. Jeananne, outraged, snatched it back.

'Look, Jeananne, I know you don't like me and I'd really like to know why. What have I done? You and I should get on great together, we think broadly alike on so many issues, though we always end up fighting like dogs over the detail. I would really like to be your friend.'

Jeananne stared at him, and then picked up her newspaper and her coffee and moved to another table close by. She watched him out of the corner of her eye as he slowly buried his head in his hands on the table. She wasn't sure why she disliked him so much, but suspected that it was his ego that bothered her. That, and the fact that they had the same interests. She'd always been fiercely competitive.

From then on their relationship just levelled off into a plain and fairly ordinary dislike. They were both elected to the organising committee for the campaign for abortion information for women, so they had to do quite a lot of demanding work together. Each learned the value of restraint and compromise.

The women's group organised a 'reclaim the night' march to celebrate International Women's Day. Cormac and Jeananne again worked side by side on the organising committee. Cormac was not allowed to attend the march though, because it was women only. He argued this point heatedly with Jeananne and others. He felt it was separatist that he wasn't allowed to go, that the march would defeat its own purpose if it ghettoised itself, and excluded men. The women argued that the whole point of the 'reclaim the night' march was that it was just women. Women are obviously free to walk the streets day and night if they have a male escort. It is when they are alone that they are under threat. Cormac could see that, but the march functioned on a symbolic level rather than a practical one. It wasn't actually going to make the streets any safer for women. It was purely a political gesture, a showing of strength to the public and to the politicians. Jeananne lost her temper with him.

'Yes. The march functions on a symbolic level. And the symbol is of women walking *alone*, laying claim to the night. Now you are just going to have to face this if you want to stay with the group. Certain things are for women only. Right? If you want to be part of our revolution, you've got to give us space.'

Cormac went off with a hang-dog look on his face, and arranged to meet them in a pub after the march, this much he presumed he was allowed. The march went from Parnell Square to Kildare Street. A joyous celebratory affair. Candles and music and chanting. Jeananne had the loudspeaker and led most of the chanting. 'Whatever we wear, wherever we go, yes means yes and no means *NO*.'

When they arrived at the pub, the general mood was euphoric. Jeananne spotted Cormac sitting in the corner with a puss on him but after some of the women chattered to him for a while he couldn't but get sucked into the mood of the company. Jeananne had a couple of drinks, and this calmed her a little. She managed to avoid Cormac, because she knew that any contact with him would immediately put her in bad humour. She got drunk quite quickly and she started to dance. The pub was mainly full of women from the march. The dance floor was tiny, so her dervish dancing had to be contained.

Unable to relax, Jeananne gathered her things together and left the pub in plenty of time for the last bus. She leant against the bus stop, and felt a sort of general unease. A malcontent was following her around. Happiness never seemed to really happen for her. Cormac arrived at the bus stop, and they nodded at each other. They had never been in this situation before. Alone, and having to ignore each other. It began to rain, yet they didn't comment. Teeming chilly March rain that made other people dash and giggle. They stood there in silence while the rain bucketed down on them in sheets. Great drops were dripping from Cormac's nose. Jeananne could feel a small river forming down the back of her neck.

Cormac turned to her and grabbed her in his arms and kissed her firmly on the mouth. She gasped. He pushed her against the wall and pressed his body against hers, fastening her hips to the wall with his own hips, and grabbing her hair in his fist. Desperately he dug his fingers into her back, and she could feel his hands through her thin jacket. She responded to him.

Hungry. Turned on. The rain pelted down and they were both soaked through. He steered her to the road and hailed a taxi. One stopped and they bundled into the back where they devoured each other all the way to Ranelagh. They arrived at his bedsit where, panting loudly and avoiding her eyes, he poured them two glasses of white wine and turned off the light. They sat there, saying nothing, in the darkened room, drinking the wine, both of them breathing loudly. He came over to her and kissed her, passing a mouthful of wine to her which spilled down her cheek onto her neck. Then he bit her neck, hard, and when she cried out, he started to pull off her clothes. They had ravenous, desperate sex. They crucified themselves with desire. As Jeananne drifted off to sleep, she could taste the blood in her mouth where she bit her lip when she came.

Cormac was still wide awake. He could not believe his behaviour at the bus stop. What had he done? Who the hell did he think he was? He hadn't intended to do it, it was completely unpremeditated. God! It was something he'd never done before. If he'd been wrong, he didn't know what she might have done. He'd fancied Jeananne since the first day he met her in tutorial, and he simply couldn't understand her attitude to him. She was much more tolerant of the other guys. He had done a bit of discreet research. Apparently she didn't go out with guys. She appeared to actually dislike men, and was contemptuous of them when the opportunity arose. She was definitely not gay. If she had been, she was the type who would be political about it. Now it seemed that she must have been interested in him all along. Funny way of showing it. As she slept beside him, he thought that she looked as fragile as a small child, just as trusting and just as beautiful.

When she woke up, she was alone in the bed. For a moment her mind was deliciously blank, then she sat up, suddenly shocked. He was seated at his desk, angle-poised lamp turned on and leaning over him like a watchdog. She remembered him saying to someone that he did two hours reading every morning before he went in to college. He claimed to be an insomniac. Jeananne had always reckoned it was a fib, just to make him look glamorous. Insomnia, a real intellectual's disease.

Jeananne got out of bed and pulled on her clothes. He didn't look up from his desk. It was a very long time since Jeananne had been with a man. She lifted up a magazine and slammed it on the ground. He didn't look up. She banged a spoon off an empty cup. He didn't look up. Finally, she thumped a chair off the ground, and he slowly swivelled round in his swivel chair.

'Oh, so you want to talk to me now. You ignore me for six months, but now that I've finally fucked you, you might talk to me.'

Jeananne gathered up her things quietly and left the flat. Cormac felt awful. He had opened his mouth and had meant to ask her had she slept all right, but instead all that hostility came out. He didn't exactly know where from.

Jeananne went into college that day, but didn't attend class. Instead she went to the computer lab, and taught herself to type. She got a Wordstar typing tutorial and methodically worked her way through it. This was something she had wanted to do for ages, but hadn't got around to. She concentrated totally on it, sitting at the computer for twelve hours non-stop. By the end of the day she could touch type, albeit slowly. Only when she got home to bed did she think about Cormac and the previous night. And then only for a second. She had difficulty sleeping, so she spent most of the night reading until she finally collapsed into sleep.

The next day she saw Cormac at tutorial. He was nervous and uneasy with her. She was totally calm and controlled. The others in the class noticed that Jeananne was for the first time behaving with civility to Cormac. They were astounded. So was Dr Oestes. Cormac, however, found it unnerving. Everything went smoothly for the first half hour of the class, until a point of dissension arose. Jeananne and Cormac once again laid into each other. The fight was even more vicious now. Jeananne got totally worked up. The rest of the class became very uneasy. It looked like she was going out of control. She wanted to thump him. She walked over to his chair and stood in front of him, her closed fists rigid and shaking. Finally she managed to control herself and sat back down. Dr Oestes asked her to stay back after the class.

'What's the matter, Jeananne?' she asked kindly, knowing that there was something seriously wrong with the young woman. Jeananne smiled and apologised, saying that she just got carried away. That she was beginning to feel a little overwhelmed, and that she thought she needed a good rest. Dr Oestes' kindness almost made her feel upset, but she managed to get out of the room before this happened. She was in a state of total emotional confusion, almost unbearable. Thoughts raced through her brain really fast and seemed to crash into each other and get tangled. Her head felt like it might explode. Outside the door, stood Cormac.

She was going to walk past him, but she didn't. Instead she stood in front of him. He didn't say anything, just put an arm around her and steered her along the corridor, down the stairs and out onto the campus. He took her to the bus stop, where they caught a bus to his place. They still didn't speak. Cormac lit a fire, and sat her into a big old chair, and wrapped a blanket around her. He then made her a cup of hot sweet cocoa. She looked like somebody who wanted to cry, but couldn't. He read her some poetry, and finally she started to relax.

They started to chat. It was the first time they had ever had a conversation. Both were excellent communicators in the formal sense, could get a point across to a large assembly without any bother, but neither could communicate intimately. Cormac started to open up like a flower.

'I came to college in Dublin to escape my family. My father is insane. He doesn't talk. He is cold to his children, and has nothing but contempt for my mother. He talks about her to people like as though she's not there, when she's standing in the room. And she behaves like she's not there. It's as though she's so used to feeling not there that she's become not there. She wanted me to go to college at home in Cork, but I decided to save my own skin and come to Dublin. Sometimes I feel bad about that.' There was nothing untrue in this story, but it wasn't telling the truth. He didn't tell her how violent his father was, he didn't tell her how many times he'd been beaten near senseless by him. He didn't tell her that fundamentally he felt sorry for his father, a big distant tragic man who hated himself and all around him because he had been led to believe he was a king and grew up to find he was a hotel manager with a dowdy wife and six kids.

He spoke of his interest in feminism as a way out from the straitjacket of traditional notions of masculinity. Jeananne started to feel for him, to appreciate his stories, and to see where he was coming from. Cormac noticed that it was he who had been doing all the talking, and he asked her to share something of herself with him.

She found it easier to listen than to talk, but she made the effort anyhow. She told him about her interests in women's writing and feminism, about her particular liking for the nineteenth century novel. She spoke elegantly of Simone de Beauvoir. She told him about the time she won a scholarship to go to Stratford-upon-Avon to visit Shakespeare's home town. She didn't tell him about anything really. Cormac knew that she was holding back on him. She told him that she hadn't had a lover for a long time. That she didn't like men. That she enjoyed being independent. That she found relationships disempowering. That night they went to bed and drifted off to sleep in one another's arms, totally peaceful, totally content.

Jeananne and Cormac became a regular couple. Everybody said that they'd seen it coming a mile off. Their sparring matches continued, but they were a lot more good-humoured. Dr Oestes watched the progress of the two with some satisfaction. She had thought they were perfect for each other from the very first day they both walked into her class. They spent a huge amount of time together, and their studies slipped. Jeananne sat a paper for which she was ill-prepared, and only got a third. She was furious with herself, and resolved to concentrate more on her work. A new resentment of Cormac developed.

They had very unusual sex. There was something of an unleashing of furies about it. It was hard to tell exactly when this fury overspilled into violence, and who exactly started it, but both co-operated with it. They never discussed it. It was something that just happened. To begin with it was a simple matter. They played rape games. He was a little reluctant, but Jeananne talked him into it. It gave her a marvellous feeling of power. He would defile himself with his own worst nightmare for her. As he got more used to it, Jeananne could tell that his protests weren't sincere. She knew that he liked it. She hated him for liking it. She didn't exactly like it herself. It was hard to explain. To begin with, the violence was egalitarian, but after a while she became less active, and he became less passive. They both began to hate themselves for doing it, though each managed to put it out of their minds afterwards.

After a period of dormancy, the women's group became quite active again. A campaign was launched to provide better lighting on the lonelier exits from campus. A number of attacks on women had been reported. Jeananne and Cormac were automatically asked to form the backbone of the organising committee. They agreed. A massive drive was launched. This campaign was masterminded by Jeananne, though she kept very much in the background, managing to keep up her studies also. Cormac was to the fore. He was magnificent. His speeches were sharper than ever. There seemed to be an added edge to them. One day she arrived at a meeting with a black eye.

'Shit. What happened to you?' asked one of the other women.

'Oh, Cormac beats me,' Jeananne laughed in reply. The whole group laughed with her. Even Cormac laughed. The idea was quite ludicrous. Finally the college authorities upgraded the lighting. Cormac and Jeananne were the toast of the group. Everybody thought they were a great couple. So good together.

Jeananne started to work very hard again. She spent less and less time with Cormac. It seemed no longer necessary to see so much of him now that they'd moved in together. They slept together every night, but otherwise, they only met in class or in the group. Both spent long periods in the library. In the back of Jeananne's brain a discomfort was spreading like cancer. Her conscience was gnawing at her. The dichotomy between her

public persona and her private existence was growing unbearable. Cormac seemed to be more and more distant from her.
They hardly ever talked. He rose early to do his two hours
reading in the morning and turned his back on her. His cold
streak resurfaced. He hated her and he hated himself for what
he did to her. They seemed so civilised during the day, yet at
night, once the lights were turned off, their monsters emerged
under cover of darkness. She loved to control him. She loved to
monitor the amount of pain. She loved the pain. She found it
exciting. It made her feel more. They never did it with the lights
still on. They needed to hide their shame. They didn't make
love. They made hate. Jeananne refused to think about it.
Every time the subject came into her head, she simply thought
about something else. She set herself a rigid study timetable,
and stuck to it meticulously. She also started jogging in the
morning. She worked so hard that she forgot to eat. Her face
grew pinched and dark shadows appeared under her eyes. Dr
Oestes noticed the change in her, and asked her if she was all
right.

'Fine,' she said, and she believed it.

The exams were approaching, and they were working very
hard. Both were irritable and uptight. After a long day in
the library, Jeananne came home to find Cormac sitting alone
in the dark. She switched on the light, and he startled
her.

'Turn it off,' he barked.

She did so.

'Why do you do it?' he asked. 'Jeananne. Why do you make
me do it? Why?'

She stood and stared in the direction of his voice.

'We could've had a good beautiful relationship. We could
have got into the whole cosy thing, sat around drinking cocoa
and hugging each other, made each other feel warm and good.
Instead, look at what you made me do to you.'

'I made you do it? You didn't have to. I didn't hold a gun to
your head. You liked it.'

'No. I never liked it. I don't know why I do it, but it's certainly not because I like it,' and he let out a terrible groan like an animal. 'Why do you do it?'

Jeananne knew why she did it. She did it because, in embracing and controlling the monster, she disarmed it. In monitoring it, she conquered it. She liked it because it made her feel. Otherwise she felt nothing.

'I do it because it makes me feel. Otherwise I don't feel anything.'

Cormac got up and turned on the light. This was the first time they'd talked about the worm at the heart of them. It was also the first time that they'd produced the worm with the light on. They both blinked at the brightness, and blushed at the sight of each other. They were both naked.

'Jeananne. I think that you should see a psychiatrist. I think you need help. There's something wrong with you, if you like that.'

Jeananne got riled. 'Oh mister mentally-healthier-than-thou. And you're the picture of stability. I tell you, I'd rather be the victim in this scenario, than to be so bloody brutalised that I actually enjoyed perpetrating it. Not to mention the sheer hypocrisy of it, you crooning away at our women's group meetings. I don't know how you can live with yourself, never mind with me. You make me sick.'

With that she slapped him hard across the face. Cormac didn't react for a second. He just stared at her with his pale grey eyes, unblinking, unflinching. For the first time, Jeananne became actually frightened of him, really frightened of him. He stood there, stiff as a pole and stared at her. Expressionless, he turned and walked to the door. For one terrible moment, Jeananne thought she had failed, that he was walking out. But he stopped at the door, and still speechless, turned out the light.

Once the darkness had re-established itself, Jeananne felt more comfortable. Darkness was where she felt she belonged. She closed her eyes and waited for the blows to fall.

Afterwards, when she embraced him, she felt so powerful. She knew that if the lights were on, that his face would be full of remorse, that he would be crucified with it. She knew that she had reduced him to something lower than he ever thought he could be. She had made him into his own worst nightmare. The ferocious demon that was locked inside him, that shit that he had squeezed into a box, she had managed to liberate. Even now that he had confronted himself over his behaviour, she could still do it. She licked the blood from her split lip, and wondered how she'd cover it up tomorrow. Cormac was shaking now, in her arms, shaking with remorse, and Jeananne was also shaking, shaking with pent-up desire to laugh.

Cormac didn't sleep at all that night. He lay there thinking and thinking. Sometime around dawn, he resolved to leave her. He knew that they would kill each other otherwise. He made the decision and a weight like an anvil lifted off his chest.

When Jeananne woke in the morning, she perceived a change in Cormac. He was no longer ashamed. He wasn't slinking round the flat furtively; instead he was very relaxed, making her a cup of tea. Something was going on. Jeananne watched him for a while, as he pottered around the room.

They both headed off to college. On the way down the road to the bus stop, they passed a man standing on the path with two kids. One child, the little girl who looked about six and wore an oversized red coat, was whingeing. It is a noise that would break your heart. The man got tired of her and growled at her to stop blubbering. The tears increased and got louder, and then, out of the blue, the man hit the little girl such a thump, that the child reeled and fell over. The man dragged her to her feet again, and hit her a number of times more, holding her by the shoulder so she wouldn't fall over with the blows. The child's cries increased. The man's voice strained hysterically with a repeated 'would you stop that whingeing you little bitch'. The six-year-old continued to howl. Jeananne and Cormac stood transfixed and watched the scene. A red colour crept up Cormac's neck and spread over his cheeks. Jeananne went over to the man and punched him in the face. This brought the man to his senses somewhat, and Jeananne roared at him.

'How dare you hit a little kid, you big bully. You big shit, you. She's so little, you fucker.' And Jeananne's voice cracked as she

started to cry and belt him again, hysterically screaming at the
man, who held up his hands to protect his face from her fury,
while the little kid in the big red coat looked up in wonder,
momentarily distracted from her own sorrows by the scene
before her eyes. Jeananne had gone completely berserk now,
she was strong and overpowered the man, and pinned him up
against a wall. Cormac came to, and rushed over to restrain
Jeananne. The man was as white as a sheet with blood coming
from his lip.

'She's mad,' he kept muttering to Cormac as Cormac put his
arms around Jeananne who started to sob and shake. The kid in
the red coat stood on the pavement and, staring at all the
adults, rolled up one of her sleeves to fit her little arm. Cormac
took Jeananne off to a coffee shop, where she sat in silence for a
time and Cormac stroked her hand. Finally she talked.

'Last night I had this dream that I'm always having. I've been
having it for years. I'm sitting in Bewley's drinking coffee, and
this huge guy comes in and starts to throw shapes around the
place, clearly deranged. He has a hunting knife. He picks up this
kid, around twelve or thirteen years old and starts to swing her
round. The kid screams and screams, and her mother just sits
there, with her arms protecting her other three smaller kids
shouting "Somebody do something" or something like that. I sit
and watch and I am afraid. The guy then clearly gets sexual
with the little girl, and starts to stroke her body in a sexual way,
and the girl starts to scream louder and the mother is
screaming. Suddenly I stop being frightened, and I go over to
him and I say "Hey, big boy, leave the kid alone." I am cool as a
breeze, totally unruffled. I have a small flirtatious smile on my
face. "Let the kid go back to her ma. She's only a kid," I say.
"She's no good to you anyway. C'mere, I'll give you a good
going over. It'll be the best night that you've ever had. I'm very
good at it. Let her go. She'll just be a bother and cry all the
time." '

'The madman looks from me to her and back to me again.
The kid has stopped crying now. He looks from one of us to the
other again, and finally he lets her go, and transfers the knife to

my throat and takes me away. As he takes me away, I think how it is that he cannot damage me now, because the damageable bit has been dead a long time. I think of the face of the little kid smiling and playing and maybe someday falling in love and being happy and I think that we can take anything when we are old, because part of us is dead, but we should protect the little children, because it would be too terrible if they grew up like the deserts that we are.'

This was more than Jeananne had ever revealed in all the time Cormac had spent with her. It was the most that she had spoken about herself. He held her hands in his and started to cry.

'I know that you're going to leave me,' she said. 'I could tell by the way that you made the tea this morning. I may be a cold fish, but I'm observant. I don't blame you for leaving me. You're doing the right thing. But remember, I didn't teach you anything that you didn't already know. I just opened the gates. I didn't create the hounds that escaped.'

'I know,' said Cormac. 'I didn't create them either.'

Jeananne had calmed now, though the skin on her face felt very tight, stretched from ear to ear over her flesh. Cormac dried his eyes and went up to the counter to order cocoa. He looked down at Jeananne, and was struck by how normal she looked. Just like anybody else, any twenty-year-old student from any university. She looked so normal, you could almost believe she was. At that moment he loved her. Not in the way he had before, tyrannised by desire, but in a new way. In the soft sad way of pity.

They decided to take the day off from college and get the Dart out to Howth. There they would climb the hill and look out over the sea and shout and scream to rival the seagulls in a frenzy of boisterous energy. There they would feel the wind in their hair and against their faces and they would think how small they really were.

CLARE BOYLAN

Thatcher's Britain

Ten Hail Marys and he'll phone. She said the prayers slowly, trying to put feeling into them. The harder she concentrated the more the words lost their meaning. *Fruit of thy womb.* Imagine, though, if little currants came out down there. Or pink blossoms that would scatter when you ran. The reality was more devious, things running riot everywhere, unseen.

All day she had heard a baby crying from some other part of the house, like a donkey braying in a far meadow. She tried to imagine what colour it was, black or chestnut or the dry, flat brown of winter leaves. Would his mother give him a bit of bread and sugar to comfort him? Her own mother used to give her her vest to suck when she was desolate. It became a craving, after you were weaned, the taste of your mother.

Two hundred drops of rain and he'll ring. She made an effort to keep track but the blobs of water slithered into each other on the window like drunks at a dance. Wouldn't you think now water was clear as crystal? Lepping with organisms, in point of fact. Every drop of London water you drank had passed through nine people. She preferred to think it had passed through a woman than a man. The way her hand went to the phone and began to dial reminded her of a character she had seen in the pictures, strangling a woman. He did it as if his hands were nothing to do with him. There was a kind of magic in it, though. She just poked the dial and there he was.

'I miss you,' she said.

There was a small chastising silence and she listened hard, not even wishing to miss the sigh as he spoke. 'I told you not to ring here.'

'Will I see you so?'

'Perhaps. Later.'

'Will you want some dinner?' Kathleen coaxed.

'I'll have eaten.' He said it grudgingly, as if she had extracted information under duress.

'It's only that I've been invited to dine with someone else,' she quickly defended herself.

'Ah, well. Some other evening.'

'It's an early dinner. I'll be back. What time will I see you?'

'I'm afraid I have no idea.'

'I'll be back.'

To soften the lie she had told him, as well as to put in the hours until she saw him, she tied on a scarf and went out into the rain. There was a little Italian place not too far away where they treated you nicely if you were on your own and you could get a beautiful lasagne at reasonable cost. Her money was nearly gone, but she would find work now her spirits were improved. On the tube she sat opposite a black woman who clutched a parcel labelled MRS BLESSINGS OKARA. A young rabbi, seated beside her, murmured something to her and she could not quite hear, but it seemed he was advising her that you could buy very good diamonds in Harrods. Her attention was taken by an Indian family who occupied a whole row of seats and she was mesmerised by the glittering painted toes of the doe-like teenage girl. She could not imagine how they saw her. She had no clear picture of herself, having been schooled against the sin of self-absorption, but she was going to see him and she felt her happiness must be plain for all to see, stretched across her like a rainbow.

When she got to the restaurant she looked in the window and there were couples already there, early diners, discussing the menu over a drink. Her elation vanished. By the time she saw him he would be full of a dinner eaten alone or with someone else, consumed in that mannerly way he had, the prongs of the fork vanishing between his lips and then only a vague abstraction of the eye and a faint budging of his chin betrayed that any activity was going on at all. You never saw him swallowing. He had taken her out to dinner once and she knew that she loved him because she ate snails to please him. That was how they got around to sex as well. You would do anything for someone if you loved them.

She went instead to a joint with loud music. Her salad was full of hard bits, red cabbage and brown beans and sweet corn and lumps of onion. The entire nation must be consumed with the state of its bowels, the grub they ate. No wonder they looked undernourished. Rubble like this would go through you like a dose of salts. She was suddenly homesick for the salads back home, a few petals of soft green lettuce, a hard boiled egg with buttercup centre, a sliver of home-cured ham and a sprig of scallion. With her mouth full of red cabbage she burst into tears.

What was it she saw in him? At first it was what she thought of as his Englishness, his beautiful manners and the way he spoke, without a trace of harshness. She had lost her way and looked around for a respectable person to give her directions. He offered her the shelter of his umbrella, 'to protect your beautiful hair.'

'Ah, sure 'tis only old wire,' she mocked.

'Gold wire,' he said. When it was time for him to go he left her his umbrella. 'You can return it when the weather changes.' A gentleman like that would never be·unkind to you. She hung his umbrella on the mantelpiece where she could watch it from her bed, a piece of England, furled tautly as a new oak leaf. Every so often she would shake out its folds and smell its good fabric smell and know that she had left behind forever the mean little black umbrellas of home, always busted, the spokes sticking out at all angles so that they lay on the step like a mangled crow.

'Call me J,' he said. She thought of him as Jay, like a bird, but the few notes he sent her were tersely signed with an initial. She imagined he must be something very high up and secret in the government and of course, as he was compelled to mention, he had a life before he met her, all the trimmings. He could not speak about his job and was too discreet to discuss his personal life but she was content to hear him talk about things he liked, good wine, the opera, poems, books, ballet, restaurants where whole sides of beef were carved.

'Oh, I'd love all that,' she said.

'You should have it,' he smiled. There was such happiness in the assertion that she would like to have had it bottled and sent back home as a tonic, only they would have laughed at his accent.

He took her to a restaurant with candles on the table and small silver vessels of flowers such as you'd see on the altar. In fact the whole event had about it the air of a religious ceremony. When the waiter poured a sup of wine J raised it up to the light and twirled it round and then stuck his nose in the glass and swilled a drop in his mouth with a mystical look. Kathleen expected to hear a little bell ringing. 'To England!' he toasted. After he had drunk some wine he grew maudlin. He raised his glass again. 'To loved ones left behind.' She thought first of his wife and then of her mother. As always, she pictured her mother in wellingtons and a man's overcoat, her hands mottled mauve like Swede turnips, her face closed off against the danger of emotion.

She had been shocked when she arrived in London to discover the young Irish people living in derelict houses with broken windows and boarded up doors, paying no rent. She took a room in a house in Notting Hill where there was a respectable Irish family, but one night they vanished and she was surrounded by silent people with amber skin and dark-skinned people who played loud music and addressed their neighbours by shouting out the window. All the women had children and because she had no child they had nothing to say to her but she thought that inside they must feel the same as she did. The things you did at home did not apply in this unrelated landscape. There was no one to advise you. She found out that the beautiful buildings and shops in the heart of the city were occupied only by politicians and pilgrims. One day she looked out her window and the entire street was filled with foreigners, and a white man with no legs who was in a wheeled cart pulled along by a giant Alsatian dog. They were singing and cheering as if they had won a great victory and she stayed in her room all day, petrified. In the evening she crept down to the corner shop for something to eat and the Pakistani shopkeeper was giving out about the Notting Hill carnival.

She kept to herself and found work in a nice respectable coffee shop where each customer got their own pot of coffee and little pastries that were eaten with the side of a fork. The girls there were Spanish and Italian, and a Puerto Rican. They did not speak much English and spent their free time going to American films. Their lives were built around these excursions. They brought in bags of sandwiches and spoke gutturally in their own language throughout the performance, occasionally lifting their eyes to make admiring groans when Michelle Pfeiffer or Julia Roberts achieved a passionate understanding with some fellow strangely burnished beneath his clothes, as if he had been sanded and then waxed.

J never asked that of her. 'I have nothing to give you,' he said. 'I want nothing from you except to admire you.' He turned up his hands to show both their emptiness and that they concealed no tricks. She gazed with pleasure on the smoothness of his palms and his short, clean nails. At home, if a man said he didn't want a cup of tea, there was a moral obligation to brew up at once. When she pressed him to kiss her he refused before obliging her with a dry, shy kiss and then he smiled at her sadly and said, 'Oh, I must just have another,' and he began to consume her in small mouthfuls, before falling on her, like a dog on its dinner. She had been shocked by his eagerness, shocked by the whole thing, which gave her a sudden sharp understanding of her mother, but afterwards he was so grateful that she could only feel she had not given him enough. The awful thing was that although she had not enjoyed the event, it made her fall in love with him. Now instead of his umbrella, she carried around the whole baggage of his life, the plays and poems and sides of beef. J had a phone installed so that she would not have to run down to the public phone in the hall which was adorned with notices from women offering to torture men in return for money. After that he rarely called.

Sometimes she did not see him for weeks on end. She could not
tell if it was him she missed or the life he lived without her. She
was so obsessed with the thought of the things he did apart from
her that she could not be happy when they were together. 'You
must not sit around like a servant girl waiting for romance,' he
rebuked her. She tried to explain that it wasn't just romance she
craved, it was the life he had mentioned. He laughed and told
her the things he described did not belong to him, she could
avail herself of them any time she wished. He made out a list of
places for her to visit, but the galleries and concert halls were
full of sour Americans, disguised in expensive English
raincoats, and she thought that culture was a cold thing when
you could not laugh with someone at the pictures of naked men
and women or touch their hand when the music was soulful.
Once he mentioned a club he belonged to, a gentlemen's club.
'It's rather grand,' he said in that way he had, as if apologising.

　'Take me there,' she said.

　'You'd be bored,' he smiled. But he had spoken of his club
with reverence and in her mind it became the equivalent of
paradise.

　When she was not waiting for the telephone she spent most of
her time in a park, walking and sometimes talking to other
foreigners who sat on benches. It was to one of these she
confided that she was pregnant. 'Go home,' he said, not to
dismiss her, but to use his small store of English words usefully.
She longed for home but she could not go back even though
when the baby arrived everyone would dote on it. She
remembered the merriment of the younger women, the careless
slide into domesticity and how sometimes when they had had
eight or nine kids they would shake themselves off and go to
university or enter politics. The women always ridiculed sex,
removing the sting with a swipe of sarcasm. She missed their
softness that was like the softness of rain, and the knife edge of
their humour. She missed them so much it was like a sickness.
And then – lunatic – she found herself nostalgic for the men,
whose irresponsible ways meant you never had to take them
seriously. She stayed in the flat for a week counting whorls and

dots on the virulent old wallpaper and then she just stayed there because the coffee shop seemed too decorous a place for her now. She began to look forward to having a child. As soon as the notion of it became a reality she felt stronger. She made up her mind to go and look for J, although she had no idea where to find him. Then she remembered his club and looked it up in the phone book. It amazed her to think she could have gone there at any time but had only got the courage because she was at the end of her tether.

A flunkey took her coat at the door. 'Who are you meeting?'

'J', she said boldly, because she didn't actually know his name.

Like magic he directed her up the stairs and told her to turn left for the visitors' lounge. And it was kind of like a fairy tale, the big curving staircase and the ceiling dripping with chandeliers. She ventured into a room full of men in suits and roosted on a hard leather sofa. While she waited, a galdy oul' lad with his eye on her bust asked her would she care for a spot of bubbly. She was looking around her all the time to see would J come in and her new friend urged her to relax. But she couldn't. She didn't fit in. She could tell from the look of the club members that dowdiness was *de rigueur*. People were staring at her dress. The champagne arrived but they hadn't the proper glasses and put big silver tankards on the table.

'Are they pure silver?' she asked.

'Not exactly,' the old lad said in his buttered shortbread voice. Not *exactly*. Tin more like. And then she had to jump up and tell him she needed the toilet.

Ah, now, that was beautiful. She had an urge to write home to her mother about that toilet. The long mirrors were like looking into a lake. There were flowers and little bottles of water, like Lourdes water only they were for drinking, and ladies who dabbed their noses in a very discreet way, as if it was an act akin to wiping your bottom. The women had a vegetable look, like something grown underwater or nurtured in a walled garden. There wasn't a mark on them. Their bland bosoms had been sketched in by some artist with averted eye. She went into

a cubicle to check and, sure enough, her aunt had arrived.
Already there was a mark showing on her brocade skirt. She
patched herself up with toilet paper and poked out her head.
'Has anybody here got a sanitary towel – the loan of a sanitary
towel – please?' The women said nothing although one of them
smiled at her. Possibly they had a different arrangement down
there, or had found some long-term method of coping with it.
'Thank you anyway,' she said. She could feel them watching
the small scarlet stain shaped like a star when she left. Probably
they would think she had been shot in the arse. She couldn't go
back into the big room for she felt certain that whatever the
ladies might think, the men would know. She was sorry about
her gentleman, left alone in all that stuffy grandeur to drink
champagne out of tin mugs.

She walked around the city for hours, not caring that she was
bleeding, bumping into tourists who were looking for strange
women to sleep with, and lonely foreigners with zombie eyes.
When the night had consumed all its leftover souls she stood
alone in some big gaunt place that was marked by a monumen-
tal arch. She leaned against the arch to rest and there, beneath
it, was a little bundle rolled up in a pink blanket. 'Oh, a baby!'
she cried. Someone had left a baby. As she pulled back the
blanket she thanked Saint Anthony for finding a replacement
for her own little lost baby. A girl, barely teenage, reared up her
head. She was rickety thin, her face as grey as nuns' porridge.
Kathleen gazed, first in amazement and then in pity. 'Oh, you
creature!' she said.

The girl eyed her sleepily. 'Got any money?'

'What you need is nourishment,' Kathleen said firmly. 'You
need a proper place to sleep.'

The girl told her to fuck herself. Her little sparrow's wrist
struck out and while Kathleen was nursing her face the girl
snatched her handbag and vanished like a skinny demon into
the dark.

Once, on the underground, she heard this announcement: 'If
passenger Pavelzciek is on this train, would he please proceed to
Trafalgar Square, where his mother is waiting.' Everyone

laughed except Kathleen who closed her eyes and felt with Pavelzciek's mother the panic of recognising no one, of being left alone with the guzzling pigeons, afraid to move from this seething spot in case you never again laid eyes on the only thing you knew.

The most shaming thing was that he wasn't even married. A few weeks afterwards she spotted him getting into a taxi and she followed in another taxi. She knocked on the door of a house in Marylebone that bore his name beneath a bell and barged in past him, into his flat, and without a word she had poked into everything, into his fridge with its little tinfoil ashtrays of frozen meals for one. 'You haven't even got a wife,' she accused him.

He defended himself, holding up his empty palms in that way he had. 'I never said I was married.' He was watching her with an odd sort of gravity and it took her a minute to realise that she had hurt his feelings. 'I'm very fond of you,' he said. 'Don't think I have been hiding anything from you. Quite the opposite. I have been sparing you. You and I have shared a remarkable happiness in spite of our differences but as far as my life is concerned, darling girl, you would be bored and unhappy.'

She tried to make sense of this but she was confused. She had imagined his flat would be very grand but it was shabby, not with the respectable dowdiness of his club but in a lonely way, as if life was dwindling around him. Kathleen thought that even though she had made it out of the sticks and got herself a man with a very high up job in the government, the subtleties always eluded her and possibly she wasn't really very bright.

She ate a little bit of the red cabbage from her salad and some brown bread and butter. The rain had stopped and black taxis, shiny as eels, hissed on the wet road. A weak sun put a halo of mist on rooftops and a faint tinge in the sky, a delicate lemon yellow like ladies' pee. She walked back, thinking of a dog she once had, a wall-eyed creature called Scrap, which had no idea of its function as sheepdog and stole a lamb and smuggled it into its bed and nurtured it after its pups had been drowned. She bought a bunch of anemones, thinking they would catch the last rays of sun through her window and draw the eye away from the wicked little sink with its pipes exposed, like a spiteful beggar showing off his deformities, but the sun had gone down and the Jamaicans had begun to fight and she had set herself the task of counting stars as they took their places in the sky by the time she heard the doorbell's peevish drone. 'Terrible day.' He kissed her cheek. 'You don't know how I envy you your simple life.' He kissed her lips in a fatherly way and she began to relax. There wasn't anything devouring in his kisses. They weren't even exciting. They made her sleepy. When she was in his arms she couldn't imagine why she suffered so much when they were apart. He lowered her onto the bed and his jacket grazed her face. It smelled of wool and had a hard edge like a rope. His legs grew restless and he grasped and pulled at her as if he was trying to get his footing on a cliff face. Something about her – not her personality, she knew – had tripped a switch, and he was off on his demented quest like a prisoner trying to dig a tunnel with a teaspoon.

To make the time pass she thought about a Russian she had met in the park. He was beautifully dressed but had the look of a refugee. His sad face gave her permission to sit down beside him, and to break the ice she asked him why he had come to London. It was the phrase 'Thatcher's Britain', he said. It made him think of a pleasant place with thatched houses and fields of hay and employment for all. She asked him if he liked the city. He said nothing but stared ahead and she thought that behind that gaze, both blank and intent, he still saw a sun-warmed scene of honest labour and contentment. 'What do you like best?' she persisted. When he told her the rats' kitchen, she thought it was a joke – some dosshouse he was staying at – but she could see he hadn't a sense of humour. Actually, it was interesting. It was an attraction they had at Regent's Park zoo, a cage that had been equipped with chairs and tables and utensils and every manner of home comfort to see how the rats would adapt to domestic life, and they lived like lords, in and out of their kitchen, holding little tea parties. 'It is proof,' said the Russian, 'that any creature, given a chance, will improve itself.'

One of these days she would go to Regent's Park to see for herself the rats' kitchen but in the meantime she got pleasure from taking out the notion of it now and then and turning it over, the finicky little creatures entering this minefield of a cage, full of obstacles and breakables. She pictured them puzzling over the cups with their dainty little claws, gnawing at the legs of chairs to get the feel of them. Had someone given them an inkling, a bit of training, perhaps, in the correct use of knives and forks, or had they to bash along like everyone else? She saw them seated around the kitchen table sipping their cups of tea, arresting the crumbs of cake on their plate with tiny little silver forks, perhaps making small talk in rat language and scarcely able to believe their luck.

VINCENT BANVILLE

The White-Walled Men

Quentin A. Howard, in his thirtieth year, swinging down to
mass in his Sunday best, thinking – Harmony, that's it,
that's what's needed. The harmony of the spheres. Swing me in
the cradle of the deep heavens. Why not wish upon a star,
makes no difference who you are. That's a laugh. Initiative, the
advertisement said. So I think, why not start it off with a joke?
Arrive on stilts and say with a merry laugh, One way of going
up in the world. Old sobersides, ties, white shirts, buttoned
down faces. Or another tack: Me Da went down in a welter of
blood on the steps of the G.P.O. in 1916. Fighting for Ireland?
No, doing his bit for Harry Thompson's public bar and lounge.
The grandda too, he had the gun under the bed, along with a
few other things besides. No? So give the job to Pimply Peter,
recommended by Father McJoab, endorsed by Brother O'Battle,
signed, sealed and delivered by the green-eyed, unicorned holy
men of the Knights of Columbanus. And I thought of writing a
letter to the paper when I came home: a hymn to Ireland. How
invigorating to the intellect it is to be living in Ireland now.
Now, when great nations have reached their apexes and are
sliding down into mediocrity and stasis. Ireland is on the
upswing, great things are happening, great changes are taking
place: slowly, certainly, but oh, so surely. Its long incubatory
period is over and the foetus is becoming recognisable.
Liberality in the arts, lessening of curbs on the people and the
clergy, new outlooks, new horizons, new . . . oh bullshit. It's
empty, and so am I. Empty of friends, empty of responsibilities,
empty of sexual impulses. But you're full . . . full of self-pity.
Look at all those empty shining people. With missals in hands,
pointing like bird-dogs, sniffing towards the twin churches.

What do they expect to find there? Is it just routine? Or are they believers? Let me in among you, please. You don't think I'm serious? Cross my heart and hope to die. Here comes Major O'Warrior, nose as bright as a Belisha Beacon, arms whirling, windmills of correct carriage. Good morning, Major, fought any good wars lately? Mind the car! Jesus, me heart. All of them gazing out at me. A benediction of smiles. Mr O'Dough driving, delicately lifting a left cheek to break wind. His bone-hard wife, maintaining the set grimace, in spite, or maybe because of, the vile odours rising about her. The back full of piggy-wiggy children. Mr O'Dough, as you make your way, not too carefully, through these pious mass-goers, do you ever get the urge to mow down a few dozen of them? To smash them against concrete? Bright glinting nuts and bolts, buckles and knobs littered all over the roadway. For they surely have no red blood in them. Robots all. A Sunday newspaper? Why, certainly. Strikes, rumours of strikes, no place for the unborn, no solace for the poor, no food for the hungry, no sympathy for the faint of heart, no tears for the fucked-up. As we file in through the imposing brass doorway. Money in the box. Flick money-stained fingers into the holy water. Throw a little of it about. Sorry, Miss Prim. Look on it as seed of the Holy Ghost. Another immaculate conception. With both legs down the same leg of her tights, it would have to be. In the name of the Father and the Son and . . . Great suffering Jesus, I forgot to genuflect. Look at that old biddy glaring at me out of red rheumy eyes. Envying me my youth. If only she knew how old and sad I really am. Turn solemn face to altar. Here he comes. Kneel. No, stand up. No, kneel. All that ritual, signifying . . . what? Who put sand on the pew? Me kneecaps are on fire. Rise a little to ease it. Altar boys and boy scouts, angelic, quiffs and scrubbed shining faces. Why dress them in long shifts? Neuter gender? Should cover them completely. Just leave the tip of the prong showing. It's not for stirring your tea with, you know. The new liturgy. Peace on earth to men of good will is now peace on earth to men who are God's friends. Hello there, God, heard you had a seventy-five yesterday. That'll shorten the old handicap. What will you have? A ball of malt's your only man. And a medium of stout to chase it down. Ah, that's lip-smacking good. Will you cut it out! Do you want him to strike you down? Rub me forehead. Is it there? Sinner, etched in letters of fire. Or the white-walled men. Now where did that come from? Someone just walked over my grave. Oh, Christ, the sermon. Get more comfortable between the two cliffs of female meat. Look straight ahead. Nod at the sound of the holy name. But keep your thoughts to yourself. Deportment is all. Keeps them at bay. More ejaculation is needed. Less suppression and more emission. Widen it yawningly. Let it gape. Here they come, the white-walled men. A great surging tide of them. Like the second coming. Sweeping over the land, arse to mouth. Human daisychains, smothering haste, worry, ulcers, lacerated nerves, piles, pimples, constipation, all the trappings of modern man. Sweetness and light and a holy chaos. I believe in what? Charity, sounding brass or a tinkling symbol? God, do something, let me know you. A cry from the heart, a lonesome bark floating on a tide of pale futility. Bells, just three and –

Quency had a brother. His name was Paud. One morning when Paud was young he hid from the Bogie Man beneath the blankets on his bed. There, in the fluffy darkness he discovered a warm, slightly asthmatic home, and he never did come out again. It was as if he were imprisoned in another dimension and only his voice could filter back from beyond the membrane. First he was supplied with lighted candles but, after a number of conflagrations, these were replaced by flashlights. For Paud did a lot of reading, but only of authors who were already dead. Quency would sit watching the undulations of the hump beneath the blankets. At such times he thought of many things, but mostly he imagined man's first inarticulate strivings to rise from the slime. That is not to say that this particular moving bump was inarticulate. An unending monologue rose and fell. When he was not reading aloud, Paud was talking. He spoke with the characters in the books, or he railed against the dead authors, or he recited long prose poems composed of bits and pieces of doggerel that made no sense and had no particular rhythm. But he never replied to any remarks made by living people. He was quite a showpiece, and people came from far and near to gaze and to wonder. When admission started being charged, however, a complaint made its way to the proper authorities, and Paud was taken away.

– it is twenty minutes to eleven on a wet and windy Sunday morning in late September. The trees in the churchyard whirl their heads about like dervishes. The chapel doors bang open and Quentin A. Howard emerges like a shot from a shovel. Leading the pack, he is halfway across the yard before he realises that the weather has changed. Frantically, he claws at his flapping coat and he thinks, Jesus, Mary and Joseph, caught again. He waves a fist at the angry sky and scampers, like a ruffled hen, out through the gates and down the hill. Across the street he goes and along by the side of the Malt House. The Garbage River is in boiling ferment, and an old man on the far bank is going mad, jumping up and down and shouting incoherently into the streaming wind. Our hero veers sharply, pretending not to see him. He dashes around a big tree and loses his balance in the slick mud. And there he goes, all dignity lost, scuttling along on his arse into the vale of tears – or to be less poetic and more exact, into a bed of nettles bordering the bank of the river.

Quentin A. Howard, reclining in the calm of his chlorophyll-ous bower, thinks, Ineffable, now there's a fine word. From the Latin, I suppose. God made man in his own image and likeness. Can you have a clumsy God? One who keeps falling in, on and over things? We poor, priest-ridden Irish. Now, that's the easy way out. Surely it was divine retribution. Or can he take time off from more important things? And just because I didn't want to get involved. How do I know what complications might have followed if I had stayed to help the old fart on the bank of the stream? Anyway, what right had he to let misfortune trouble him? He was as old as the hills. Calm resignation towards the slings and arrows, that would have suited his worn grey hairs

much better. Did you learn it, you old Roman Juvenal? Enlarge
my life with multitude of days, you implored. If you wanted all
those days then you must have had something to fill them with.
How does it work? Or does it ever? My brain is like a fried egg.
Utter and complete stillness, I should imagine. To sit gazing at a
wall . . . and to see it? No pictures, no recollections, no hopes,
fears, longings, wishes, desires. Wrap me around myself. The
human chrysalis. To prevent ossification of the brainpan, feed
in abstract variations on a theme by Nihil. Heh, heh. Thought
you had me there. Be off, you pixilated pale ghosts. Is pale a
colour? Save it for later. We shall arise and go now. How many
doppelgangers in a clone? Such questions, questions, questions . . . Be nonchalant now. Even though mud-stained, sorely
stung and mutely chastened, if the centre holds and the seam is
invisible, you might just about make it. Yes, my good man, you
see something of interest? Kindly swing those bulging, blood-
stained orbs of yours somewhere else. Nearly there, now.
Christ, the ma! Off with the raincoat. Into the dustbin. Aha, yes,
indubitably. What nasty things are deposited in the streets
nowadays. Keep the home towns tidy. Keep the lines of battle
clear. Sweep it under the carpet, up the leg of your trousers,
anywhere, just get it out of sight. A touch, the barest, of
incredulity. Mud! In my hair! Should I try a joke? Must have
been a flying cow. No, better not. Not the kind my traditional
Irish ma would appreciate. Sidle around her now. Keep staring
her in the eye. Close the ears to the mounting tirade. Keep those
filthy, mud encrusted trousers out of sight. Ah, the good old
family pet. Down, dog. Sniff there again and I'll tear the
danglers off you. Safety, bang the door, turn the key in the lock.
Strip down to my pelt. Rub down with rough towel. Hee, hee,
nurse put cotton wool on it that time. Met her in the street the
other day. Fine double meaning talk out of her. How's your
scar, says she. Would you like to see it, says I. What for, says
she. To see how naked and defenceless you left him, says I. O ho,
says she, is that the way the land lies. It's not lying, says I, it's
standing up and taking notice. Be careful I don't give it the side
of my hand, says she. It'd prefer a taste of your tongue, says I.

But then I go and ruin it all when I say rapturously, Oh, Miss Bedpan, how your moustache quivers when you pout. In her white uniform and black cape. Little hat perched on top of her glossy curls. And the growth on her upper lip. Excites me. Like eating a fuzzy peach. They say you've never been kissed until you've been kissed by a man with a moustache. What about by a woman with a moustache? Who cares where. All right, all right, I'm coming. Come? Did you come? Did you come good? Did you come at all? Me? I only went.

And Quentin A. Howard descending. All done up in his green corduroy britches with the wide belt. White shirt, brown pullover. No underwear. Stopping to admire himself in the long narrow mirror at the foot of the stairs. Spots pimple on nose. Groans. Inside, the da is stuffing red corned beef into his mouth. Molars chomping, spittle flying. It's like a hailstorm in there. Seats himself. The three of them, constituting the bosom of the family. Sitting warily in front of a mountain of food. Then eating their separate ways through it to emerge at the other side, blinking.

Did you hear, the ma says. Poor old Martha Gurgle. Her that never did harm to anybody. And then to be taken like that.

Quency and the da eating away. But all ears.

Sitting in the outside water closet, she was, the ma continues. And down the whole lot goes into the Garbage River. Drowned, she was: all blue and swollen when they fished her out. The poor old husband was beside himself. Said people kept passing him by and wouldn't lend a hand. And them on their way from mass . . .

An unmerciful belch from the da. Quency keeps the head down.

You'll do yourself an injury one of these days, the ma says to the da. I don't know why I waste my time talking to you. What are you at, Quentin? Saying your prayers?

That'll be the day!

Inside, reading the paper. Rattle of crockery from the kitchen. The da already asleep. Sunday afternoon rain beating on the windows. Greyness . . .

Nothing for it, the bed is the only place.

And then slipping away from consciousness, dreaming . . . Soft childhood land. The eye of the mind moving down from a sky filigreed with cloud. Through branches, apple blossom, to ground level and the crushed smell of grass. Two boys, sun-bleached, coming forward. Close-up. Warmth of sweat-stained flesh. Youth, young skin, unblemished yet blemished, small scars and scratches. Minds free, full of sunlight, dancing shadows round the edges. As it was then. Butterflies like multi-coloured tears. Gadding cows. Movement everywhere beneath the stillness. Stopping, kneeling. Water silvering down through interlaced small fingers. So cool. So sweet. Then day's clear even light muting into dusk. Banks of midges floating, rising and falling above sliding river murmurs. Ethereal images in mushrooming heat lightening as the sun goes down. And the hoarseness of one lone corncrake as the young Quency wanders homeward. Wafted along in the echoes of his friend's goodbyes. Past the yellow blooms of windows in the purple twilight. Drinking up the odours of the folding day. No fear yet. Content inside himself. No need to touch with trembling consciousness the responsibilities of growing up. Stop!

And Quentin A. Howard sitting bolt upright in bed in the lateness of a September evening, thinking, The things I haven't done. A nice little square house with a neat little garden. And a wife full of tender little children. Who'd call me Daddy even if I didn't deserve it. As I back out in my mini-car. Noticing the weather. All bundled up in hat and scarves in winter. open necked shirt and tanned pulsing neck in summer. Waving at the neighbours. Saying, Hi, Tom, and, Morning, Sarah, and, Up yours, McManus. Working all day happy long at my routine little job. Music in my heart, a song on my lips. Dashing across wet pavements under parcels on leisure Saturdays. Rain-disfigured faces of kids pressed trustingly against car windows. And the feel of another human being in bed beside you at three o'clock in the morning. Come out. come out, wherever you are. Don't hide your face from me. It's nearly as difficult to give in as it is to go on. I'm halfway, hitting the point of no return right on the button. Like the bell you ring at a carnival when you test your strength. Bong! Okay, here we go. My aching head. Dash a little water into the face. Dry it off, hitch up the trousers, spit on the hands. Could sneak out the back. But it takes courage to hurt people. Yes, Ma, no, Ma, three bags full, Ma. Into the car. Out with the choke. In with the clutch. As dark as the inside of a hole. Cement road. Trees in the headlights. Closing in. Now where the ass stuck its head over the wall that time. Frightened the living daylights out of me. All those crosses where people died. Remember him like that. Only he's not dead yet. In through the gates, swing around in crunching gravel. What was that game he had seen them play? Ring a ring a rosy. And we all fall down. Old young men. All dressed in grey. Clasping hands. Living in the dreaming. Sitting now in echoing waiting room. All rooms painted white. White walls. Waiting to go in. To see. Him.

And Quentin A. Howard sitting between his mother and father, at the foot of his brother's bed, thinking, If I climbed in beside him, would I find it. And if I did, would I know it. As it is now.

Bread, I Said

I was standing in the mobile looking out the window and thinking how much bluer the sea looked this year, how much whiter the sand, when he said, 'You don't like it, do you?' I could see his mouth moving some distance away from me but the sound seemed to follow later, coming in spasmodic bursts, like sperm. His words hung there, suspended like a sentence that awaited a main clause. He acknowledged my silence by saying, 'The name, I mean.' I chose not to answer him still. He knew I didn't like it, that was clear from the way he phrased his words, a conclusion he'd arrived at long after the arguments were over. I just listened to the sound of his words which lingered, and imagined it all so clearly. The child's clothes slumped in a heap at the river bank, her fat body splashing furiously where the water was shallow. The next time I saw her she was older and fatter, her adolescent body hidden beneath jeans and sloppy yellow tee shirt which seemed to bake and grow hard in the hot summer sun, the remonstrance of some painful emotion flickering in her eyes. And all the while she watched the thin girls swim free and unimpeded by the consciousness of an overweight body.

This vision of her had been growing steadily over the summer months like my overstretched and impregnated body. I thought of the child inside me and felt guilty because I knew her shape and size would be as immutably fixed as a quantum reality. And all because of the name Macy. He had chosen it as a tribute to his mother, Mary Catherine MacCarthy, who died on Bloomsday, and offered it as a compromise, a restricted sort of choice.

'Well,' he said, and then I didn't see his mouth move

anymore. I knew he was waiting because he didn't say anything or do anything, just waited, as if it were something to be done, an act in itself.

'Bread,' I said, thinking aloud in answer to his demand. That's when he said,

Jesus.

Woman.

What.

Has.

Bread.

Got.

To.

Do.

With.

It.

But it had, because somewhere out of the distant past an image was forming of a young girl repeating over and over again the words, 'It looks like bread, it tastes like bread, but it is not bread, it is . . .' and somewhere between the repetition of the words and the child I stood remembering the difficulty I had even then in ever thinking of the word as anything other than bread, a difficulty that was born not out of the concept, but out of the word. I wanted to tell him that there was something soft and corpulent about the name Macy, a sound that echoed an indulgence, a superfluous thing beyond bread, beyond words, beyond his understanding, that this was an age of superfluous things, of corpulent appetites and attitudes, that there was some organic affinity between the name and the substance, unchangeable. Like bread, promising a forlorn sort of destiny, imbued with a need for fleshy things. But I knew I wouldn't. He seemed to have changed his position now. He was standing near a green door, not erect, more hunched in a subdued sort of way. I tried to create the image he would have of me if I said that and for a moment I was standing somewhere outside of myself, like upside-down on the ceiling with an overhead view. I stayed there watching the words that spilled forth from my lips, and associated the sounds with words like, disturbed, hysterical, absurd, vague, woman. I knew from up there he would never fully appreciate my relationship with words, their sound, colour and substance. So I said something hurtful to him instead, like, 'You don't need to immortalize your mother, you know.' I had to say something. Something intelligent that would guarantee the ebb and flow of words between us.

'What the hell is that supposed to mean?' he said.

'I mean isn't it sufficient that she died on Bloomsday, it's got to be earned . . . like Joyce.'

'What has?' he said.

'Look', I said, 'what's the point in burdening our unborn child with a name like that. It's not going to make any difference to your mother now.'

'No,' but it does to me,' he said, 'I can't see what your problem is with the name.'

'I just don't like it, do I have to give a reason?'

'Yes.'

His head seemed to be tilted backwards, and I imagined him drowning, not in the sea, but in a stagnant pool of green leafy things and water reeds near a weeping willow, and out of every corner of the dark woods behind him, their mouths green from dockleaves, crept forth men upon their hands, for their legs would not bear them, looking like anatomies of death, speaking like ghosts crying out of their graves.

'Well?' he said.

I could only say again, 'I just don't like it'.

'It's my mother, isn't it, you never liked her, no matter what name she had, 'twould be all the same, wouldn't it.'

'That is not true.'

'Sure seems like it to me.'

I knew this line of argument was sick, a careless use of words. But we had gone with the flow, unable to stop in mid-stream. I didn't want to hurt him, but I knew I did.

'If you loved me . . .' he said, and then he turned away from me.

But I did. It wasn't a question of love, but a question of words that were now deceiving us, were playing us like pawns on a chessboard, were creating the dividing lines, black and white, fencing our playing fields. Somewhere a door banged while I was watching the windows' linear shadow on a green floor and wondered at it. I thought about Yeats, his image born out of the shadow, but yet not of the shadow, that bore some relationship to the linear lines. And I pondered on what he said about Wisdom and felt sad. There was something comforting in his image that I wanted to prolong, to suspend *ad infinitum*, but in the corner of my vision a shadow moved, and when I looked again the image had vanished. I noticed a dark cloud move across the face of the sun, and on the green floor there was no shadow to wonder at anymore.

He was listening to Beethoven's Fifth while I was opening out the window, and drawing on the sea air, wet with spray that came up from the strand. While he was listening to the movement I was thinking about Oscar Wilde and the summer of sixty-nine. White light intensified on white pages in a meadow, and Wilde pondering on the name Earnest. Rachael Houghton went to Barbados that summer and came back tanned. Julie went to Ballybunion and met Ian. I stayed in the meadow in the dry white heat of an inland summer thinking about the name Earnest, my own name Margaret all orange, hot and agitated like fizzy orange in a wet glass. There was something inevitable about the name ... a forlorn sort of destiny that was immutably fixed by its sound, colour and texture. There was some organic affinity between the name and the substance, unchangeable. When I thought of Margaret I thought of bread, ordinary, mundane and plentiful. Julies and Rachaels were synonomous with a blue indolent sea, white foam spuming on the surface, full of mystery, promise and hope.

I must have said something disconcerting to my mother that summer. I don't remember what she said exactly, something portentous about Saint Margaret Mary. But it was the forlorn look in her eyes, reflecting the mundanity of her summers, of bread and ordinary things, that saddened me. So I didn't listen then but retreated into English class drawing rooms, with Oscar and Earnest, Emily and Heathcliff, and knew my destiny to be as indelible as my mother's impressions of Saint Margaret Mary.

Now Beethoven's Fifth moved through my mind; I thought of him inside in the blue room, and missed the melody that once gave feeling to our words. That was a long time ago. Long, long before I was born. And over the indolent sea I imagined a million tears glistening on the surface that had a texture like crushed ice. Somewhere in the distance a dog barked. I saw his face and heard sea water lapping. I said the name Macy and imagined the fat child running along the beach towards me, her flesh pink and taut from the salt water. I reached out my arms to her and the child in my womb moved. I knew that I would go to him and relent. This year I was different, older and wiser. I knew life to be about compromises, about bread, about love, about us. I turned slowly away from the window, confident of the path I had chosen. The sand this year seemed whiter, the sea a deeper shade of blue. Sure what's in a name I asked. I looked back and saw the swell. I heard the shrieks of a million Jews in the name Hitler, I heard the agonizing pleas of an Irish nation in the name Cromwell, I felt something warm and tender move inside me.

As I walked the length of the mobile, a great weight bearing me down, I knew that this child inside me had come together in that primeval throw. A tiny life-speck that had traversed the ages in the blood of her ancestors had borne the scars of a great famine which now echoed its last cry of remembrance. She too would live to listen to the eternal lessons that whispered in her blood and know that bread is blessed.

The Rembrandt Series

We have our own Rembrandt. A small one, to be sure, of doubtful attribution, but this is Dublin. An old man with a flowing white beard. I often used to visit it with McGrane, in the days before he was persuaded into early retirement. I never shared his lifelong obsession with the great painter, but I admired how he could relate that bearded old man to other bearded old men in galleries throughout Europe, in the cities where he passed his holidays. For the civil service he was an intellectual, which is why, I suppose, he never got farther than Assistant Principal, and why the delicate balance of his nerves forced him out by the time he was fifty.

I have his notebook in front of me, with its jottings on art and other matters, from here, there and everywhere. It is all I kept of him after we emptied out his flat near Leeson Street Bridge. It was the cleaning lady who found him, a day dead. I involved myself as an old friend and former colleague. He had been an only child, and there was little family left to come up from Sligo. I doubt if he had ever considered marriage, not because he was unattractive to women or they to him, but for his own reasons. There was, besides, the sweetness of his nature, as if something childlike had never been overcome in him by the rough and tumble of life the rest of us were accustomed to. He was, as they used to say around our corridors, one of nature's gentlemen.

The notebook. It has a hard blue cover and yellow pages, unlined. The handwriting, recognisably by the same person, transforms itself over the years from the uncertain scrawl of the first pages, to the devil-may-care lostness, the near illegibility of the last entries. In between, in varicoloured inks, are the steady and the shaky, the bits written in the silence of a hotel bedroom

somewhere in Europe, and the unsteady jottings made in more
public places. Trains, cafés. I know this for a fact, since I was
sitting opposite him in a compartment on the night express
from Amsterdam to Berlin, in September 1961, when the
earliest entry was made. I had just annihilated him in a chess
game in which my own aggression had surprised me, and the
flat landscape was darkening as we barrelled east towards
Hanover, two students on the long summer break, acquainting
ourselves with Europe. The blue cover, the yellow pages, are
what connect me now with that moment long ago, that
landscape. But the mental horizon of the notebook entry itself is
another matter.

September 1961
The Hague. Mauritshuis. Rembrandt self-portrait as a young
man. Buttoned up in white collar, waiting to be unbuttoned
by life. Energy, sensuality, in the full lips, the redgold hair.
20 September 1961
Amsterdam, Rijksmuseum. Rembrandt 'Jewish Bride'. Two
betrothed, in ceremonial cloth of gold. His hand on her
breast. Proprietorial, but with grace, gentleness. A study in
chastity. Her. Him. The wedding photo on our mantelpiece in
Sligo, that I grew up with. And later The Other One, brought
so brazenly in to join us for supper. A foursome, painfully
eating in silence. My childhood.

Later, T and I along the canals, the chill streets. Women in
the windows, tapping for attention. Acres of images, there on
the shelves. Girls copulating with dogs on drawing-room
floors. Horses in stables, being fellated. Man with a light
moustache and artificial tan asking me, as a fellow friend of
liberty, if I wish to see the harder stuff at the back of the shop?
As if the bottom had dropped out of my mind, and something
dark had risen, to unbalance me . . .

Listen, T laughs at me later, over soup with an egg floating
in it, if you lived where I live around Leeson Street, you'd see
it every night of the week. It's just that you're not used to it.

*

Strange years. The Berlin Wall had just gone up, while in Ireland, for the first time in decades, barriers were collapsing that had kept us from the rest of the world, in the claustrophobia of our extended childhood – mine, McGrane's and the nation's in general. I was able, for the first time, to drain a long glass with the girl who later became my wife, in the smoke of public bars, though she still had to resign her job in the civil service when she married me. A few years later, with new money and freedoms flowing into the country under Lemass, and we might not have bothered with the civil service at all. I might have gone into business, McGrane become something in the Fine Arts. But we were the last of the cautious generations. Old hungers and deprivations, or the memory of them transmitted through our parents, still pushed us into the safety of state offices.

Five years later, just before I got married, McGrane and I went to Paris for our last holiday together. Actually, there were three of us. Meagher, my deskmate in Finance, had decided to join us. We found ourselves in a cheap three-bedded room in a hotel in the Arab quarter, near Gare du Nord. Half my reason for coming had been to scout out Paris as a possible honeymoon destination, but I still remember that Easter as a time of constant rain which kept us off the streets, sprawled on our beds, getting on each others' nerves. As always when there are three, someone becomes the butt of the others' moods. That, as it turned out, was McGrane. I still regret some of the things I said to him then, considering his state of mind at the time, if I infer it correctly from entries like this:

27 April 1966
Paris, the Louvre. In the Rembrandt room, Hendrickje Stoffels, his mistress, the dominant presence. High breasts, strong legs, mature folds of the stomach – a nude Bathsheba, having her feet washed. Watched by Saskia, the dead wife, from the opposite wall, with the aged painter himself, all bulbous nose (overdrinking?) and incandescent skullcap, in his framed self-portrait, at a safe artistic remove.

The doomed triangle. Mother. Her endurance, back then.
And the Other One, brought into our house, making free in
front of me, with her big white body.

Later, the women behind Les Halles. Leaning in doorways,
out of the rain. Aged faces, beneath high bouffant hairstyles.
Plump bodies, in openwork tackle. We do the act together
two flights up a wooden stairs, as if time had stopped, in
frozen emotionless space. It is still there in my eyes when I
meet the others, back at the hotel. You're fucked up, that's
what you are, McGrane, T sneers at me. I'd do it myself, says
Meagher on the other bed, if it wasn't for the disease.

I admit it. Early marriage, as is so often said, brings on a kind of
smugness. Is it the freedom to indulge, as often as one likes, in
socially acceptable sex? Perhaps. But in a sense, those were
smug years for everyone in the country. There was money
around, a sense of optimism, infinite possibility. McGrane and I,
in our different areas, moved steadily up through middle
management, at times even refusing promotion because it
seemed to lead in the wrong direction, and because there was a
certainty that something better was just around the corner. We
bought property, I out in Dalkey, a house for when the first of
our three came along, and he the flat at Leeson Street Bridge
where he lived to the end of his days, his Old Master
reproductions on the walls, his shelves crammed with art
books.

At the time, though, I regarded him as a slightly pathetic
figure. I made remarks at the dinner table which my wife – my
then wife – sharply corrected. I see it all differently now, of
course, in the light of circumstances. But good times make you
blind. Only misfortune opens your eyes. For a while, McGrane
dropped out of the picture altogether. I had other friends,
politicals leaning to the left, espousing a nationalism I now feel
embarrassed by. Our high point, perhaps, was marching with
the crowd through Dublin, on that day of driving rain in
January 1972, to chant outside the burning façade of the
British Embassy. We looked at ourselves in the mirror of the

times, and saw that our hair had curled and grown an inch longer. McGrane, on a rare occasion our paths crossed, said I reminded him of a Rembrandt from the middle period – curliqued and complacent, as he put it, amid the trappings of prosperity.

It didn't last, for me or the country. Suddenly everything froze into the beginnings of that long disillusionment, that depression that has stayed with us, on and off, to this day. I got stuck at the same grade for over a decade, in a monotonous section, under an ill-disposed superior. My sense of myself began to buckle. Trapped, I womanised. At night, my car joined those streams of lonely lights cruising the leafy precincts off Leeson Street, seeking a fleeting moment of escape. All this might have passed had I not, one night, out of what reckless-ness or desperation I don't know, brought home the woman I am still with now. I didn't need the horrible scene with my wife, or the hellish weeks of moving out that followed, to lay bare the truth of things. One look in my children's eyes was enough to tell me the marriage was over.

In this, my blackest hour, McGrane reappeared like an angel of mercy. For six months I lived with him in the flat at Leeson Street Bridge, in that terrible interim between the collapse of my old life and what, if anything, was still to come. I got to know his art books well, the bachelor quiet of his rooms, his sweet nature. I got to know the stretch of canal above the bridge, and my face reflected in its weedy waters, the ripples merging with the new deep-set lines, the etchings of experience, of middle age. We lived together like two bachelors, not intruding on one another, forging the basis for that newer, later friendship, so full of warm unspokenness, that lasted until his death. And was it delicacy that took him off for two weeks towards the end of our time together, and left me and my lover the freedom of the flat at that so-important time for our subsequent life? I will never know, and his jottings in the blue notebook around that time cast no clearer light:

9 April 1981

London, National Gallery. Late Rembrandt self-portrait,
dated 1669, and portrait of Hendrickje wrapped in white
furs, strings of pearls. In both, maturity touched with the
prospect of death. They stare at each other, from opposite
walls, the 1669 painting a clear variant on its Paris
counterpart. Her plunging neckline, inch of cleavage. She
came into his life with a full cargo of experience.

Two months ago, turned forty. Visit Her often in Sligo now,
with Him and The Other One long gone. I know it clearly now
– the types I seek are Her in disguise. In first-floor rooms off
Drury Lane, in backstairs cubbyholes in Hammersmith and
Bayswater.

Honesty that comes with middle age. Compassion, towards myself as well. The loneliness replaced by self-
sufficiency. Is it work that saves me?

Rembrandts. It is the selves, the wife, the lover that matter
to me. Crises of sex and death, in those reds and golds, those
dark oils.

My logjam finally cleared in the early Eighties. I moved out, at
last, from under the shadow of my superior, into the grade of
Principal Officer. I started to travel more, and the terrible
blockages of the Seventies left me. I can't say things in the
country got much better, but by then I had stopped thinking of
myself as in any way political, other than in the matter of
pragmatic advice, the text of a reply to a parliamentary
question. I was a man doing a job, and trying to keep the rest of
himself on the rails.

Bit by bit, my private life resolved itself. After a spell when
financial ruin stared me in the face, my ex-wife and I came to an
arrangement, cold to be sure but manageable, that allowed me
to set up in a two-room flat in Monkstown with my woman
friend, as she prefers to be described. I had access, again, to my
own children, and the younger two forgave me. But the eldest
boy, Patrick, took the whole thing to heart, and though we see
each other from time to time and our conversations are always

civil, his nervous depressions, his problems at school and then at university, and his tendency now to solitude and introspection must be laid at my door.

Patrick was lost to me, but McGrane was restored. Once a week we met for lunch at Merrion Square, in the restaurant of the National Gallery. I got to know a little of our own painters – Jack Yeats, whose wild colours put me off, the Roderic O'Connor nudes, which I fancied discreetly, and the Walter Osbornes, which I could imagine on our walls out in Monkstown. Upstairs were the Dutch, their winter scenes and spicy tavern interiors, and that old, old man of Rembrandt. Only recently had I developed the patience to look and to contemplate, though with nothing of McGrane's practised eye. Sometimes, instead of looking at the paintings, I looked at McGrane looking at them. His hair was greyer than mine, and his face was lined. His gentleness, his lack of ambition, had got him no higher than Assistant Principal. It was as clear to his superiors as it was to me that his real life was elsewhere.

When the Berlin Wall came down, he was on the phone to me from his office. It was thirty years, almost, since we had been there, and the lid was off again. He was excited, for his own reasons. Art reasons. He was already planning a trip east. The Dresden Rembrandts were ones he had wanted to see, to get the complete picture. Not that Dresden had ever really been off-limits, but like many of our priest-ridden generation, he had held aloof, almost superstitiously, from entering what we had been told, too often perhaps, was enemy territory. The following autumn, when the fuss and euphoria had died down a little, he flew to Dresden, stopping over for a couple of days in Berlin. It is all there – what little there is – in the notebook, which still, despite all those years of odds and ends, has a third of its pages unused. The pages of unlived life, if life is measured by some natural span of seventy years instead of being a self-completed entity, as some say it is.

2 November 1990

Berlin, Gemaldgalerie. Rembrandt self-portrait as a young man, 1634. Society fop in feathered tricorn. Thirty years back, I didn't notice. But why should I have?

A Hendrickje, leaning in a window. Chaste presence. Heavy folds of red and gold, on a dark background. Companionship, not sex. A woman to turn to, after the end of marriage, before the last aloneness.

With time, understanding. With understanding, forgiveness.

4 November 1990

Dresden, Staatlich Kunstsammlungen Gemaldgalerie. Tricorned fop again, this time the young married successful Rembrandt. Self-portrait with wife, Saskia, turned pertly round as she sits on his lap in what appears to be a brothel or public house. Laughs, in complacent superiority, raising his longstemmed glass to us, as if in answer to our toast to the happiness and success of his life, its sex that is both licentious and licensed by society. Young marriage.

And that other Saskia, two frames away, dated 1641. Probably the last before her death. All life withdrawn to the eyes, and the hand extending, as if from beyond the grave, a flower. To Him who will continue, in another life.

Outside, freezing dusk of Middle Europe. City of stopped time. Trams clang past, through the gloom of Hapsburg streets. A solitary meal, to the tunes of a jazz band from fifty years ago. Innocent society, like our own, about to be thrown open to the big, bad world.

No nightlife. But I need no distractions now.

Freedoms began to blow our way too, at the edge of Europe. It was as if, after decades of dirt, the sandblasting of our public life was at last under way, even as the public buildings of the city I walked through daily were being blasted clean. New forces were gaining the upper hand. I was too old to be marked by them, other than the hope I might some day divorce properly, but I saw them at work in my children, as they moved unafraid through open worlds charged with energies no one could predict the future of. The younger two passed out of university into good jobs in the private sector. Patrick, after much hesitation, followed me into the civil service, where he remains, clever, enigmatic, inert, on a lower rung of the ladder, showing no ambition but covering the cost of his independence in the small flat he rents on Anglesea Road, living alone, as far as I can determine, and only in touch with his mother.

Overnight, McGrane aged terribly. It was the death of the only person who really mattered to him that brought it on. The benign remoteness at work, the dress-sense slipping, the inability to get things done. I had seen it all before, a thousand times over. The father, I knew by now, had been out of the picture for many years. I said what I could, given the reserve and discretion that governed our friendship, and what I said amounted to the suggestion that he take the lump sum and get out early, that his stint was done. I knew by the way he allowed me to pay the bill for lunch, something he almost never did, that he agreed with me the time had come to let go.

The last entry is no different from the others, a casual jotting, breaking off into nothingness. But was it any different for Rembrandt? I hold these written scraps to myself for the same reason, their sense of a life with its central tensions, through time and experience. What else has anyone to leave? Here it is, then, scribbled somewhere in the Rhineland, where he had gone two months after retirement, against the advice of his cardiac man, to chase down one more Rembrandt.

16 May 1994

Cologne, Wallraf-Rickartz Museum. A half-lit face, vanishing into the earth-brown night of its own background. Old, stooped, beaten, cowled in a gold wrap. On the face a half-smile, looking back at me. Asking for what? Forgiveness?

Reconciliation with the father (as in the Leningrad 'Prodigal Son'). Alright, then, I forgive Him, wherever He has got to, on this side of the grave or the other.

Humid night over Cologne. But the fresh breeze down by the Rhine. Wide water, threaded with river traffic, slipping past in the darkness. Trains coming in, glow-worms of light, across the trestle bridge to the station. Alone, but not lonely. At peace.

We all vanish.

He must have got the gas-ring lit, for it was still going when they found him. If he had got his saucepan of soup onto it before the attack came, the smell of burning would have brought someone sooner. But he was sitting on the kitchen chair, emptying the tin into the saucepan when it hit him, according to the inquest. Massive, instantaneous, fatal. He knew nothing, and he was still in the chair, head slumped over, when the cleaning lady let herself in next day.

One more thing. The tickets. Bus tickets, Metro tickets, train tickets, from all over Europe and Ireland too. Stuffed in the back of the notebook, interleaved among its pages. He collected them, and one or two of them I recognise. The faded rectangle of a Dutch Railways ticket to Berlin. The yellow stubs of Paris Metro tickets. And this one, Coras Iompair Éireann, fifteen years back, before our friendship resumed. It was Easter. We had bumped into each other at Connolly Station, exchanged politenesses. He was carrying a large, giftwrapped cake. He was going home, to Sligo. To his mother.

DAVID MURPHY

Lost Notes

Aengus's eyes momentarily widened with alarm. Too wrapped up in childish things to notice that I had steered off the road merely to park, his gaze returned to normal as the wheels of the jeep settled into the soft roadside.

Anyone watching would have thought we were to spend the afternoon in pursuit of fish. Rods in the air, tackle bags on shoulders, we left the jeep and walked north past uniform lines of fertilizer bags puffing out their chests with turf. To our left, a solitary snipe strained its neck and stared at us with beady eye and long, straight bill. It knew we were not fishing for fish, but then snipes know everything. I broke eye-contact with the bird and walked on. The wind rose, so did the land. I looked up, fearing showers, but the western sky was clear. The hill was steep, steeper for smaller feet.

'How much farther?' asked Aengus.

'Not far.'

I took his hand as we jumped over a turf-walled trench deep as a grave. Not easy for him; not easy for his father either, plodding over sods that concealed ankle-twisting holes. Bog-cotton waves prettily, beneath it the detritus of ten thousand years opens up. Not easy, rods in hand, bags around neck; balance came hard, breath came hard. A stream gurgled to our right. It should not have been to our right. I hoped it was not *that* stream, the one we should be keeping to our left. Crest of hill confirmed that it was.

A blue-brown lake slid into view as if some unknown god had pushed out a massive, panoramic drawer from the wedge of hill beneath our feet. The drawer contained a mirror sparkling between mountainy folds of heather. My eyes soaked it up. I knew that more than nature was at work here. Magic permeated the air. Not the cheap, illusory tricks of gameshow conjurors, but *magick*. I breathed in great lungfuls of it. It seeped, percolated, inebriated – in, through, up, down – filling my senses until I looked at the lake and knew for certain that down in its dark underbelly something waited.

Lough Natragh, *Loch na Tráigh*, Lake of Beaches. Two of them, white-sanded, lay at the eastern end. Small, separated by the merest spit of bogland, they might as well have been miles away. Correct stream, wrong side. To our right an impenetrable gorge; rhododendroned, steep-sided, not for adults, much less children.

Below us a marshy bank. Heads bowed predaceously, we slunk to within casting distance. A trout rose invitingly. I ignored the fish and cast out quickly. My red rose sank and snagged. I stood up straight and pulled it free. It snagged again – too many rushes spoiled the retrieve. Eventually, I reeled in my ragged flower and glared at the rushes. Then I looked at Aengus. He was waiting to be rigged up. I glanced at the rushes once more. 'Let's go,' I nodded to the western end. 'Looks clearer down there.'

He shrugged and sighed a little.

'Best find a good spot before settling down,' I added, consolingly.

Ours was a circuitous route because we had to climb another hill – a reed-infested quagmire down by the shore saw to that. Footholds were difficult; solidity a rare commodity in these parts. I heard Aengus's ragged breath behind me, matching his jerky steps. When I heard him struggle no more I looked and saw it was because he could not keep up. I waited for him. He soldiered on gamely, once or twice catching me with that familiar look which asked why do I have to do this, or, more to the point, why did *he* have to do it. I had no answer to that, so I turned around and marched on.

Ten paces later we reached the top of the hill. With no warning the ground jumped up a metre. Luckily, only one of my legs dive-bombed into the bog-hole, otherwise who knows what depths I might have plumbed. I pulled my sore and sodden leg out of the morass, then smiled ruefully at Aengus. I checked for damage to the rod and reel that fell with me, and looked down at the lake. 'Damn,' I muttered, cursing my eyesight. Rushes were abundant here as well. I should have seen them sooner. Now we would have to slog our way around the far side. 'There,' I used my wellington as a pointer while I emptied it of bogwater, 'about halfway along, there's a place we can cast from.'

My steps were more prudent now, not just so Aengus could keep up. The terrain was firmer on this side; huge folds of peat corrugated the land, making walking difficult. Stiffness slithered up my legs. Aengus's breath was still jerky – not entirely from exertion. 'Nearly there now,' I told him, knowing that his irritability was justified. I promised him milk and chocolate, and told him joyously that the water was free of reeds. Soon we reached the chosen spot. I checked my watch. Fifty-five minutes since we had stepped from the jeep.

I gave him sustenance, cast my line, and rigged him up. By the time he made his cast I looked for my bubble float – it was not there. Hope fluttered briefly, then sank – the wind had merely blown the float back to the shoreline.

We cast our bubbles with roses attached – he with three, I with two – for five minutes while he finished his refreshments. Then I broke the dreaded news: 'It's no use, Aengus, the elements are against us here. Our flowers keep floating back in. But down on those beaches, we'd have no problem – the wind would carry our bait out far.' With trepidation I mentioned this; I was fearful that all our setbacks might turn my son against that which I must teach him to do. But the sustenance strengthened him, and he reeled in compliantly. Anyway, he knew I could not rest until we were in the right place.

Ten more grudging minutes took us to where we should have been in the first place. Now we stood on a little white beach, wind at our backs. I rigged us both up, carnations this time – we had learned that rose petals disintegrated too readily in these conditions. Aengus cast ten metres; I twice that. Length did not matter as the wind carried our flowers out.

We stood on the beach for an hour casting and waiting. Occasionally our bait grew soggy and slipped beneath the surface. Wet carnation, slowly sinking, sometimes works – but not here. We tried different colours: pinks, reds, whites. Nothing took, but we were patient, knowing the object of our pursuit was wary, nervous, and utterly unpredictable.

Aengus no longer asked the time. He came under a spell and so did I – the beauty of our surroundings guaranteed it. No trace of man here; no looping wires, no roads, no fences. Only God's own mountain, lake and bog – and man and boy.

Time passed. The sky turned kinder. Clouds chased higher, whiter. No threat of rain now, the wind died as Lake of Beaches became Lake of Glass. Even birdsong ended. A stillness came. It took the wildness from the wilderness and replaced it with an anticipation not conducive to smalltalk. The world was pregnant now, and the time was near.

I lay my rod upon the sand, forgetting about the beautiful invitation sinking beneath my float. Nature, magick, prayer invaded my spirit. I felt renewed, at one with the universe, at peace with the world. Invisible to Aengus, I shook off the shackles of the world the way a newly-hatched mayfly shakes the water from her wings.

Aengus noticed it first. 'Father!' he shouted. 'Look!'

Nothing raises the weary spirit, nothing lifts the sinking heart, like the sight and sound of a line going taut. It whipped across the surface like a water boatman gone mad, shooting out into the middle of the lake, a tiny wake spreading behind it. The rod-tip strained before I could bend to reach; it jerked toward the water before my hand was on it. I grabbed the butt-end just in time, striking quickly. In my fingers that glorious feel, that momentary resistance which signifies but one thing. I reeled in furiously. It fought a little – a living force, an elemental weight – I could sense it thinking about diving back into the darkness. Then it surrendered.

My son stood to the wrong side, net in hand. He has a lot to learn. Wary of losing momentum, and my catch, I decided not to waste time asking him to move to the correct position. 'I'm going to beach it,' I yelled, knowing it was very close.

The lake exploded two metres out. Something golden broke the surface, then disappeared as I pulled hard on the rod and gave the reel one last, mad twirl.

It erupted onto the beach in a fiery cascade of water and sand. There it lay flat, gasping and helpless as a premature babe. Aengus dropped to his knees and huddled over it. Overwhelmed with curiosity, he scanned it up and down with great swoops of his eyes. Unable to take his gaze from it for an instant, he asked, 'What is it?'

I plucked the carnation from its golden-brown head and watched its azure wings stir a little. I lifted and separated them, blowing lightly. Aengus looked at me this time. With a great gulp of breath he demanded to know.

'Listen,' I whispered, and the wings began that frantic, flapping action of the newborn. 'Just listen,' I whispered again, and he did.

I gently lifted the golden creature from the sand. A tremor ran through it, ran through me. Aengus and I knelt on the shore, my arms offering a frail, nascent gift to the fading light of day. I stretched up my hands to the sky above, to the red orb of the sun, and to the stars beyond. I bent my head in worship. Aengus instinctively, respectfully, did the same. In the palm of my hand a tiny heart beat.

The weight lifted from my palms and soared into the sky. More than rhythm to its wings now, the creature sang as it flew. There was music. Sacred music. At once new, and forever ancient, it filled the mountains with notes of serene beauty. It redefined the space between mountains. Its resonance plumbed the depths of lakes, rebounded below, and echoed back up with a cosmic sonar that broke the surface, making our hearts tremble. Its chords would have felled trees, if there had been trees here. A song to die for, it made the setting sun go slowly supernova until its burgeoning orb reached out, finger-pointing us with bright, red rays. The ground trembled beneath us, the

lake shimmered, as if a giant plectrum had come from
somewhere and played the landscape.

All too soon it was gone, free, released. The bearer of
trebles to make us tremble, of bass notes to touch the hiding
places of our minds, had soared so high its notes were lost in
cloud. The music faded, the chorus ended, and the sun's
glorious rays diminished as the sun itself slipped behind the
mountain.

'I know what it is!' Aengus got off his knees and jumped up
and down, as if jumping might bring him nearer to the sky and
he might hear the lost notes again. 'It's a song!' he yelled. 'We
caught a song!'

Reluctantly from Loch Natragh we trudged. Mindful of
bogholes, mindful of music beyond compare, we made our way
to the jeep without mishap. Aengus was full of mountains, lakes
and exotic things that sing as they fly. In his eyes I saw a look
which told me he would spend his life forever in search of that
which we released today. For that I was glad, for someone will
have to take over from me when I am gone. I knew then that
Aengus would be that person, and that is as it should be, for he
is my son.

But ·we were back in the realm of humankind, with all its
frailty and distractions. We drove on tar steamrolled long ago,
past electricity wires long since hung, down to a wider road.
There we joined a stream of red tail-lights wandering aimlessly
through a concrete environment. We came at last to a
driveway. No lakes or mountains here, but at least our home is
surrounded by a rampart of broadleafed trees.

Aengus ran to the figure in the doorway, the story gushing
from him. 'We caught a song!' he yelled. His mother smiled and
patted his head. Then she took him into the kitchen, heated his
supper, and listened patiently while I went out to the yard to put
the rods away. By the time his story was over I was bolting the
shed. Before I had time to turn I heard the discreet click of the
backdoor latch. My wife stepped out. She checked that the latch
was secure before walking across the yard. I knew from her

look that she had news. I do not know how she knows, yet she always does and she is never wrong.

'There was a suicide off the railway bridge,' she whispered. 'A young girl.'

'When?' I asked, knowing her answer.

'Before sunset.' She put her hand on my shoulder and lifted her head. Together we looked up. Clouds had gone and there were stars.

I like to think a new star shone that night, the light of a soul released. But there were too many lights to count. I like to think that the music Aengus and I heard out at the lake was played by Gabriel on his horn, or by angels on their harps, and that the vocals were the joyous notes of a soul singing in celebration. I silently thanked the stars for giving me the key to unlock these tortured souls, and I put my arm around my wife. We stood there stargazing, secure in the knowledge of our destiny and our task, and secure in the knowledge that there was someone to follow us. Enough for us now to hear him sweetly singing in the kitchen, and enough for him, at his tender age, to think we are merely the fishers of songs.

URSULA DE BRÚN

Life in a Cracked Cup

The party was in full swing when the lights suddenly went and they were plunged into darkness. Undaunted, Joe's da, well on his way to being pissed, struck up 'One Fine Day' from Madame Butterfly – his only claim to erudition; most of the time he listened to racing results and read cowboy novelettes. An omen, Joe thought, as consternation surged around him.

'Would someone check the bloody fuses?'

He peered into the hallway. One of his uncles was holding matches to the fuse box as, one after the other, they extinguished themselves on his thick, awkward fingers. An omen, Joe thought again, refusing to be drawn into the rising hysteria.

'Da, shut up, will ya!' His sister Liz's voice screeched a major crescendo over the babbling and gabbling relations.

'I knew it,' she whined, the shadow of her fiancé hovering behind her. 'I knew something would ruin my engagement party.'

Joe sighed. Typical of Liz. Everything boiled down to just one thing – herself. He didn't bother to point this out, Liz had enough of a skin collection under her nails, garnered from him over years of squabbling. And she was at it now, squabbling with anyone who dared to squabble back. He lounged against the sitting-room wall. They were a family of squabblers who wore themselves out watching each other's every move, every word, every nuance, ready to pounce. It bothered him to know that.

He felt his way towards the kitchen, wondering where his ma was. These things were her territory – fuses, plugs, banging the telly in just the right way to get a decent picture. She'd usually arrive, elbowing them all aside, full of purpose. He pulled open a kitchen drawer; she'd know where to find a fuse, if there was a fuse. His hand was sifting cold castors from the old suite, twine, loose, crumb-coated birthday candles, when the lights suddenly came back on and there, just outside the back door, was his ma in the arms of Uncle Robert, who wasn't really an uncle but a friend of his da's from way back.

It was Uncle Robert's fault that he'd been doing all this 'thinking' lately. Uncle Robert had got him on the Fás course. He knew someone, who knew someone who bumped his name up the line, or so his da had said. His da loved Uncle Robert: now, obviously, so did his ma.

He saw that her face and neck were flushed and before she could look into the kitchen he slunk out, bumping into Liz.

'It was a bloody fuse,' she said. 'You said that, didn't you, love?'

Her fiancé, the 'Wimp of Walkinstown', gave her one of his mealy-mouthed smiles and wrapped his arms around her, making her giggle and softening her sharp face.

'Where's Ma?' she asked.

'I'm here,' his mother said, coming into the hall. 'I was out at the rubbish.'

Oh, yeah, Joe thought, just the word to describe Uncle Robert. He looked down at his mother. She gave him a quick dart of a smile. There was no indication in her soft brown eyes that she knew he knew.

In the sitting room, his da was still singing, only by now it was 'Kevin Barry'. 'In Mountjoy Jail one Sunday Morning . . .'

Who'd end up in the 'Joy,' he wondered, if he told his da what he had seen? Decisions. Decisions. Decisions. A few months ago he'd have had no problem about what to do. He'd have gone bald-headed for Uncle Robert, defended his ma's honour; torn her from his arms, frog-marched a terrified Robert into the sitting room to face his da.

At least, that would have been the fantasy. But now, thanks to Uncle Robert and the Fás course, he was thinking differently. Actually, if he was honest, he was just thinking, not something that was often indulged in at home. Too much thinking can get you into trouble, his da always said. Maybe he was right: Robert could be classed as a thinker.

Joe bit the inside of his lip. Was that it? The fruit of Robert's thinking? Was that Robert's 'Master Plan'? To put them all, his da, Liz, the twins, on a Fás course, learning to think, so that he could have his way with Ma? It was a worrying thought and when Uncle Robert finally reappeared and poured his mother another vodka and orange, he gave him what he hoped was his surliest look.

He had given that same look to the Personal Development woman the first day she had arrived in the classroom. They had said nothing to him about having to delve into his 'innards'. He was being paid to learn to search for a job, even when everyone knew there wasn't one. He hadn't minded that, a few bob was a few bob. But then Norrie had arrived.

She sat them all in a circle and made them breathe. In, out, slowly. Some of them sniggered, making comments like how breathing would help them in their extra-curricular activities – like riding. She never batted an eyelid, just sat, waiting, until eventually everyone just got fed up and went on with their breathing. The first time Joe did it, it made his head light; but after a couple of sessions he found he liked it, not that he dared admit it.

He did it now, the breathing, trying to calm himself. It wasn't every day your ma 'got off' with someone. She was cool about it, he'd give her that; cool enough to puck his da for shoving cocktail sausages into his mouth three at a time.

Joe looked around the room. Here they all were laughing, joking, drinking, celebrating (outwardly anyway) the engagement of Liz to Tommy Grehan, shoe salesman. Everyone killed pretending how great it all was; nobody mentioned the 'bump'. Even with fancy, glittery leggings and a matching, oversized top, Liz looked exactly what she was – pregnant. Another disaster for the Byrnes. But then, what did they expect, Joe wondered. His ma and da were more ill-fated than Anthony and Cleopatra; and a lot less in love. A thought washed icily over him: no wonder his ma was cool, she was pleased about Uncle Robert's kiss.

Joe looked over at his father. Someone had given him a big cigar and he was mimicking a rich plantation owner. Unlike Robert, his da considered anything not connected with the pub or the bookies as 'women's things'. Joe wasn't much into women himself. His dream didn't stretch to marriage or anything, just one of those non-existent jobs so he could earn enough to travel with the lads for World Cup '94, providing, of course, that Jack delivered the goods. Otherwise, he'd go to Ibiza.

'What are you so serious about?' His ma was smiling up at him.

He shrugged and smiled back. He was her favourite, he knew that. And he loved her too though he could never see himself telling her. When he was working last year he'd put a few extra pounds in her wages one week. She had made a right song and dance about it.

'Son, I think you've given me too much this week.'

'I didn't,' he'd said gruffly, mainly because he was embarrassed, but also because she had this habit of going on and on, grateful, like an abandoned puppy who finally got someone to pet her.

She was still beside him, smiling. 'It's going well, isn't it?'

He nodded, feeling a lump in his throat. 'I have to go to the toilet,' he said.

He took the stairs two at a time. It was as if sometimes her feelings surged out of her body and poured all over him. He knew she was sad a lot of the time. He'd watch her at the stove, jiggling the chip pan, a real 'fed up' look on her face, a droop to her shoulders. She didn't seem to hear them sometimes, not even when the twins banged the table with their forks demanding their dinner. She was away somewhere in her head and nobody missed her. It annoyed him that most of the time nobody really saw her. She was just Ma. I'm never getting married, he told himself as he shut himself into the cool and quiet of the bathroom.

*

The toilets were where half the Fás class disappeared to when they had Norrie and Personal Development but Joe didn't join them: he found himself curious. For two weeks she had been having them look at their family dynamics – not a pretty sight from where he was sitting. Then, yesterday, they were back in a circle, eyes closed, and she was talking quietly.

He liked her soft voice. It was the first time he'd come across someone who knew they'd be heard without roaring at anyone; it fascinated him.

'Picture a beach,' she said. So he saw himself on Dollymount.

'Feel the white sand under your feet . . .'

He'd had to move himself to the beach in the Bacardi ad.

'Palm trees are waving in the warm breeze that caresses your skin . . .'

He shifted in his chair. Were they supposed to be nude? All of them?

He sneaked a look over at Rosie. Her eyes were closed and there was a soft smile on her face. Rosie nude. On a beach . . .

'You walk to the water's edge. The beach stretches for miles and miles on either side of you. In front is the ocean. This is the Ocean of Life . . .'

He felt his gut tensing.

'There are people on either side of you for as far as you can see . . .'

He couldn't visualise Rosie anymore. He felt alone.

'You are holding a container so that you can take from the Ocean of Life. What kind of container are you holding?'

His heart began to thump.

'Is it a jug? A bathtub? A swimming pool?'

He felt panic grip him. He was holding, no, clutching a cracked cup.

He had gone home depressed. There was a hammering on the bathroom door. One of the twins thumped up and down outside.

'Hurry up, Joe, I'm bursting.'

He didn't want to go back into the hot, smoke-filled sitting room so he let himself out of the back door to get some fresh air. And there she was, outside again over near the shed. His eyes scanned the garden for a possible skulking Uncle Robert but his ma was alone, staring up at the stars. If she'd heard him come out into the yard, she didn't acknowledge it.

He watched her, feeling a queer tug around his heart. She hadn't stopped going since the day before yesterday. Cooking, cleaning, organising everyone so that tonight would be a success. She wore a new dress that made her look quite slim and younger looking. She looked lovely and it dawned on him that none of them had told her. Maybe Uncle Robert had; maybe that's why he'd got the kiss from her.

He wondered what kind of a container she had had at the Ocean of Life when she was his age. Was it a mixing bowl she had? Or was it a pipe-line? He felt his chest tighten. What if it had been a pipe-line feeding her dreams of love and laughter and somebody had turned the tap off, and the supply had been slowly cut off, until there was only the merest drop to keep her going.

He felt another surge of panic; if he ever managed a pipe-line, would someone turn his off too?

He coughed. 'You'll get your death out here, Ma.'

She didn't answer so he lit a cigarette, sure she'd swing around and tell him it was a disgusting habit and a waste of money, but she didn't do that either. It struck him that it was like the fight had gone out of her, and yet it hadn't.

'What are you doing out here?' His da was standing in the light of the kitchen, weaving from side to side. 'They want to do a toast or something.'

'I'll be in in a minute,' his ma said quietly, still not turning around.

His father was about to argue so Joe steered him back towards the noise.

Uncle Robert sat on a straight-backed chair, hands hanging between his knees, like a deserted island in a sea of confusion. Guilt, Joe thought, resisting the urge to place a hand on his shoulder and tell him he had nothing to be guilty about; he'd put a sparkle in ma's eyes, a stillness in her body.

Hands wedged into his jeans, Joe refused a limp sandwich from his auntie May.

'Suit yourself,' she said.

He only wished he could. He looked around at his family. Liz was hanging out of Tommy, her hairstyle slowly caving in, a soppy smile on her face. The twins were in a corner surrounded by plates of cakes, laughing at some private joke. His da stood alone; bewildered over the choice between having to make a toast or start up another song. His ma was still outside.

He felt very much removed from them all. He was being slowly cut adrift and no one even noticed. They still thought he wanted what they wanted but he didn't. Not that he knew what he wanted; not exactly. All he knew was that he suddenly and desperately wanted to stand at the Ocean of Life with something more than a cracked cup.

MOLLY McCLOSKEY

Mythology

It was the week the black cat died that we almost made a go of it. We found her on the road, an untrafficked stretch of laneway in the country, not far from home. We were passing in the car and Charlie slowed down. I saw only the small white slippers of her paws, crossed daintily, and knew. Her blood had stained the tar and she appeared to have been dragged a short distance.

I thought we were safe here, I said to Charlie.

We have had four pets, Charlie and I. Three of them are dead. We aren't people whose animals will limp around our feet and trip us up. Old, feeble, and signs of something lasting.

Charlie got the spade from the shed and headed back down the road to where the cat was lying. The spade was propped against his shoulder and Charlie's chin hung towards his chest. Like he was heading off to some forlorn day of communal work.

Afterwards, we cried and stretched out on the sofa together. He seemed like a hero to me then, attending to the more painful and grotesque aspects of our lives, so that I wouldn't have to. Saying to me in the car: don't look.

I really believed there was still a chance.

In the days that followed, we were kinder to one another. Attending to the smaller, more easily forgotten needs. Remembering things. We talked about the last cat we'd buried, the white one. They'd given her a shot at the vet's and rather than have her die on the strange cold table, we took her home and laid her on her favourite rug. Then we sat there and watched the life just leave her.

With speed that surprised us, she stiffened into a C-shape, her body locked and hard as wood. I carried this curl of an animal up the back yard and placed her in the hole that Charlie'd dug. We'd only just moved in, away from the city, our minds full of plans. That was one of our first memories in the new house. But we needed better memories than that.

Rain, like needles, clacks against the window, and Charlie and I make love as best we can. With manners and a mindless attention to detail. In textbook terms, we 'please' one another. We don't need inspiration or passion or even much interest, just that we be physically present, that we perform with precision. I lie there wondering if there is anything else in the world quite like sex, the way it drinks in insult and transforms it.

Around us in the room: a coat rack, a wicker chair, a stack of magazines layered in dust, wardrobes. This bed I've slept in, solid underneath me. The relentless innocence of our objects. I look at Charlie. Already, I see, he has acquired that sad beauty peculiar to people to whom we are lying.

This is where nostalgia starts. Because, of course, we haven't always been like this, and it's worth keeping that in mind. In the slack, grey periods that are coming at us faster and faster, the only place we can go for comfort is the past. Where had we been happy? When? What were we doing?

There is a lake in our town, and the sea, too. A time we made an effort. Raking the sand for cockles or trawling in the shallows for mussels. We liked to turn into the wind and get the full smell of the sea. This is an image I've held onto. Charlie with his sleeves rolled up, his thick arms submerged, wrenching a shell from a rock. Talking over his shoulder to me about wine and butter. Says he can taste it already. He kisses me before we head up to the car. There is a tang of salt water off his lips, and his unshaven face feels like a burn against my skin. We look in our bags. We're all excited. Like kids with a booty of Hallowe'en candy. It was silly, but that was how we were. Anything we shared, we treasured.

If we can just get back there, we think, we'll be OK. But whatever it is we're counting on is failing us. The bright patches that used to stretch for months have become pinpoints of light.

And in between, there's just this dull grey. What is disappearing is a sense of contrast. There are no seasons, no peaks, no valleys, no midnight sun, nothing.

It isn't what we say that troubles us. We can clutter up the air with words to keep other words out. There are household chores to be divided, home improvements when the weather cools. We hang out laundry and marvel at the hot, hot sun which is melting the tar on the roads, the sense of mirage everywhere. We make dates to meet friends and talk about a long break in November. A nice hotel, somewhere south of here. As long as we can plan, that means we're safe. Once we start looking only backwards, it'll be over.

A wind has risen in the valley, relentless and hounding. It forces its way into our thoughts, so that we speak of cold and warm air pockets, the long unbroken flight of condors, hot air balloons and hang gliding. Anything at all. We're out, having a drink. I look at Charlie's profile. If you've ever seen an American nickel, the head's side, then you'll know what I'm talking about. A set jaw. Strength. I look at Charlie and what I see is his dogged approach to each day, his stoic ironing of shirts, the way the world really does baffle him. How he wakes up angry too many mornings. I feel like reaching out and touching him. There is the thigh I once coveted, the shoulder, the forearm, between his legs. This is the worst of it, feeling the residuals of love, like embers it's too late to stoke.

And yet, there are times we brave it. Eat dinner by candlelight or take a picnic to the beach. We spread our wares on the blanket and focus on the sailboats stabbing the horizon. Sundays, we go for long walks through the woods. We do what is expected of us and await the desired effect. But these acts are forms of cruelty. They only serve to expose what's gone missing. If we can't love each other in the moonlight, what chance have we got?

This morning, we're drinking coffee outside. Charlie looks at the sky and says to me, I think it's going to be OK. He's talking about the weather – the day – but we both catch his unintended meaning. He smiles, sheepishly, almost pleased with himself. I can't help it. Charlie, I say, do you remember Croyde? That beach that stretched for miles?

I remember that beach alright, he says.

I'm not talking about the beach.

Then what're you talking about?

Afterwards, when we went inside. Do you remember that?

Should I? Charlie says, studying the sky again.

Well, I do. I wanted to make love before we went out. Just for a change. You know what you did, you scoffed at me, like I'd made a corny joke. And then when you saw how angry I was, you tried to pacify me. You said we'd make love when we got home that night. And I said, We'll be drunk when we get home.

Charlie shakes his head and doesn't look at me. I'm not sure I remember that, he says.

We weren't even married very long, Charlie. We were supposed to be lovers, not people who found the idea embarrassing.

I wait, to see what his response is.

I was reading in the paper there yesterday, he says finally, where people who don't know they're HIV positive live longer than people who get early treatment.

Imagine, I say.

I don't pursue it. I'm not interested in reminiscing. It's just that I want him to know. I want it entered in the record. That the turning points were times he doesn't even remember.

Our neighbour, Mrs Harrington, is lamenting the assault of weeds on her garden paths. She is passionate on the subject of their eradication. Charlie goes to our shed and roots out the sprayer. Mrs Harrington straps the cylinder gamely on her back, and in a hunched-over position, shoots poisonous liquid along the ground. She wears a mask and sunglasses, and looks like she is engaged in some sort of bizarre, not altogether legal activity. When she returns the sprayer to us, it is with an air of great triumph. Why, I wonder – when her house falls down around her, her husband drinks and goes missing, her children cry – does she spray the weeds?

Simple, Charlie says. Control.

I notice: our own garden let go, clothes flapping on the line for days, that I don't often look out the windows anymore; the little grave with the stone to mark it, that one of the first things we shared in this house was death. In bed, we try not to touch. I keep quietly, stiffly to my side, and he to his. Making love has become an idea as strange to us as violence.

We are stretching away from one another, pulling painfully apart, like a string of taffy. The space between us elongates and disfigures, and yet still manages to contain elements of us. It can accommodate things we never thought it could. Failure. Other people. White lies. Our bedroom doors, now separate and closed, like two combatants facing off across a hall-way.

We take gentle stabs at the tangibles. What's yours, what's mine. What you have come to love, what I have. Who can bear to give up what. It should feel concrete, material. But it feels more unreal than real, as though we are speaking in a foreign tongue in which neither of us excels, or using profanity, when we don't even feel anger. We shake our heads as though we really can't believe it.

It is this meek acceptance of our failure, our almost benign embrace of it, that seems most profane. But that was always our problem, that we were elderly before our time, that the silence between us was a silence we hadn't earned.

There are boxes heaped in the spare room, waiting to be filled. Charlie and I, we pretend not to see them. We pretend we have not collaborated in this most odious task of gathering cardboard cartons from the supermarket. It shames us to see our suffering reflected in such ordinary acts. Every time I go to fill them, I stop.

All around, there are reminders. Roads it seems I'll never drive without thinking of him. There are buildings, butcher's shops, wrought-iron gates, bends in the road, lay-bys in which we stopped to view the exceptional days. There are directions of wind, times of day, foods on the shelf, animals. And water, always water.

There is the tall tree, the island, the jetty, the buoy, the rusty red and white boat, not moored where it was last year. The lake itself, his dream of living on it, the way I'd seen him slalom through it on one ski, cutting an arc of spray behind him like the plume of an old ink pen.

All these things belong to our mythology.

One evening, while mowing the lawn, Charlie discovers a plum tree in an overgrown corner of the yard.

Look, he says, what we have.

He is standing in the doorway, cradling plums in his arms, like some kind of windfall. A few of them drop and hit the floorboards in the hall, so ripe their skins split on impact.

Get a bowl, he says, and we'll pick them before they rot.

The sky is searing red on this particular evening. Charlie leaves the lawnmower humming low on the grass while we gather plums. More than we can eat. As we hoard them, greedily, I know that they will rot, most of them, in their bowls on the kitchen counter. But for a brief moment, we feel rich, in love again. We feel there is a chance. There is joy, fruit, a late summer sky. Tears smarting in my eyes.

I go back inside and dutifully wash plums, sorting out the bruised ones, and picking a few fleshy ones to eat. I sit down at the window and watch Charlie push the lawnmower back and forth in the fading light. That old urge to touch him. That pinpoint of light. And then it's gone. I can see it. I see how tired and preoccupied he looks, and I know what he knows. That nothing is ours anymore. We don't have anything.

JULIA O'FAOLAIN

Rum and Coke

I expect at any minute to hear from the nursing home where my wife is due to go into labour. They thought I was making her nervous, which is why they asked me to leave. I can't blame them. After all, what could they know of our – what? Anomalies? So now I sit by the phone, thinking of the boy – we know it's to be a boy – and of how he'll be called Frank in memory of my father: Senator Leary, whose death, to quote the obituaries, was such a sore loss to his country. Soon there will be a new Frank Leary to take his place. Symmetry and *pietàs*. He'd have liked that.

He laid out his principles for me on the day, not long after my nineteenth birthday, when I took up my duties as summer barman at the Moriarty Castle Hotel. He'd got me the job. The Knights sometimes held functions there, indeed were holding one that weekend, which was why he drove me down. My mother came in her own car and stopped off for lunch. She was *en route* to Galway where the League to Save the Unborn Child (SUC) had organized a rally. She's one of their officers.

While she settled my father into his room I introduced myself to the head barman, who said he'd show me the ropes in the lull after lunch. Then back came my parents and my father asked me to pour him a drink: Coke and rum. That surprised me because of his being a teetotaller. He grinned and so did my mother: a benedictory, parental grin. Declan's an adult now was what it decreed; then he made his speech. You could sum it up to sound like hypocrisy – until you remembered about *that* being the tribute vice pays to virtue. Anyway, his principle was simple – although its workings turn out not to be! He said he wanted me, during his stay at the castle, to do what trusted

barmen around the country had been doing for years: slip a
sizeable snort of rum into his Coca Cola but charge whoever
was standing drinks for the coke only. Later, he would drop by
and pay the difference. The common interest came before that
of the individual. And he, a man in the public eye, must neither
alienate voters nor weaken his own influence for good. What
the eye didn't see didn't matter.

'But Father, surely drinking wouldn't alienate many Irish
people?'

'As a politician I can't afford to alienate any. For the sake of
the causes I support.'

As this was one of the times when the Right-to-Lifers were
making a push to stop creeping Liberalism, I guessed he meant
them. 'But what,' I objected, 'about your conscience?'

'That,' he cut me off, 'is between me and my God.' Then he
said again about the general good coming first. 'Abide by that
rule and you can do what you like. Obedience,' he smiled,
'makes for freedom!' And raised an eyebrow.

I laughed.

He believed in having a sense of humour. The obituaries
quoted him on how disarming it could be. It was, he liked to say,
a tempering mechanism. Also, that conservatives must strive to
surprise and dazzle so as to steal the opposition's fire.

It's been odd reading about this clever, shifty man. To be
sure, some of the reminiscences went back to his schooldays –
and how could he have stayed the same? Ironically, though,
change was a bogey of his. One writer described him as 'a man
whose unwavering aim was to preserve on our island a state
faithful to the more orthodox teachings of the Roman Catholic
Church.' To do this, as he told me in the Moriarty Castle bar,
you had to fight unethical innovation. Unchristian practices.
Unseemly publications. You needed counter-seductions. Wit
and paradox. Nonchalance. Panache.

No-one denied he had *that*. Too much? Maybe. Maybe he
ended up seducing and bamboozling himself? *I* certainly can't
be trusted to judge. He was fifty-seven but looked younger, in a
Cary Grant sort of way: silver wings to his hair, white teeth, big

frame, flat belly. He had a good tailor and could, as the saying goes, charm the birds off the trees – or, discreetly, pull birds. I was proud of him but apprehensive as to what he expected of me – or believed in really. My eldest brother has for years been a missionary in Ecuador, and it would be a mistake to suppose this pleased my father. According to him, most missionaries nowadays were crypto-Communists. Indeed, now that the official Communists had collapsed, they *were* the last Communists. Priests – which may sound odd from a militant layman – were dangerously gullible and monks worse. He'd sent me and my two brothers to school to the Benedictines with advice to take what they taught us with a pinch of salt. He wanted us to have a grounding in religion, yes, but also to be able to take the world on at its own game. And for this, the Benedictines, he was sorry to say, were insufficiently robust. They were considered classier than the Jesuits, but lacked the nous to spike their Coke with rum. Or their red lemonade with whiskey, which I should also be prepared to serve. Likewise tonic with vodka. Doubleness was all. I guessed that the job as barman was meant to sharpen me – and was happy about this. I had been reading Stendhal and thought of Moriarty Castle in terms of his great houses where raw young men learn amatory wit. My second brother was in Australia. As an uncle of ours put it, he and my father were too alike, and two cocks in one barnyard upset the pecking order. My sisters were married, so on whom could my father's hopes focus if not on me? I might have resented this if I had been surer of it. As it was, I was desperate to impress him.

*

I've rung the nursing home again. They're to let me know just as soon as I'm needed – and are undoubtedly being patient because of whose son I am. In this city you are never anonymous, so may as well reap the benefits, since there are drawbacks too. It's odd: I haven't thought so much about him for months. Not since the last panegyric was read and folded

away. Maybe when the new Frank Leary is hogging attention
I'll forget the old one? Come to think of it, I'll *be* the 'old' Leary
then. Old, worldly and not quite twenty-one! Maybe, God help
me, I'll burst out in my fifties!

*

The drawbacks? Well with women for a start. Feminists. His
name was a red rag to them, so I could never take things on
their own terms. Every choice meant being with or against him
and I always chose to be 'with'. I had – I admit – a girlish
admiration for his manliness and saw women as rivals.

Away from home though – I spent three summers abroad,
learning modern languages – all this changed and by my
second week in Italy, when I was fifteen, I was sharing a tent
with a Danish girl. The tent was a tiny thing and dyed bright
orange so that hunters would not shoot in our direction. I loved
that: colour of flame and folly! I was over the moon to be out
from under my Irish camouflage. Our parents, of course,
thought we were in a hostel, but we simply moved out and after
that I swear it was the difficulty of communicating – we talked
pidgin Italian to each other – which made it easy to be together.
I conclude that the answer to that old conundrum as to which
language Adam and Eve spoke in Paradise may be 'none'. Not
being able to ask questions eliminates the tripwires of shyness,
class, and wondering whether what you feel for each other is
love or lust. As for the one about using 'artificial contraceptives', Vinca was on the pill and had a container with a
dial which clicked forward a notch each time she took one.
Streamlined and sage, it made me glad I couldn't tell her of the
preserved foetus which my mother's colleagues toted to their
lectures on the ills the flesh is heir to. Silence was golden in our
Umbrian olive grove – and we left chatter to the crickets.

But to return to Moriarty Castle: as I wasn't yet, strictly
speaking, on the staff, my father asked if it would be all right for
me to sit down to lunch with my mother and himself. Later,
such privilege would be off limits, like the swimming pool and

the nine-hole golf course. Teasingly, he made me try a rum and Coke.

Then my mother left and, as he and I strolled back through the lobby, he introduced me to the receptionist, a Miss Sheehy.

'This is my son, Declan,' he told her and she gave me a funny look. I told myself that I was imagining it and took her hand in a forthright grip. She was one of those slim, quivery girls who shy like deer and have a curtain of dark hair for hiding behind. I guessed her to be my age or maybe a bit older. More importantly, she was a beauty. My Stendhalian summer partner? Why not?

Later, after the barman had shown me how to mix drinks, I came back to the lobby. She was still on duty.

'How does it feel to be the son of a famous father?'

This annoyed me, so I countered with 'How does it feel to be a knockout beauty?'

That got a blush. I walked off regretting the balkiness of words. With Vinca and her summery successors I had rejoiced in their absence. Maybe it was auricular – Christ, *there's* a word! – confession which poisoned them for me? All that talk of 'bad' thoughts. Maybe I should become an explorer and live in the Amazon jungle: steamy heat, warm mud, bare-breasted Indian girls and, above all, no chat! I kept thinking of Miss Sheehy though. That hair had a tremulous life to it. Like seaweed. Now I'd got myself uselessly excited and should maybe take a run around the tennis courts – unless they were off limits too. I wondered, was Miss Sheehy?

As it happened, I had no time to find out because carloads of Knights started arriving and soon the bar was abuzz and I was kept busy. I wondered whether the Castle chapel was off limits to staff too? This seemed unlikely, so maybe I'd be able to watch them next day at their mumbo jumbo, robing and disrobing, in imitation of the Crusaders donning armour to fight the forces of darkness and fornication. I wasn't sure how close my father's connection with them was. They favour confidentiality and infiltration and he might be their man in the Senate. He didn't appear in the bar.

I finished work after midnight. There was no sign of Miss Sheehy. I fell on my bed and slept.

I was awoken before daylight. My mother wanted me on the 'phone. Or rather, it turned out, she wanted my father. There was some decision to do with the rally which only he could take. Neither she nor the other Pro-Life ladies took decisions. They were there to make it look as though *women* were opposing the feminists but were puppets really. She apologized for waking me but said she'd been ringing him since last night.

'Your father's not answering his phone,' she told me. 'It's off the hook. I think maybe he knocked it off inadvertently and now he'll miss all his calls.'

So I pulled on some clothes, took the lift to the guests' part of the hotel, and arrived at his door just as Miss Sheehy emerged from it – or rather just as she started to emerge, for when she saw me she ducked back in. That was hard to misinterpret and froze me in my tracks. I mean if she had said 'Hello Declan' and that she had been answering a room-service call, I would have believed her. I would have accepted any plausible story because I was thinking of her in terms of my own designs, not his – but, instead, she turned tail on seeing me. For perhaps a minute, I stood transfixed. Then, as I turned to go, out she bobbed again.

'Declan, can you come here, please. Your father wants you.'

I bolted. Unthinkingly. Or rather what I was thinking was that I didn't want to know any more of his secrets.

Back in my room I started making faces at my mirror and told the clown grimacing back that I was a prize ass. Obviously he was ill and she *had* been answering a room-service call. Why, though, had she bobbed away? Clown, so as to tell him his son was outside. Clown, clown! What would they both think of me now? Worldliness, where were you? I had failed the test! Fallen at the first fence. Could my father, I even wondered, have set the thing up deliberately? I had heard of British Foreign Office candidates being tested like this on country-house weekends.

I wasn't surprised by the knock on my door. It was Miss Sheehy to say that, just as I'd guessed, he was ill. Alarmingly so. Her manner had grown agitated and she was asking for my help. 'He can't walk and we can't have the doctor finding him in my room.'

Her room? I was so flustered that we were at its door before I remembered that, just now, they had been in his. How had he got here?

She brushed away the question. 'Look, he's passed out. We should get a doctor. It could be serious! A heart attack even! But he can't be found *in my room!*' Her voice had an edge of hysteria.

She opened her door and there he was on the carpet. I saw the urgency then. Jesus, I thought. Christ! As far as I could tell, his pulse was all right. Or was it? I tried, clumsily, to compare it to my own – but it's hard to take two pulses simultaneously.

Miss Sheehy became impatient. 'Take his shoulders,' she directed. 'I'll hold the door. Can you drag him to the lift? Or hoist him on your back?'

'Supposing we're seen?'

'We'll say he began to feel ill in your room. Then, when you tried to help him back to his, he fainted. I'm here because you rang the front desk.'

Good enough, I thought with relief, and gave myself to a frenzy of activity which kept my feelings in check. He was heavy but I'm strong and was able, like *oius Aeneas* fleeing the wars of Troy, to carry my father down the corridor, into the lift, then down another corridor to his room. By then, she had rung the doctor who was on his way. As I laid him on his bed, she divulged some facts. They had, she admitted, been quarrelling and her invitation to me to enter his room had been a move in the quarrel. When I left, she had rushed off, whereupon he, thinking she'd gone after me, followed her.

'He's terrified of his family finding out about us.'

'Us?' I asked stupidly.

'Him and me.'

You, I wondered dourly, and how many others? I was in a sweat of filial guilt: unfounded, to be sure, but my feelings had run amok. My father's poor, vulnerable, open eyes stared glassily and saw neither of us. Oh God, I prayed, don't let him die. Not here. Not for years! Please, God! At the same time I was furious with him. For what about my mother? Did she know – I recalled her tolerance of the rum-and-Coke – that as well as trusted barmen 'up and down the country', he also had – what? What was Miss Sheehy? His heart's love or one of a team? A team of floosies? If so, how big? Basketball five? Hockey eleven? She, no doubt, imagined him to be in love with her. Might he be? I felt obscurely flouted, and confused.

The doctor, when he came, quickly changed my mood.

'It's serious,' he warned. 'He's had a stroke. I'm going to call a helicopter and fly him to Galway.'

He told us to stay in the room while he went to make arrangements. For moments we sat in silence. Miss Sheehy was as pale as paper. My father's eyes were closed now and his face was grey.

'How long have you – been with him?'

'Three years.'

'So why the quarrel now?' He would not, I was sure, have misled her with false promises. He would never leave my mother. A Senator! A militant Catholic layman! Never in this life!

'I'm pregnant,' she blurted and began to cry.

'Don't cry!' I could have slapped her. Hysteria, I thought. Then: could he be such a fool? 'You mean you didn't use anything?' Condoning the use of artificial contraceptives led, said the League to Save the Unborn Child, to condoning abortion. Changing our legislation would open the sluice gates. I knew the arguments by heart. But what about the principle of what the eye didn't see? *Her* eyes were getting scandalously red. 'Don't cry,' I urged. 'The doctor will be back in a moment.'

'And he'll take him away. To Galway. Listen,' she clutched my arm, 'I must see him, get news of him. But he'll be in intensive care. I won't be let in. Only relatives will be. Will you help me?'

Red-eyed, feverish mistress! Outcast, beautiful Miss Sheehy. I kissed her and it was she who slapped me! Ah well, some outlet was needed. The doctor may have heard the slap for he gave us a look as he came in the door. Two paramedics were with him and in no time had my father on a stretcher. We followed them down the familiar corridors and out to the lawn where the helicopter was waiting. They loaded him on. Blades rotated; wind moulded our clothes to our bodies; then up it whirred into a misty dawn, turning silver, then grey, then fading to a speck.

I thought of 'the rapture', the bodily whisking of people up to heaven in which certain Protestants believe – ex-President Reagan for one was, I'd read in some magazine, expecting to be whisked aloft. Holus, bolus, body and bones! It was an inappropriate thought. But then what was appropriate? Maybe I was in shock?

Miss Sheehy's hand was in mine. Would I help her see him, she begged, or at least keep in touch? Yes, I said, yes. I'd be leaving for the hospital as soon as I could explain things to the management here. I'd phone her this evening.

'I have this weekend off,' she told me.

Ah, I thought: they planned to spend it together. Poor father! Poor Miss Sheehy!

'What's your first name?' I asked.

She said it was Artemis. Her parents had wanted her to be a huntress, not a victim. I made no comment.

*

I've had a call from my mother. From the nursing home. No need for me, she says, to worry. First babies are often slow to arrive. She should know: a mother of five and a four-time grandmother. My sisters have been dutifully breeding. She's in her element and hasn't been in such good spirits since my father's death.

*

He never regained consciousness. When Artemis came in on the Friday evening, I dissuaded her from seeing him, arguing – truthfully – that he'd have hated to be seen with drips and needles stuck all over him.

She acquiesced, noting, with an unreadable little smile, that she was used to *not* doing things – not writing to him ever, nor ringing him up. Not at his office. Not at home. Nowhere. She always had to wait for him to make the contact. I looked appalled and she said defiantly, 'When we were together, it was pure delight. Like wartime furloughs. Utterly without ordinary moments. We met sometimes on a friend's barge on the Shannon, once on a yacht in Spain, once in a flat in Istanbul. Never for long. But he was so happy at being able to do what he never ordinarily did . . .'

Christ, I thought, he'd raised negativity to a mystique! He was a one-man cult and had brainwashed her good and proper. I suddenly realized that I disliked him deeply and had, unknown to myself, done so for years. No wonder my brothers had fled to Australia and Ecuador.

By now I had spent three days in the hospital with my mother – the stroke had happened on the Wednesday morning. There was nothing to do but wait, talk to doctors about their scans, filter their pessimism back to her, hold her hand. The staff, predictably, was assiduous, so I had a lot of help.

'Such a fine man,' I would hear them murmuring prayerfully to her in corridors and guest areas. 'What a tragedy!' Sometimes they went with her to the chapel. One of the nurses was a member of the League to Save the Unborn Child. She, she told my mother, rarely questioned the will of God but found it hard to see a clean-living teetotaller like my father struck down when the town was full of drunks whose blood pressure seemed not to give them a moment's trouble. 'God forgive me, I'm a desperate rebel!' boasted this docile mouse, trembling under her blue, submissive veil.

These conversations, I admit, gave my mother a lot more consolation than I could provide. Communicating with her has never been my forte. She was younger than my father and totally his creature. They were what's called a fine couple. She's five feet ten, graceful, blonde speckled tastefully with grey, dutiful, cheerful, plays tennis and bridge, takes pleasure in her volunteer work for his causes and has never, in my presence, revealed a spark of even the mild brand of rebelliousness favoured by the blue-veiled nurse. None. My sister's opinion is that she's been emotionally lobotomized. By whom?

I went from time to time to look at him. He was semi-paralyzed and his face was badly askew: mouth twisted up and down in a vertical, Punch-and-Judy leer. Doubleness had finally branded him. Nobody but me, though, seemed to have had such a thought. At least nobody voiced it, and neither, to be sure, did I. My mother kept putting her hand on his brow, murmuring coaxing endearments and kissing his convulsed grey face. She hoped something might be getting through. This must have drained her emotionally for, in the evenings, she went back to her hotel and was served a meal in bed.

This left me free to dine *en ville* with Artemis Sheehy, whose weekend was, I reminded myself, available and blank. Despite my advice, she yearned to do precisely what my mother had been doing: put her long-fingered hand on my father's brow and kiss him well.

I decided – in retrospect it is impossible to disentangle my motives – to let her. From hope? Pity? As aversion therapy? How can I say?

We had by now had a row, or rather we had had another. Our relations from the start had been edgy. Why, I queried on Friday evening, as we sat waiting for the baked Alaska – I had, since she refused to drink with me, had a bottle of claret to myself – why had she let my father cast her as Patient Griselda, while he played the Pillar of the Irish Establishment? A PIE, I mocked, that was what he was, a po-faced Pie! An escapee from the novels of Zola and nineteenth-century operetta! Old hat! Self-serving! A canting humbug! My jealousy revenged itself on his charm – I now thought of it as smarm – and on his unassailable advantage in the minds of my mother and Artemis: his poignantly stricken state. The new-felled Knight!

'Can you,' I harried, 'deny that he is – was a hypocrite?'

What could she do, in all decency, but throw down her napkin and leave? I, waiting for the bill, had to let her go – and, anyway, knew I had her on a string. I was her only connection with him and so could let her stew. Greedy from anger – and satisfying one appetite in lieu of another – when the baked Alaska arrived with the bill, I ate her portion as well as my own. It struck me, as I walked morosely back to my hotel, that I was beginning to act like him. Ruthless and masterful. I hated myself. Still – I licked the last of the baked Alaska from my lips – it would be pointless to forgo my advantage by capitulating too soon.

Sure enough, she rang me next morning. Triumphant – but hiding it – I was sweetness itself. And contrite. She must, I begged, see how hard it was for me to hold my mother's hand by day and hers in the evening? I was painfully torn – as no doubt my father too had been. Instinctively, I was blending my image with his: an anticipation of what was to happen when obituaries appeared with photographs of his young self, looking, as was universally noted, disturbingly like me. But, to go back to my conversation with Artemis, I now made a peace-offering, which was that if she really wanted me to, I would take her to see him this evening, after my mother had left the hospital.

She accepted and, as I had tried to dissuade her, could hardly blame me for the shock. His skewed mouth dribbled. There were tubes in his nose. He looked worse than dead. He looked like an ancient, malicious changeling put together from that grey stuff with which wasps build their nests. Or ectoplasm or papier-mâché made from old, pulped Bibles. These conceits swarmed through my head as I watched, then, from pity, ceased to watch her.

She was devastated, disgusted, guilty; a mirror of myself. Did she also feel that hot rush of feeling which, for days now, had been distracting and perhaps healing me? The urge to fuck, which is a pro-life remedy for death-fears? People get it in wartime and, notoriously, in graveyards and during blackouts and other foreshadowings of mortality. I let her look her fill. I even left her alone lest, like my mother, she wished to kiss him. I don't know whether she did.

I waited in the hospital-green corridor, not hurrying her

adieux which, whether she knew it or not, were what they were. He, the doctors had told me, would be a wreck if he lived but was unlikely to last the weekend. I hadn't told her this, but guessed she knew. Then I took her on a drive along the coast, next for a long, twilight walk along a stretch of it, and finally to a small seaside hotel, where we spent the night comforting each other and conjuring away ghosts.

My father died that night, which was just as well for all concerned, especially her. If he had lived, what would she have done? Gone to somewhere like Liverpool to have her child, then given it out for adoption? Or raised it in resentful solitude on the income he would feel frightened – if *compos mentis* – into coughing up? Taken an 'abortion flight' to London? Instead, once we had faced my mother with the *fait accompli* of our runaway marriage – registry office in London, followed by a conciliatory Church ceremony back home – Artemis became part of the household which, for three years, she had been forbidden to phone. Sometimes, she tells me, she used, in her loneliness, to dial the number anyway then listen, silently, to our irritably convivial voices.

'Hullo! Speak up. Who is it? Press Button B! Oh it's the heavy breather again! What do you want, Heavy Breather? If you're a burglar, we're all at home so there's no point trying to break in!'

Now she *is* in and the noses of my sisters' children – none of them Learys – are put out of joint by the glorious prospect of Frank Junior's birth. Any minute now my mother will phone with news of my new brother's entry under false colours into the Leary clan. Brother masquerading as son, he will be born under the true Leary sign of duplicitous duality.

And I? Well, I'm in law school and active in the student union. People ask whether I'll go into politics and my fear is that I may find myself turning into a carbon copy of my father. I am, after all, living by his principles and can't see quite how to break out. Drinking claret instead of rum in Coke seems an inadequate gesture, and my support for Family Planning, Abortion and Divorce has been hailed by some of his cronies as the sort of forward-looking thinking to which he himself might well have subscribed had he lived. Times have changed, they say, and we must march to the European Community's tune if we want subsidies for our farmers. After all, providing the option to use contraception, etc., obliges nobody to avail themselves of it. And anyone who does can repent later. God is good and there's no point being simple-minded. So, they would have me think, opposing the letter of my father's laws is a way of being true to their spirit.

Maybe. It's hard to tell. Double-think is the order of the day.

Of course I rejoice in Artemis's love, though here too a shiver of doubt torments me: does she see him in me? Am I two people for her? To be sure, it's foolish to probe! We're happy and . . . there's the phone! Alleluia! Where are my car keys? Frank Junior must be on his way.

Street Magic

But Tomas was never in the humour for convincing Paula so she just heard over and over, 'It's a long story.' He told her no more than that he was waiting for a thing that was soon to come, a mindblowing thing. He spoke of this with borrowed eyes that fixed a distant judgment in the grubby sunlight. Then he'd sort of twinkle and take her hand and press it and, say they were on their way to a bar, it was like they owned the road the way they drifted over shadows of fugacious clouds. She wouldn't quiz him on his big break. She knew enough – what business he was doing. One day months before she'd seen him walk to the quay. She'd hung back and watched as he stood outside the jakes. His face, when she caught sight of it in the day's sticky dazzle, had a bare simplicity. It seemed delighted to splash for hours in the dirty shade rippling at the entrance. She wasn't disgusted: it had burned her up with desire.

Inside her she thought: Shit, what a difference in him! They'd been waiting for the spring to be happy in Dublin, but when they'd first arrived it had freaked him out. For months he'd walked around on his own and sat moodily and she'd promised herself they'd give it till the summer. Now that it was May, a great rotting ball in the sky, he was himself again, making eyes, carefree. 'We're gonna be reekin' with money soon,' he gladdened her. 'This crap's only a bad spell. Right?'

He was there some days by one to catch any lunchtime business and the trickle of scumbags just out of bed. Or sometimes she'd glimpse him later when the action must have slowed to a pause, waiting, chatting on the quay to another randy angel, leaning over the wall, maybe spinning rays of spit to the river. This wasn't his scene, it was a brief mad buzz he and she were on together. As for the surprise outcome, she would go along with that, she thought, for a bit. Because it wasn't like it was too much hopefulness that had dashed them to the capital from their town further north with its hankerings amid chimney smoke and winds of manure, its concrete glazed with dreamlife: it was too much need for it.

Paula had protection from disasters, she'd seen it again and again. So she felt safe enough, and she felt he was just too shy to do anything heavy. Anyway, she trusted him. He'd even told her what he was doing was dodgy, just hadn't filled her in. He wouldn't tell a cruel lie. It was his good nature she'd fallen for, more manly than the malice and jittery sinews of Fran, a guy back home whose lack she saw more clearly than ever when Tomas came out with things like: 'It's all your fate, you can't change it, believe me Paula.' Her former guy was an acidhead. And he was that lapsed cliché, couldn't permit faith in anything because faith sounded Catholic. And besides, while he'd blown her welfare on tripledips and cans and kebabs, now in Dublin Tomas was coming back with scores and tenners scrunched up into beads. When she took them she pictured those scumbags' yellow thighs, but she was down-to-earth about it. She thought, and she was on the point of teasing him in the bath once as she kissed a patch of grime: 'Where there's muck there's money. Right?'

And their unhappiness was okay. They went to nite clubs. They sat in chippers like they were waiting to make new friends. Then one day Tomas brought in one of the guys from the flat below theirs. They discussed in front of her, just messing. Men were individual but women weren't that evolved. She gave out: 'D'you believe that, you?' She tutted. 'No.' He straightened his face. 'I like girls.'

He was called Fish. He wore tracksuit bottoms with pin holes burnt in them and pointy slip-ons and had snarled hair. Soon they all started sitting up late in his flat drinking and talking over videos. Fish had lots to say about his life while his cousin Sammy had no personality, he was an unphysical boy, half made of light, it seemed to Paula, maybe constantly conversing in an invisible style with the dead. Fish talked intensively about 'great friends' and people with 'dead-on personalities' in a way that excluded his cousin and involved Tomas and Paula. She sat with her finger in his fist. Scratching his miraculous Medal, Fish entertained, recollected the first time he plucked a crab off him when he was fifteen – he was so outraged he'd kept it lusting in an upturned glass. Paula just listened. He produced hash. And with him it was no paranoid buzz, now they got on top of hash. He told them what bars to hate, what clubs to obsess. He was into reggae. They mellowed out and giggled a bit. He asked Paula did she know who to borrow from. She said no. He started rolling another and said did she want to hear a story about how his granny had got that wrong and lost her fingers. She had come here from America, a really nice woman. Paula was happy to get all this suss. She said, 'yeah,' and made Tomas listen. Fish was good at talking.

He explained how when his granny died a gang walked right into the funeral parlour and cut her fingers off to get the rings. 'But she was only in a coma, right, Paula?' He flicked the spliff with his nail and bit off the twist. 'She opened her eyes. The gang nearly died of fright. Dropped her fingers and legged it. Can you see it, Paula?' He held the spliff ready to light while he finished describing how she'd climbed out of the coffin and wandered home a bit dazed. 'Me old one had a heart attack when she saw her.'

'I don't believe that,' laughed Paula.

'It's true.'

'How is she now?' Tomas asked.

'Grand,' he said. 'She sells up town.'

As time went on Tomas's tongue loosened too. Once or twice when they were walking through town he came out with stuff she'd never heard before in her life, weird stuff about pentacles and wands and meditating and planets. 'Stop,' she said with a laugh, using one of Fish's words. Yet there were other moments when Tomas's certainty was infectious. Like every time she kept him going about a proper job and that gaze would train on something behind the glare. It was like he could picture a sparkling horizon lapping at the backs of the high moth-eaten, dove-possessed buildings on the quay. Or a moist dawn about to break on the dull red streets behind that were always full of fumes and warm shade and where odd cars cruised in the early afternoon.

As they waited she got hooked on their life, on all the stupid things: like waking on stains, sometimes late, to distant lorries rumbling and a bluish-grey haze that stuck to things in the room. She was hooked on the way they played as they dressed, on the feel of his bare foot on her cunt, even on nipping out for white bread and milk to the shop on the corner among fresh dust and birdsong. They'd have evening breakfasts. Then when he threw his jacket on she'd maybe delay him by giving his tongue a suck. 'What're you doin', Paula?' 'Kissin' you, you prick.' When he went she'd spend her time on the big streets going into cafés, asking for a job. She'd hold her head up as she walked and breathe in buses and warmth and crowds and splinters of sun. Kids sat about begging in rags. Sometimes she ran into friends of Fish: Snakey and Donna with people whose names she never knew. 'What's the story, Paula?' the slimey smackhead would say and she'd go to bars with them and join in some of their chat.

'Where's Tomas?' She'd tell them what he'd told her to say: 'He's makin' good moves, stockin', drivin' cars.' They liked you to talk yourself up.

One late afternoon she walked from them through rising heat and a smell of tarmac to a bar to meet him. There was a fat beat from a top window. She hated her own sweat as she waited inside the bar. He turned up smiling. 'How's the business?' she began. He said it was cool. Then she thought she'd ask him about that opportunity. He shrugged.

'It was bullshit,' he said.

'You said you were certain,' she reminded him softly.

'I was wrong then.'

They drank and leaned against each other and he reassured her this was just a run of bad luck. Then they reeled home to bed while it was still light.

She brought up the subject of the bullshit again one night in bed.

'Forget it,' he yawned.

'Tell us.'

So he told her the whole story, disjointed, mumbling. Told her how in early May he'd met a guy. They'd got talking, he'd sussed that Tomas needed money. He'd called himself a Druid. 'He was a mad bloke,' Tomas told her, 'into all mad things.' For a minute he didn't say any more and Paula realized she was gripping his cock with her gentle fist. She slapped his thigh.

'Go on.'

'He was a mad bastard,' Tomas tutted. 'He said he could get me loads of money and all. I asked how.'

'How?'

He sighed, mumbled, 'He did a spell or somethin'.'

'Did he?'

He rolled on his side away from her. 'So now you know.'

She whispered, 'What did you have to do?' He didn't speak. She tried to coax him. His cock was curled up asleep now. He wouldn't say more.

She lay and wondered. If there was one thing that should be true, it seemed to her, it was a spell, because there was no way to change your life without one. She remembered how when she was younger she'd kept seeing a boy when their parents had all been against it. She'd said to him, 'We can make it happen, Dessie, with the power of thought,' and nodded to him with confidence and her ponytail tapped her from behind. The more she'd persisted the more unlikely obstacles popped up. After that she'd stopped trying to make things happen at all, she'd started waiting for whatever was meant to come. Nothing ever came. Her mother had told her, 'You can never beat life,' and she'd realized that was dead right. 'But you have to keep tryin'.' Before she and Tomas had left with excited reluctance for Dublin she'd tried once again to get her act together. She'd applied for courses, she'd tried to get work as a waitress in every farflung and scabby snack bar and canteen, she'd applied for jobs for Tomas. It was like pushing a wall. As she looked at him sleeping now she thought: We were born poor, we're fated to live among shit. To want to change your fate was right. It was well right. And she burrowed her fingers through his and lay and heard him mutter once, twice.

After that they both felt down for a bit and didn't talk much. Tomas and Fish spent a lot of time together. A flavour of crap was getting in the flat from the street like the brightness gone bad. She started wearing her hair up. Then one evening Tomas broke some news. 'I have a job!'

'What?'

'Come on, we're goin' out.' And they went to a bar. Paula asked more. He just said a guy was getting him a job soon.

'What guy?' she asked.

'A guy, right?'

'Where did you meet him?'

'It's a hundred per cent fact, Paula.'

'What job is it?'

'Don't believe me then, I don't care.'

So she didn't ask more. But a few weeks later when she was in town one day she had another squint across the river. The buildings were shimmering and fawn. Dazzle moved on the quay like spirits, maybe disappointed to find out what their relatives were at. She could make him out talking to tough-looking guys with cropped hair while boy scouts went in and out. As she stood now she wasn't imagining his various filthy blisses, she was thinking about the million lives going on alongside his which she never saw, the ordinary lives of young guys on the road with moustaches or shoulder bags, lives folding around them as they walked away. More subtle lives. More real. Guys nodded at other guys and she wondered what they knew. Then she wondered: Could it be that they seemed happy only because they hid the crap in their lives and didn't fight it like her and Tomas?

A nervous tramp came up to her and asked her directions. She shook her head, walked away. She pushed herself through the almost tropical summer and made herself feel good by pretending Dublin was a much more interesting place, an unknowable city. She ran into Fish on a big road lined with dusty palms. He wore a baby's shades. 'You're one of our own, Paula,' he said, 'Let's get *there*, let's get *home* . . . to a bar.' He blessed himself passing a church.

Fish, it turned out, wasn't all Irish, and she sat imagining somewhere in Egypt. She asked where he got money. He settled more into his seat. He said he lived off a claim he'd got when he was eighteen for fifty-six thousand: when he was a kid some cleric, handy with cuffs on the ear, had administered a freak one, concussed him. Paula didn't drink much. Soon they walked to a hotel bar. 'Take my hand, right?' he said. 'For luck.' There she had coffee and he drank more. Later when they stepped out on to the street he tried to coax her to go somewhere else, she said she couldn't but walked a little way with him. She held his sinewy arm. 'You'd suit your hair short,' he said. They parted. She strayed back to the flat past kids burning a tyre and went to bed. She sweated too much to sleep.

Later Tomas came in, a bit spaced. She rolled over with her arse sticking up so he would pat it. He talked in bed thinking he should cheer her up. He told her a story. When he was younger and at home, he giggled, he'd been sitting on his bed wanking with his eyes closed and a Walkman on. He giggled a bit more and then carried on. When he'd opened his eyes there was a mug of tea on the bedside table. 'My old one,' he said, cracking up laughing.

She didn't react. She'd never known him so talkative, it wasn't like him. The early morning traffic had begun, aeroplanes on their way to places. 'Why should that guy give you a job?' she said.

'D'you not believe in friendship, fuck it!' He rolled over. She threw another blanket off them. She decided: I'll give it till September.

And she saw Fish in bars in the afternoons. There was nothing to do but talk and pant and drink. Europe was on tongues: how could Danish porn ever defeat the spinster virgins who marched around town jerking posters – 'Porn Causes Rape' stencilled on the sides of cardboard boxes. She asked Fish

was Tomas going on about anything these days. He thought
and answered vaguely how he'd told him they should be
positive and make things go their way or something. She knew
there was something there that Fish had never thought about.
He wasn't into it, he was already talking, telling her about his
cousin. Sammy was actually one in a million or one in ten
thousand or something. Froth put a little moustache on Fish. At
one time, he confided, he'd been thinking that his cousin might
have been queer. And there was a point when his cousin started
thinking this too, but he wasn't sure. Fish paused. He picked his
teeth. She loosened her sleeves. He went on. He told her that
he'd come to the conclusion at last that his cousin was asexual.
He asked her with a laugh had she ever heard of that. 'Not
really,' she said. On his own his cousin had actually found out
that this was the case from a doctor. Fish began to snigger. 'And
he thought this was really like a tragedy, right? D'you know
what I'm saying, Paula?' Sweat rolled on his cheek like
hysterical laughs. 'But at least he knew!'

'Is he really that?' Paula asked.

'What?'

'Is he what you said?'

'One in a million,' said Fish.

At last it rained. One morning in September when Paula and
Tomas woke up the garden was drenched. She recognized the
smack of wet phlox. They had tea and caramel eggs and she
said lightly, 'When are you gettin' that job, Tomas?'

'It fell through, the bastard,' he said.

She nodded and smiled. 'You're a bastard,' she told him, and
the rain started pouring inside her eyes as well. 'You're full of
shit.'

Now she didn't know what to do. She went out and got a bus
into town. I'm spiralling down, she thought. A woman passed
her in the street, crying. To give herself a purpose she went and
got her hair cut. She wanted to pray, she believed in praying,
praying would be playing her last card – but it spooked her, God
was so negative. He would only give relief from pain, never
anything positive. A few times in the past she'd begged for

something she wanted from a guardian angel she pictured behind the air. The result had always been dramatic, but the answer was cruel. Very rapidly she'd got what she'd asked for, but with something mischievous tagged on. She remembered the clearest example and she related it to Fish that evening when they met. For many years while she was at school, she explained to him in the corner of a crowded snug, she never had a boyfriend. 'It's true, Fish, I was really depressed.' One night she was specially low because she had to turn up at a party on her own. On her way through the garden to the flat where the party was she was psyching herself up and she made, she explained, this great intense plea that she would meet someone there. Fish bobbed his head. One of her mates was at that party, she'd been thinking about trying to fix Paula up. She introduced this boy to her. He had freckles and ginger hair. They got talking. 'I think Paula's a lovely name,' he'd said. 'My sister has a friend called Paula, she's dead quiet, so she is.' He was better than nothing, she'd thought, at least he had a mouth she could kiss, a body she could touch. Fish bounced closer. At one point in the party, she went on, he took his hand out of his pocket to secure a crisp bag on his lap while he picked from it. The hand was deformed. His fingers were like crushed toes. With corns. The first thing she'd thought was: It's a message that I shouldn't be so selfish and want a body.

Fish shook his head, 'Oh don't say that, Paula, that's stupid.' And he started stroking her hair. She went along with it.

She didn't any more, she told him. Now she didn't have a clue, she just wondered if it was simply meant to stop her getting her way. 'You know if you're a bastard,' she said, 'it all falls in your lap. But you see if you're sensitive . . .'

Fish was stroking her hand. Maybe this time Tomas was right to believe you could have your way if you were positive. Fish slid his arm around her. 'D'you understand it, Fish?' she said. 'Life?' Suddenly he put his lips on her cheek. She waited, smelling his Guinness.

When she turned to face him he was examining her mouth. She kept thinking as his hand went up her blouse. She couldn't deny what she thought. It seemed to her life would always go against her needs. Cruelly and deliberately. And she knew that if there was a God he would have a long maroon tongue, toad legs, bat wings. She didn't tell Fish how it ended with that boy with a hand like a foot. She'd actually gone out with him. It was the rumour that his arse was freckled that decided her to blank him. Now Fish was scratching her back.

'I hate me,' she muttered. 'I do . . . being me . . .'

'You're not,' he said into her neck.

They walked back to the house together with their arms looped and she wondered was his hand on his hip. When Tomas saw her he looked at her hair. 'Where were you Paula?'

'Job huntin', right?'

He shrugged.

But a week later, without mentioning, she moved out. She finally decided Tomas was no good. A poxy but cheap bedsit had come up. She was going to get a job in Dublin or she was going to go back home. But either one of these seemed like the wrong move. One morning Fish called out there. They ate Toffee Crisps as they waited for the bells of a cathedral to stop. She hated those mangled bells like the voice of a devil. When there was quiet he told her that Tomas had left the flat and moved in with some bloke. She sat down sneering. He looked at his wrapper. And now he sort of almost proposed to her, he asked her would she move in with him. She stood up. She paced up and down. 'Would you?' he said. He took her hand, tweaking her fingers.

'What about your cousin?' she asked.

'He's dead,' he said. 'Did you not hear? He was in a crash, there was metal touchin' his brain. Oh, it was terrible. They had to cut him out of the car and all, so they did . . .'

'Is that true?'

'Yeah.' He folded his arms. She stared at him. 'What?' He laughed like she was picking on him.

She took herself for an evening roam somewhere she'd never been, around high towers of corporation flats, deliquescent, sensing Heaven. Every face seemed ugly, with too much detail, cheeks were too big. She wasn't imagining some other city now, because she couldn't think of anywhere more unknowable. Dublin had gone bogey on her, the thing to do was leave. A fat leaf fell on a burnt-out car. Yeah, I'll move in, she thought.

From then on she tried to forget about Tomas, and every time she was in town she made sure she didn't look across the wet distance at the quay. But one day on her way to meet Fish she ran into him again. Now he had cropped hair that didn't suit his clothes, made him look violent. His jacket was an elegant shade of grey that matched the sky. 'What's the story?' she said, a bit blown out by the gear. He looked like he was well into it these days, getting big money, reeking with it. 'Have you cracked life?'

'Well, I know what I think,' he said moodily. 'I know now everyone just fuckin' uses everyone, right?'

'Yeah?'

'Life's evil, Paula, that's my opinion. You have to be evil for this world.'

'Are you right this time?'

'It's a hundred per cent fact, Paula. Believe me, you have to be clued in.'

As they walked their separate ways she didn't let herself get upset, she told herself that Tomas was in the past, a better time was coming. She joined Fish and laughed as they walked across the river to a bar. Everywhere there were salty bus fumes and pigeon shit and empurpled passers-by. Fish knew something was up so he gossiped, talked about anything to keep her glowing. 'You just don't believe in anything,' she kidded him as they drank. Soon she relaxed and she decided to tell him the whole story of Tomas's spell. She took her time over telling it, embroidering most of it and buzzing off him as they drank.

Pandora's Box

He was a good forty metres past the hitcher before his foot pounced on the brake pedal and shocked the swift Audi to a standstill. He eyed her in the rear-view mirror, noticed her indecision. He thought to reverse but palmed the horn instead. *BEEP-BEEP!* Yes, she was coming. He adjusted the mirror a fraction to take in her sauntered approach, also using his wing mirror.

The hitcher opened the door and peered in. 'Hi,' she said, two-handing a cascade of hair behind her ears as she ran a mental check on the driver.

'Hop in.'

'How far are you headed?'

'Cork. All the way to Cork.'

'. . . Mmm . . . Yeah, okay!' she decided, and she made to get in.

'Throw the knapsack in the back.' He signalled with his head.

She did this and then she moved nimbly into the spacious front seat. The Audi slipped away into the sun.

Chris Mulvey usually had no time for hitchers. He passed thousands of them in any given month as he journeyed to check on his chain of betting shops. Loads of buses and trains – let them fork out. There was too much sponging going on; that's what had the country the way it was. It couldn't last.

That July day, though, on the road out of Thurles, some chord of need had sung in his head; had stopped him in his tunnelled tracks, had him framing a stranger in his mirrors.

It was now ten minutes since he'd picked up the hitcher and few words of consequence had been exchanged – small talk, the normal stuff. He fidgeted with the radio buttons as if seeking some new station, some diverse sound. Finally, he returned the dial to its old mark and again hit the 'off'.

The Audi surged towards ninety as he fished in his pocket for cigarettes and steered one between his lips. This was another rigid rule he was about to break: smoking while driving. He was aware of this and he did hesitate but then his thumb moved sharply to engage the car's lighter.

'Smoke?' he said, showing the open packet of Dunhill to the hitcher.

'Ahm, is it okay?' She meant the No SMOKING sticker and he knew this.

'It's okay. Work away, it's okay.'

'No-no, you're fine,' she said. 'I'll go for one of my own.' She pulled a pouch of Golden Virginia from the breast pocket of her lumberjack shirt and started to make a roll-up. She was good at the job, real handy.

'Hmmm,' hummed Chris Mulvey, a peeled eye settling back on the road.

'Thanks all the same. I appreciate it.'

The Audi eased back to seventy, but soon the speedo needle was creeping again towards dangerous figures. Chris Mulvey tapped a pellet of ash onto the floor and then he pulled open the ashtray and used that. It was packed with his wife's butts from the last time she'd accompanied him on a drive to Galway. Long butts – half-cigarettes really.

'Gawd, the countryside looks magical,' mused the hitcher aloud, her eyes drawn by a pair of frisky chestnuts galloping in an isolated paddock.

Chris Mulvey stared straight ahead, the great flats of road melting into mirages under the burn of the sun. The speedo now said a steady eighty.

'What part of America would you be from?' he asked suddenly.

'Georgia,' said the hitcher. 'Athens, Georgia.'

He stabbed the Dunhill into his wife's butts. 'Athens . . .

Georgia . . .' The drone in his voice suggested a flounder through murky geography.

'You got it,' said the hitcher, absently caressing her weathered mane.

'Athens. Athens. Now that doesn't sound American to me.'

'Well, it sure is. Don't ask me how it came to be called that because I ain't got a clue. Something to do with the Greeks, maybe.'

'The Greeks?'

'Yeah, the other one in Greece. Capital city.'

'Oh aye, aye, that's right. I knew there was something.'

The Audi slowed as it hit the outskirts of Cashel and Chris Mulvey rolled his window down, rolled it right down, sent his arm out into the sun.

'You see that up there?' he said, pointing towards the imposing fortress which lorded a local hill. 'That's the Rock of Cashel.'

'Ugh-ugh.'

'It's famous, you know.'

'I bet,' said the American, using her hitching sign to fan her face. He brought the Audi down another gear and gazed up at the Rock – almost as if *he* were the tourist. He pinched his aquiline nose.

'Do you want to take a photo of it?' he said. 'I can stop. No problem.'

'Not really,' said the American in a tired drawl. 'I ain't much into all that *dead* stuff.' The way she leant on the word 'dead' indicated a disdain for all matters historical, a punky V-sign to the past. 'You understand?'

'I do, I know what you're saying,' said Chris Mulvey, rolling his window slowly shut before pushing the Audi into a higher gear.

The snug town of Cashel seemed to shimmer in the midday heat, folk going about their business all leisurely and lightly clad. Chris Mulvey kept the Audi at a crawl, his fingers interlocked, prayer-fashion, atop the padded steering wheel, his eyes scouring left and right.

'Cashel,' he said. 'This is the town of Cashel.'

'Downtown Cashel,' said the American.

He glanced across at her and smiled weakly. When he looked away, after a lingered moment of acute awareness, he felt a rare stirring in the stilled canals of his blood. So subtle, a feathery sting.

Leaving Cashel behind, they moved on through the fertile pastures of dairy country and Chris Mulvey lit another Dunhill. He drove in silence now, his eyes fixed like radar on the bad bends. He thumbed the radio back on and a woman could be heard talking about the wild private life of Mozart. He got a pop station then but that was worse. He sighed as he switched off.

Later, much later, he lit himself yet another Dunhill, took a few drags, and pianoed his left fingers along his left thigh.

'You're very quiet there,' he said.

'Yeah,' said the American. 'I guess I'm a bit wasted.'

'*Wasted?*'

'Yeah, wasted,' she chuckled. 'Not enough sleep and stuff lately.'

'I see,' said Chris Mulvey, directing his eyes back to the snaky road. He sucked more smoke out of the Dunhill. 'Do you have a name?'

'Sure I have a name. Marilyn. Marilyn Goldwater.'

'Goldwater.'

'That's the one.'

'Goldwater, Goldwater . . . Wasn't there a politician–'

'Yeah-yeah,' cut in Marilyn. '. . . *Bobby.*'

'The very man. You wouldn't be . . .?'

'Nope. No kin to me. Never knew him, never wanted to know him.'

'A gangster, was he?'

'Dunno. Who cares? Who cares about all that stuff?'

'Hmmm, I suppose you're right,' said Chris Mulvey. He drew the last out of his Dunhill and eased down through the gears.

'A student, are you?' he persisted, indicating to pass a lorry that was stacked high with baled straw.

Marilyn inhaled deeply and gazed at the plushly-padded roof of the car.

'A student?' she said. 'Yeah, I guess you could say I'm a student.'

Chris Mulvey waited for her to say more but she didn't say more. He took a hand off the wheel and wiped it on his kneecap. The load of golden straw grew smaller and smaller as he watched it in his rear-view mirror.

'Have you friends or something in Cork?'

'Can't say I have. It'll be a whole new vibe for me.'

'You'll like it. A grand spot is Cork.'

'Magic.'

'A grand spot,' he repeated, angling his hairy wrist just enough to show the face of his watch.

Marilyn set to making a roll-up, her head swaying ever so slightly to a private beat. Chris Mulvey sent an eyeball left. He saw the faded jeans, a sunflower patch on her near thigh. He saw her tongue the cigarette paper.

'You wanna try one of these?' she said.

'No-no,' he said. 'No.'

'I can roll you one.'

'You're all right, work away. Would there be drugs in that now?' he said a few moments later, pincering his nose in his fashion.

'Just good ol' Golden Virginia.'

'Hmmm . . . The drugs are a queer boy.'

'A queer boy!' cried Marilyn. She burst into giggles, coughed on smoke.

A longish silence followed and Chris Mulvey thought of repulsing it with the radio but he stuck it out. He wiped an imaginary eel of sweat from his lined brow and then he asked Marilyn if she slept in a tent. 'When you're touring like this, I mean,' he explained, visibly flustered.

'Hostels,' she said. 'I prefer to use the youth hostels.'

'All bunked in together, I suppose.'

'Sorry?'

'In these hostel places. Would the lads and lassies be together, like?'

Marilyn Goldwater worried the Indian beads about her throat and pondered what reply she might give. 'Yeah, I guess they could end up together,' she said. 'Do you have a problem with that?'

'What do you mean, *you guess?*' said Chris Mulvey. 'Either you know or you don't know.' He reached for another Dunhill.

'Sure, I know,' said Marilyn, a teasing lilt to her voice. She comforted herself deeper into the Audi's soft seat and lifted a sandalled foot onto the bare shelf of the dashboard.

'Just asking,' said Chris Mulvey. He jetted smoke from the corner of his mouth and veered a peripheral eye onto the roosting foot.

'Sure. You're just curious. Right?'

'Not curious, just asking. Anything wrong with that?'

'It's a free world, man, a free world.'

'Someone has to pay for it, though,' sneered Chris Mulvey. He tamped his half-smoked Dunhill into the packed ashtray, instantly wishing he hadn't.

'Pay for it? Pay for what?'

'You know what I mean.'

'No, honestly. Come on, man.' The tanned foot arched sharply, relaxed. Chris Mulvey said no more, far too bristled to elaborate. End of chat.

A few miles before Mitchelstown, Marilyn started to hum a snatch of an old Carole King song. Very low, very sweet. She smiled dreamily as she hummed, the smile of a traveller making good time, seeing good tomorrows.

'Are you married?' she asked suddenly. The question was a dagger slicing through the tent of Chris Mulvey's silence; it stunned his head around.

'Am I married?' he said.

'Yeah. Don't mean to be personal or anything.'

'I am,' he said with slight hesitation. He looked back at the road and saw another mirage in the distance, a melt of phantom water.

'Why do you ask?' he said, after a few long seconds, seconds in which he was trying to formulate answers to further imagined questions.

'Dunno,' said Marilyn. 'Idle curiosity, I guess.'

He then remembered his Dunhills; he lit one and smoked it right to the butt before speaking again.

'You're not married yourself, I suppose?'

'Nope. I sure ain't.'

'Mmmm, I thought that.'

'It works for some, it don't work for some. I ain't the gambling type.'

'I see.'

'Too much pressure. Too much space for lies and hurting.'

'How? What do you mean exactly?' Chris Mulvey's tone was challenging.

Marilyn raised her foot above the dashboard, settled it back down again.

'Go on, I'm interested.'

'Naw, I ain't up to it, man,' she said languidly but with an undertone of annoyance. 'Not today. Sorry.' She teased a bit of tobacco from her pouch, evened it deftly along the paper and gazed out at a shimmering hillside of tremendous colour – a crop of rapeseed ready for the shiny blades.

Chris Mulvey angled his head and gorged on all he saw. Dragging his eyes away he chewed on his upper lip and checked his watch. He quietly inflated his lungs to bursting point as he readied to speak.

'We could pull for a drink up ahead,' he ventured. 'It's roasting.'

'Sure, if you want,' said Marilyn, 'but I gotta be pushing on for Cork.'

'Just a quick drink.'

'Thanks for the offer but I gotta pass on it.'

'Whatever you say. Just asking.'

'I know,' said Marilyn, studying the finished roll-up abstract-
edly.

The Audi devoured the good road into Mitchelstown, the purr
of its engine hardening towards a whine. The speedo needle was
hovering about the eighty five mark when Chris Mulvey sucked
the last out of his last cigarette. His left hand dropped onto the
gear shift then to ensure he was in 'top', the movement
mechanical but edgy. Even driving had lost its simplicity.

He brought the car to a halt in the centre of town, thumbed
the hazard flashers on and unbuckled his seat belt.

'Won't be a minute,' he said. 'Just going to get fags.'

'That's cool,' said Marilyn, stretching her arms wide, watching him go.

Back outside the shop, Chris Mulvey stood in the shade of the
awning and lit a Major – they didn't stock Dunhill. He gazed
down the street for long and private seconds, eyes focused on
the car with the blinking hazards. He tossed the cigarette aside
then and strode forward, viewing his reflection in a butcher's
window as he went.

'Now,' he said, sitting in and belting up.

'Nice little town,' said Marilyn.

'Mitchelstown,' he said, as he eased the Audi away.

'I guess we're in Cork already.'

'. . . What?'

'In the county. Somewhere in the county. Right?'

'Aye, aye,' he said testily. 'The very north,' he added, a
moment later; his tone soft, grudgingly apologetic: hoping to
draw the earlier sting.

On the twisting incline out of the town, a heavily-laden lorry
slowed the Audi to a crawl. Chris Mulvey nosed out and in, out
and in, mad for road.

'Come on, come on,' he said to the lorry, pulling the
cigarettes out of his pocket and stabbing one between his lips.

'Here,' he said to Marilyn. 'Try one of these.'

'You're okay, I'm fine.'

'Go on, they're different ones.'

'No-no, really.'

'Come on, come on,' he said to the lorry again.

'I guess it's going as fast as it can,' said Marilyn. 'Whatever's under that canvas sure must be heavy.'

Chris Mulvey kept a still eye in his wing mirror as the lorry groaned on up the hill, gear changes punctuating its smoky climb.

'Pandora . . .' thought Marilyn aloud.

'What?'

'Pandora,' said Marilyn again, pointing. 'The sign on the truck. See?'

'Hmmm.'

'Strange name for a haulage company. Maybe that's why it's labouring so hard,' she chuckled after a moment.

Chris Mulvey gaped across at her, his face a taut mask of blankness.

'Pandora's Box. You know the one. The huge weight of all those miseries and dreads and stuff waiting to break free. I guess–'

The sudden swerve and thrust of the Audi cut Marilyn's drawl, the lorry quickly left far behind as the open road beckoned. Chris Mulvey powered up through the gears, his jaw set hard. The speedo needle hit ninety, kept on going; the blossomed whitethorns became woolly spectres on the margins.

'Are you afraid?'

'Afraid? Naw, not a bit,' said Marilyn. 'I get a hit off speed.'

'She's only cruising, you know. This lady has a lot more in the tank.'

'Sure.'

'Cruising,' said Chris Mulvey through viced teeth. 'Only cruising.'

There was no more talk then and Marilyn Goldwater was happy to have it so. Keep hitting the gas, mister, she thought. You're doing real fine.

She smoked a roll-up, her cheek nesting against the wing of the seat. It was such a comfortable car; the hum of its engine settled about her brain, an aural cocoon. Had she not been so fatigued, she would have reopened the channel of conversation – if only for kicks. As it was, she drifted into imaginings of Cork and the good time that would surely await her there, as it awaited her everywhere. Cork: she liked its single syllable roundness. Names held occult meaning.

Chris Mulvey, meanwhile, thanked Christ the law weren't out with a speed trap and now took it cautious and slow: a steady fifty. He didn't look to his passenger, nor in his rear-view or wing mirrors, didn't look anywhere but at the road ahead. He knew he'd made a show of himself, behaved like a miffed youth; he wondered what the hell came over him. The deeper he mined for reason the more ridiculous he felt. He imagined Marilyn having a muted giggle, pitying him maybe. But there was nothing he could do to reclaim an ounce of pride, nothing. And the car, it was so fucking hot. Like a sauna. He teased loose the noose of his tie and made to wind his window down but stopped himself at the last moment. Her smell, that's what stopped him. So long he'd been breathing it in, unaware, nasalling it down to his core. He was aware of it now, wouldn't let it escape or be diluted.

The stubborn silence eventually came to remind him, fleetingly, of those rare occasions when his wife sat for hours in the hitcher's seat. Thinking her own thoughts, cut off from him as if by a glass wall. Chain-smoking to beat the band, pondering what she'd buy in some pricey boutique at their journey's end. Their lives a forked road, a sham of suburbia.

A few miles before Fermoy, Chris Mulvey fished a Major from his new packet and braced himself to speak. Something light. *Anything.* There was no cause for this awkwardness, he reasoned. 'Twas ridiculous.

Marilyn Goldwater's shadow entered the corner of his eye as he waited on the car's lighter to heat. Her cedarwood-oil scent lured his every sense.

'You're getting the weather anyway,' he heard himself say, his voice all shackled, without fluidity. No response issued from the so close seat. 'It makes all the difference,' he continued. 'Nothing to beat the bit of . . .'

Three or four telegraph poles of silence flashed by before he angled his gaze left. He stayed his gaze until the lighter popped, the sound stout as a rifle report in his head. The hitcher was fast asleep, a sleep so quiet her very breathing seemed suspended. Her roll-up, half smoked but now gone out, horned from between her limp fingers; her foot high on the dashboard, naked inside its sandalled cage.

The Audi eased back to fifty, forty, slowed to thirty where it began to jolt in need of a lower gear. Chris Mulvey glanced in his mirrors, glanced at the sleeping figure. His heart drummed inside his tight chest.

The unlit cigarette was still in his right hand and, realising this, he dispatched it to his pocket, squashing it in his fumbled haste.

Wake up, wake up, he pleaded mutely. Inner warnings, choking fears.

He came to a picnic area on the rim of a wood and saw knots of people seated at the ash-slab tables and he kept going. A juggernaut droned past, horn booming, its slipstream pressing down on the crawling Audi.

He ran his palm across his brow but there was no sweat there, though his whole body felt sickly hot.

Once more he stared across at the hitcher. He winged an arm towards her, one eye on the road, one eye not, then held his shaky hand no more than an inch above the sunflower patch on her lean thigh – almost as if in warming a frozen hand over a single ember.

He ached to touch her, to cross the bridge of that last, pulsing inch.

Numbly he stared into his rear-view mirror. The eyes that stared back at him, the dreadful truth in those eyes, shocked him to the point of nausea. '*Jesus,*' he whispered. He said the word again, inflecting it with the full horror of a mind suddenly forced to acknowledge its deepest and darkest twistings. Icy relief rode on the back of the horror; the nausea remained.

The speedometer said forty when he looked at it. He checked what gear he was in. He trembled the squashed Major from his pocket, saw he couldn't smoke it and got a straight one. After a few drags he felt the pounding of his heart slow somewhat. He pushed the Audi up to sixty, was afraid to go faster. His hands gripped the steering wheel, paled claws.

On the straight coming into Fermoy he forced an eye to his left but drew it back sharply. Again, he palmed his brow for sweat. He thumbed the radio on. He turned the volume up, turned it right up, then lowered it.

'Wha-wha?' cried Marilyn Goldwater, starting awake. '... *Oh* ...' She whipped her foot off the dashboard and peered at her watch and, with a degree of discomfiture, looked across at the silent driver.

'Gawd,' she said. 'I can't believe I . . .' Her voice tailed off and as it did she shuddered. Her whole body shuddered, as if a spectre of intuitive menace had shadowed the route of her thoughts.

Chris Mulvey mumbled something but didn't risk looking across.

'Where exactly are we . . .?'

'Fermoy.'

She stared out the window. She wanted to ask how close they were to Cork but she didn't ask. Gradually, her panic faded; she again trusted the sun.

'Gee, I'm sorry about dropping off like that. Anti-social, I guess.' No response from the driver. *Damn*! She eyed him with faint sympathy. Aw well. what's done's done. No crime in sleeping.

Hitting Fermoy, the Audi slowed and stayed slow. Duffy's Amusements were in town – the roller coaster going full tilt in the fairground – but Chris Mulvey had eyes only for the central junction up ahead. 'I have to let you out here,' he said, pulling sharply in to the side, grimacing as he felt a hub cap graze off the high kerb.

'Oh?' said Marilyn, glancing across. 'Yeah ... okay.' She
noticed the iron set of his jaw, the rigidity of his posture, the way
his hands clawed the steering wheel. 'Thanks anyway,' she
offered, feeling for the clasp of the seat belt. A sliver of unease
had revisited the pit of her stomach.

'I can't bring you further.'

'Sure,' she muttered, pushing open the door.

Chris Mulvey's grim gaze stayed fixed on the junction.

Marilyn eyed the back of his bony head as she leant into the
rear of the Audi and yanked her rucksack out onto the
pavement. Sighing a deep sigh, a sigh of bemusement and ill-
defined relief, she stepped forward a pace to the front door.
'Thanks again,' she said, hands tight on her thighs as she
stooped to look in. Nothing from the driver, nothing at all. She
shrugged, and eased the door quietly shut – almost as if being
careful not to rouse the trance-like figure within.

Chris Mulvey angled his gaze. The hitcher was gone, already
busy checking the signposts, searching for the town with the
auspicious name. Only her smell remained; undiluted, palpable
as fear.

The Audi moved away slowly, quickly picked up speed. It
shot through the junction in a jangle of gears and followed the
main road towards Cork. It gained more speed as Marilyn
Goldwater shouldered her rucksack and drifted after it, her
blonde head rocking, weighted with puzzlement, rocking until
the furious whine died on the distant air and another car slowed
to a halt before her absently rising thumb.

KEVIN CASEY

Photographs

When Stoner discovered that his mother was removing photographs from old family albums, he felt an immediate sense of loss as if memories, images, particularities of place were being taken from him. The empty spaces on the pages, dark rectangles that had once been covered by examples of his father's artless photography, were like tombstones. Some evoked almost total recall; others were anonymous as if their inscriptions had been worn away by time and weather.

There was no evident logic behind the selection of the photographs that were missing. Of those that Stoner could remember, some dated back to his mother's early years. They showed the house in the middle of the fields in which she had been young, her overweight sister, her mother dressed in black, her graduation day. Others had been taken on golf courses, on promenades or in front of modest hotels. In one of the later albums, in what seemed like an act of aggression, an assault on his past, she had torn out ten or twelve photographs of Stoner and his brother. Some of these had been taken in their back garden but most dated from a summer holiday and showed the two boys on a beach. Stoner, at eight or nine years of age, had been fair-haired and very thin, his ribs evident and startling as in some anatomical illustration. His brother had been sturdier and, in various stances, more obdurate, the focal point of the photographs.

Stoner's mother was ninety-two years old, an almost embarrassing age. She lived in the mews of her elder son's house, surrounded by items of ill-matching furniture that had once belonged in the family home. When Stoner visited her, some piece of the past always thrust itself on his attention: the dining-room table at which he had eaten so many meals, the piano on which he had practised, a particular chair. These associations were not always positive. The objects occasionally prompted feelings of unease as if they were joined by lines of tectonic stress to tremors in his childhood.

Sometimes, during evening visits, before the lamps were switched on, the room became blurred in grey light and his mother's face softened as if she were the much younger woman who stared out from the earliest album. It was like a return to a past that he had never known, his mother as a single woman, getting ready to play golf or to go for a drive in the country, flirtatious in her silences. They would sit there with little to say to each other that had not already been said; she relied on repetition. A clock that had ticked through the years of his childhood ticked through these moments of monotony. Outside, past the entrance gate and across the road, the sea stirred against a breakwater, shifting stones.

'Do you realise that there are photographs missing from these albums?' he asked her one afternoon.

'What?'

He repeated the question, observing, with irritation, that she could hear him quite easily when she wanted to do so.

'I don't know where they've gone,' she said, in a slightly accusing tone, as if she suspected him of having removed them.

'You didn't give them to anyone?'

'What?'

'You didn't give them to anyone?'

'Who would I give them to?'

The reply had an apparent logic that was difficult to refute. She had outlived most of the people who might have been interested in even seeing the photographs. His brother had had no doubt about what had happened. 'She tears things up. She's always tearing things up. There's nothing else that could have happened to them.'

'There's no one to give them to,' his mother said emphatically. 'Anyway, I like to have them. I was looking at them the other day. There are some photographs of people that I didn't even recognise. I don't know what your father was thinking of when he took them in the first place.'

Stoner drank tea from a large china cup that had once belonged to his great-grandmother. The tea was weak and indifferent, as it had always been and, as usual, his mother had asked him if he took sugar. On hearing that he did not she had stared at him as if he had revealed some shameful weakness.

'It's just that you've forgotten who they are,' he said.

'What?'

'You must have known them once. The people in the photographs.'

'Maybe I did,' she said, as if humouring him, 'but I certainly don't know them now!'

Her hair, which had not lost any of its colour until she was into her eighties, had now faded into an indeterminate greyness. Uncombed, it surrounded her head like a deranged halo.

'Some holiday photographs of me as a boy are missing,' Stoner said, attempting to keep an involuntary tone of grievance out of his voice. 'I was on the beach, looking up towards the promenade. Do you remember how you used to call to us from there to say that it was time for tea?'

'What?'

He felt a stirring of love in the remembrance of a time when she had defined the movements and the limits of his days, her voice calling to him, her hand closing around his as they walked towards the hotel. His brother would walk beside their father and engage in a conversation that deliberately excluded him. He remembered his mother's dress and the pieces of jewellery that she wore and her reassuring insistence that he was not freakishly underweight. Now she sat there as if waiting for some reassurance that he could not offer to her, her fingers plucking restlessly at an unseen thread in the pocket of a cardigan that she had knitted for herself during some unrecorded winter, turning banal hours into something almost permanent. Her eyes were bright yet oddly without expression, her lips drooped into a sardonic look of disapproval. He wanted to reach out and thank her for old kindnesses but it was impossible. Although she sat within arm's reach there was the illusion of a great distance between them.

During lunch with his cousin, a clergyman from another country, Stoner referred to the photograph albums. His cousin took an informed interest in the history of the family, reaching back to small triumphs in the past as others might reach into the future with hopes for the achievements of their children.

'When you visit her this afternoon get her to show them to you,' Stoner said.

'There are at least a dozen pictures of your family. I'd say that you were four or five years old. They were taken in a garden. There's some kind of bench. And an arch.'

'I think I can even remember your father taking them,' his cousin said. 'It was a holiday. We had called in somewhere for lunch.'

'They're in an album with a brown cover. At least, I hope they are. She's been taking out photographs and losing them.'

He felt guilty at this disloyalty to her, at exposing her to disapproval, but his cousin didn't seem surprised.

'I've come across that kind of thing,' he said. 'Older people can do it as if it's part of some unfinished business. Maybe you have to get rid of the past before you can embrace the future.'

The idea that his mother might be acting compulsively was both new and disturbing to Stoner. It hinted at the long and friendless days that she spent alone with her memories. It had been easier to regard the matter as a minor if irritating eccentricity, a habit to be deplored rather than understood.

His cousin had the breezy manner of a man who dealt in certainties. Faith had left his face almost free from doubt; his beliefs had resulted in no evident anguish. He looked questioningly at Stoner, silently urging a resumption of the conversation. Stoner looked away.

Later that evening he dialled his mother's number, prepared, as usual, to let the phone ring and ring until she happened to hear and respond to it. She must have been in her bedroom because she answered almost immediately.

'Has Peter gone yet?' he asked.

'What?'

'Peter. Has he gone?'

'I don't know anyone called Peter.'

'Your nephew. You've always particularly liked him. I had lunch with him today, then he was going out to visit you.'

'There was a man here but I don't know who he was. A tall man in a dark suit. He had grey hair.'

'That was Peter. You must have recognised him!'

'What?'

'I asked him to look at the photograph albums. There are photos of his family that I knew he'd like to see. Can you remember if he looked at them?'

'I have no idea what he looked at.'

'Try to remember,' he said irritably. 'Please just try. It's important to remember.'

He regretted, almost immediately, that he had used a tone of voice that would be inordinately disturbing to her. He didn't even understand why the photographs mattered so much to him. They were nothing, after all, but accidental memories; children in a summer garden, boys on a beach.

'I'm sorry,' he said.

'What?'

They remained silent for ten or twelve seconds, then, in an anxious voice, his mother asked, 'Are you there?'

It was as if she were calling to someone who she feared might be lost, her voice thin and distant. 'Are you there?'

He didn't answer her. He couldn't think of anything to say.

Beyond the Walls

I was thirteen, at boarding school in Ballaghaderreen, when I first heard French. From then on I couldn't get enough of it, devouring everything I could find about France. I trawled my history books, geography books, and the encyclopaedia in the school library to feed my hunger. I went around speaking French to the other girls and became the laughing stock of the school. At night I would lie in my cubicle savouring the delicious sounds. Even the nun who taught French was suspicious of my obsession, sensing the French weren't God-fearing enough. Although she had never read Zola or Flaubert, she knew she was giving me the key to a world far beyond the convent walls. I believed that I looked French too, dark and petite with well-turned ankles, and I always managed to add a bit of style to the school uniform – a red velvet ribbon in my hair or a brooch borrowed from my mother.

From boarding school I got a scholarship to go to college in Galway. There were a hundred or so girls and five hundred lads; it was the early years of the Free State and there was a spring in the nation's step. I shared digs with three other girls, and there was an endless stream of fellows calling on us with invitations to dances and parties. The others complained that I worked too hard. I couldn't understand how reading great literature could be called work. It opened me to the poetry and music of life, took me soaring beyond the walls of convention, revealed to me the world of the spirit. I trembled to each line of *A la recherche du temps perdu*. I raced around Paris with Balzac and roamed the fields of Normandy with Maupassant. *Les Fleurs du Mal* taught me about sex and I learned about love from Stendhal. By the time I finished my degree, the streets of Paris were more familiar to me than the streets of Galway. On leaving college I went straight into a teaching job in a small market town in Leitrim, but I knew from the start that I wasn't cut out for teaching. I was so nervous about standing in front of a class that I used to get sick in the staff toilet. I was teaching French grammar to First Years, girls from small farms who knew French would never get them the big houses and fine dresses of their dreams.

At the weekends I used go dancing. The hall was an old airplane hangar, a cold building made of corrugated iron. We'd stand against the wall, shivering, waiting to be asked out. The farmers would cross the floor unsteadily. 'Would you like a dance, Miss?' Too drunk to dance to the music played by the band, they shuffled you around to some inner noise of their own. Later, they would push a bike as they walked you home, and the bike would be carefully placed against a wall while they rammed their hard bodies against you, the heavy porter breath signalling the kiss. Next day they'd cross the road to avoid you.

I met Con on a visit to Galway. He was the cousin of a friend, and had come from Dublin to work as a civil engineer with the County Council. He had Julien Sorel's Roman nose and dark eyes. Con was younger than I was and he would listen with great concentration as I talked about French Literature. He, however, was trying to find the underlying principles, the laws of literature. 'It is itself, Con,' I used to tell him. 'If you break it down, it will cease to be itself. You would be understanding not it, but something different.' And I'd read aloud to him so that he could hear the music of the language.

We married after three years of courtship and we bought a house I had long dreamed of living in. It was a Victorian farmhouse, covered in ivy, a few miles outside Galway, standing alone on a small hill beneath which was the great ocean that roared down to the western shores of France. An elderly Protestant couple had owned it and it lay abandoned after they died while their will was contested by some relatives. I was so happy when we moved in. I used sit in the garden for hours, staring at the sea and dreaming. Con said I did the dreaming for the two of us.

I gave up teaching when I became pregnant with Eileen. She was a big lump of a girl who cried when she was hungry and stopped when she was fed. When she wasn't feeding, she slept peacefully. The nurses said how lucky I was to have such a contented child.

It was about two weeks after I took her home that it started. I would set out on the road of a sentence and suddenly the road would get slippery and I'd go skidding all over the place. Down boreens, through stone walls, or I'd spin right around, not knowing which sentence I had started. I might want to say to Con 'I read an article on de Valera today,' but with all the slipping and skidding it would turn into 'I read that de Gaulle was beaten by the Helvetians and he broke the ice to have a swim'. I'd wake Con in the middle of the night begging him to hide because I could hear the engines of the Black and Tan lorries coming up the hill to take him away. I wouldn't answer the door when I was alone during the day because I was sure it was the Protestants come to take the house back. I couldn't cook or look after the house. There were too many important things happening around me. When Con's mother came to stay I kept shaking her because she didn't seem to understand. 'You must listen,' I shouted. 'I had a vision we'll lose at Compiègne, the Burgundians will capture me and I'll be burned at the stake.'

They took me to St Bridget's in Ballinasloe. It was full of Connemara men, driven mad by poteen and Roscommon men whose madness was their inheritance. There was one room full of half-naked imbeciles, men and women, who wrote on the wall with their faeces. The men at St Bridget's were mad for me and I took some comfort from them.

After a while I was moved to Dublin, to St Pat's. I had a friend there called Mary, a sad woman, married to a vet from Westmeath. He'd visit once a month. 'Isn't it time you were getting better now, Mary? The children need you,' he'd say as he eyed up one of the young nurses.

'The children are embarrassed and ashamed of me,' she'd

say. She had a terrible weakness for the truth.

We'd play cards to while away the evenings, silly games like snap, so it didn't matter if my mind went on a ramble. Father John would join us if he was in after one of his benders. I knew him from home, a great one to make us laugh. It took real comic genius to get a laugh out of Mary, I can tell you.

After a few years I had a good spell and I went home. Con's mother had moved in to look after Eileen. I was home long enough to have another baby. Feargal, we called him. He was a delicate little thing, constantly crying. I held him all night long, reciting La Fontaine to comfort him.

After a few years my sentences started wandering again. I invented a new language, each word made up of a combination of French, English and Irish syllables. I'd walk about the house all day talking aloud, delighting in the new sounds I had created. Then Con's mother became the evil conspiring Cousin Bette and I would wake him in the middle of the night to tell him he had to throw her out because she was out to destroy the family.

I returned to St Pat's and stayed there for ten years. When they put us all on the new drugs I swelled up like a pregnant cow, but my sentences stopped slipping and Con's mother turned back into herself. A few months afterwards, I came back home to live. Eileen was nearly grown up and Feargal was eleven. Eileen was a big girl who wanted to study domestic science and have a family. She looked like the prosperous farmers' wives on her father's side of the family. Feargal was slightly built and dark. He walked for hours by the sea, played the piano, listened to music alone in his room. I think he was very disappointed in me – Con had told him stories about how beautiful and artistic I had been. I would see him watching me sometimes as I sat for hours with my back to the sea, swollen and silent. I didn't want to be too ambitious with the sentences. I knew I couldn't survive another spell in hospital.

I've been home now for three years. Eileen got married and went to live in Cork. Con is President of the Chamber of

Commerce so he's out almost every evening. His mother got Parkinson's disease and she had to go to live in a nursing home, so it's just Feargal and myself most evenings.

I'm afraid I upset him the other night. I was staring at the television, not paying much heed to it, when I suddenly realised that the programme was about Flaubert. When it finished, I started weeping and I just couldn't stop. The weeping turned into a terrible wailing. Feargal came rushing downstairs. 'What happened, Mam, what happened to you?'

When I eventually stopped, I said, 'I've never been to France, Feargal. That's what happened.'

WILLIAM TREVOR

Marrying Damian

'I'm going to marry Damian,' Joanna said.

Claire wasn't paying attention. She smiled and nodded, intent on unravelling a ball of garden twine that had become tangled. I said: 'Well, that's nice of course. But Damian's married already.'

It didn't matter, Joanna said, and repeated her resolve. Joanna was five at the time.

*

Twenty-two years later Damian stood on the wild grass, among the cornflowers and the echiums and the lavatera, under the cricket-bat willow that had been a two-foot shrub when Joanna made her announcement. He was wearing blue sunglasses and a powder-blue suit that looked new. In contrast, his tie – its maroon and gold stripes seeming to indicate membership of some club to which almost certainly Damian did not belong – was lank, and the collar of his shirt was frayed. We hadn't been expecting him; we hadn't heard from Damian for years. Since the spring of 1985, Claire afterwards calculated, the year after his second divorce, from an American widow in upstate New York. Before that there had been an English woman who lived in Venice, about whom we had never been told very much. When Joanna had declared her childhood intention Damian had been still married to the only one of his three wives Claire and I actually knew: a slender, pretty girl, the daughter of the Bishop of Killaloe. We had known her since the wedding; I'd been Damian's best man.

I was actually asleep when Damian walked into our garden

all those years later, and I think Claire was too. We were lolling
in deckchairs, Claire's spaniels stretched out under hers,
avoiding the afternoon sun.

'Yes,' Damian said. 'It's Damian.'

We were surprised, but perhaps not much: turning up out of
the blue had always been his style. He never telephoned first or
intimated his intention by letter or on a postcard. Over the years
he had arrived in all seasons and at varying times of day, once
rousing us at two o'clock in the morning. Invariably he brought
with him details of a personal disaster which had left him with
the need to borrow a little money. These loans were not paid
back; even as he accepted them he made no pretence that they
would be.

'Damian.' Claire hugged him, laughing, playfully demanding
to know what he was doing in that awful suit. I asked him
where he'd been and he said oh, a lot of places – Vancouver,
Oregon, Spain. Claire made him sit down, saying she was going
to make some tea, inviting him to stay a while. He was the tonic
we needed, Claire said, for she's always afraid that we'll slump
into dullness unless we're careful. A woman, somewhere, had
given him the suit: we both guessed that.

'I wasn't all that well in Spain,' Damian said. 'Some kind of
sunstroke.'

We are the same age, Damian and I, not young any more:
that day, as we sat together in the garden, we were sixty and a
bit, Claire five years younger. She's tall and slim, and I can't
believe she'll ever be anything but elegant, but of course I know
I may be wrong. When we married she came to live in the
country town I've always known, acquiring an extra identity as
the doctor's wife and the receptionist at the practice, as the
mother of a daughter and a son, the organiser of a playgroup,
the woman who first taught the illiterate of the town to read.

Damian, at the first opportunity, fled this neighbourhood. On
his return to it the time before this one he had carried – clearly
an affectation – a silver-topped cane, which was abandoned
now, no doubt because it drew attention to its own necessity,
and Damian inclines towards vanity. Although he sat down

briskly in the chair Claire had vacated for him, the protest of a joint caused him, for a single instant, to wince. His light, fair hair is grey in places now, and I don't suppose he cares for that either, or that his teeth have shrivelled and become discoloured, or that the freckles on the backs of his hands form blobs where they have spread into one another, or that the skin of his forehead is as dry as old vellum. But that day there was nothing about his eyes to suggest a coming to terms with a future destined to be different from the past, no hint of a hesitation about what should or should not be undertaken: in that sense Damian remains young.

Even as a boy his features were gaunt, giving the impression then of under-nourishment. He was angular, but without any of the awkwardness sometimes associated with that quality. In spite of whatever trouble he was having with a joint, he could still, I noticed that day, tidy himself away with natural ease. As always at the beginning of a visit, he was good-humoured; moodiness – sometimes a snappish response to questions, or silence – was apt to set in later.

If, in terms of having a profession, Damian is anything, he is a poet, although in all the time I've known him he has never shown me more than a verse or two. Years ago someone told us that he once had a coterie of admirers and was still, in certain quarters, considered to possess 'a voice' that should be more widely heard. A volume entitled *Slow Death of a Pigeon* – its contents sparse, Claire and I always assumed, for nothing about Damian suggests he is profligate with his talent – appears to represent all he has so far chosen for posterity. In time we would receive a copy of *Slow Death of a Pigeon* he promised on one of his visits, but none arrived.

'Well, yes, it was that. Something like it,' he was saying, slightly laughing, when I returned with another deckchair after Claire had brought out the tea things. He had repeated all he'd told me about his sunstroke and the lack of anything of interest in Vancouver. Yes, he was confessing now, a relationship with a woman had featured in his more recent travels, had somehow been the reason for them. There was no confirmation that the powder-blue suit had been a gift. Damian wouldn't have considered that of interest.

'I thought I'd maybe die,' he said, returning to the subject of his sunstroke, but when I asked him what he'd taken for it, what treatment there had been, he was vague.

'Bloody visions,' he said instead. 'Goya stuff. In any case,' he confidently pronounced, Spain was over-rated.

Had the woman been Spanish? I wondered, and thought of dancers, white teeth and a rosebud that was red, black skirts swirling, red ribbons in black hair. I have doctor colleagues who farm a bit, who let the wind blow away the mixture of triviality and death that now and again makes our consulting rooms melancholy places. Others collect rare books, make cabinets, involve themselves in politics, allow gardening or some sport to become a way of life to skulk in. For me, Damian's infrequent visits, and wondering about him in between, were such a diversion. Not as efficacious as afternoons on a tractor or searching out a Cuala Press edition of Yeats, but then by nature I'm lazy.

'A chapter closed?' Claire was saying.

'Should never have been opened.'

Later, in the kitchen, I decanted the wine and Claire said the lamb would be enough, with extra potatoes and courgettes. We heard Joanna's car and then her voice exclaiming in surprise and Damian greeting her.

I carried a tray of drinks to the garden. Damian's small black suitcase, familiar to us for many years, was still on the grass beside his deckchair. I can see it now.

*

The visit followed a familiar pattern. In the small suitcase there were shirts and underclothes and socks in need of laundering; and when they had been through the washing-machine most of them were seen to be in need of repair. Damian, besides, was penniless; and there was the request that if anyone telephoned him – which was, he said, unlikely since, strictly speaking, no one knew his whereabouts – his presence in our house should be denied.

When we were children, Damian and I had played together at Doul, the grey, half-derelict house where his Aunt Una had brought him up. Doul is no longer there, having been sold to a builder for the lead of its roof, and later razed to the ground. Damian's Aunt Una had drunk herself to death in a caravan. I was actually there when her head jerked suddenly to one side on the pillow, the visible indication of her demise. She'd been, in our childhood, a vague presence in that old house and its lost garden, tall and handsome yet somehow like a ghost of someone else: it was said that she was Damian's mother. People who remembered her advent, with an infant, in the neighbourhood, said the house had been bought for her by the man who'd made her pregnant, buying her silence also.

I learned all that later. When Damian and I were eight his Aunt Una was known to me as his aunt and there was never a reason, afterwards, to doubt that she was. He and I were sent away to different schools – the seducer from the past said to have obliged in this way, also where Damian's boarding fees were concerned – but our friendship none the less continued. Damian – like a scarecrow sometimes because it was never noticed by his Aunt Una that he grew out of his clothes – was easy company, hard to dislike, an antidote to the provincial respectability I grew up in. We wandered about the countryside; we hung about point-to-points; when we were older we went to Friday dancehalls if one of us had money; we dreamed of romance with Bettina Nowd, clerk in the Munster and Leinster Bank. Abruptly, our ways parted, and remained so for a long time: when Damian, at nineteen, left the neighbourhood he did not return for fourteen years, by which time his Aunt Una was dead and her house gone. It was said he hadn't written to her, or communicated in any way during that time, which was surprising because he was always fond of her. But as I heard nothing from him either it's perhaps less odd than it seems. For Damian, perhaps, the vacuum of people's absence cannot be filled by any other means. During that fourteen years he and I met only once, at Killaloe at the first of his weddings.

'You know, I'd like to see Doul again,' he said the day after he'd appeared in his powder-blue suit. So we went there, where there was nothing to see, not even the caravan his Aunt Una died in. Beneath the brambles that grew everywhere, and the great swathes of nettles, there might have been remains of some kind, but if there were the naked eye could not discern them. When we walked on a bit there were the walls of the kitchen garden, ivy-clad in places, fallen away in others.

'You couldn't build Doul again,' I pointed out when he said he'd like to. 'Not without a fortune, Damian.'

He muttered something, and for the first time sounded disagreeable. There was some kind of complaint, a protest about his continuing lack of means and then: 'The avenue . . . the gates . . .'

A fragment from a poem? I wondered. Sometimes in Damian's conversation words stand isolated and out of context, as though they do not belong in conversation at all.

'The house,' I began.

'Oh, not the house as it was.'

Claire's spaniels sniffed about for rabbits. As we stood there, the September sun felt hot. Damian believes in the impossible and when we were younger occasionally inspired me with his optimism: that nothing could be easier than poaching salmon, that a bookie or a publican would accept an IOU, that Bettina Nowd had the love-light in her eyes. It was an endearing quality then; I wasn't so sure about it being one that had endearingly endured. I felt uneasy about this talk of coming back. During the companionship of our youth there had never been an attempt to borrow money, since there was none to lend; nor was advantage taken of small politenesses since politeness was not then readily on offer. The threat of a neighbour with a fly-by-night's presumptions was just a little alarming.

'Who owns it now?' he asked, and I told him: the son of the builder who had stripped the roof of its lead.

The cawing of rooks and the occasional bark of the dogs were the only sounds. It had always been quiet at Doul; that tall, beautiful woman floating about from room to room or picking the last of the mulberries; bees in the honeysuckle.

'What?' I said, again unable to catch Damian's murmur. Still moody, he did not directly reply, but seemed to say that the Muse would not be silent here.

*

I had ceased to practise on my sixtieth birthday, feeling the time had come, although previously I had imagined I could go on more or less for ever, as my father had in this same house, to his dying day. 'What'll it be like?' Damian used to ponder when we were young, the world for him an excitement to investigate after a small, familiar town in south-west Ireland. Both of us, of course, knew what it would be like for me: we knew my father's house, its comfortably crowded rooms, its pleasant garden; we knew the narrow main street, the shopkeepers, priests, and beggars, the condensed-milk factory, the burnt-out cinema, the sleepy courthouse, the bright new hospital, the old asylum, the prison. But neither of us could conjecture a single thing about what lay ahead for Damian.

'It's all right, is it?' Damian asked me on the way back from Doul that day, his mood gregarious again, suddenly so, as if he had remembered who I was. 'Doing nothing these days is all right?'

'Yes, it's all right.'

In fact, it was more than that: all sorts of things were easier in retirement. People weren't patients any more. Met by chance on the street, they conversed with less embarrassment; while privately I registered that Raynaud's was at work or that Frolich's Syndrome would not now be reversed. In ordinary chat, awkward secrets were not shared with me; more likely I was shown an adolescent's face and then reminded I'd been the first to see it as an infant's; or informed of athletic achievements in children who had grown up, or of success in other ways, and weddings that were planned. Worries were held back, not coinage for me now, as bad backs weren't, or stitched wounds or blood pressure, the smell of sickness in small back bedrooms.

'Yes, it's fine,' I said in the bar of Traynor's Hotel. 'And you?' I added. 'Nowadays, Damian?'

Again he became morose. He shrugged and did not answer. He stared at the back of a man who was standing at the bar, at the torn seam of a jacket. Then he said:

'I used to think about Doul. Wherever I was, I'd come back to that.'

From his tone, those thoughts about the place of his youth had been a comfort, occurring – the implication was – at times of distress or melancholy. Then Damian said, as if in response to a question I had not asked:

'Well yes, an inspiration.'

He had finished the whiskey in his glass. I went to the bar, and while the drinks I ordered were poured I was asked by Mr Traynor about our son, now a doctor in New South Wales, and about Joanna, who had returned to the town six months ago to work in the prison. 'You'd be delighted she's back here,' Mr Traynor conjectured, and I agreed, although pointing out that sooner or later she would move away again. I smiled, shrugging that away, my mind not on the conversation. Could Doul have been a poet's inspiration for all these years? I wondered. Was that the meaning I was supposed to find in what had been so vaguely stated?

'I thought I recognised him,' Mr Traynor next remarked, his voice kept low, after I had answered his query about who Damian was. 'How're you doing these times?' he called out, and Damian called back that none of us was getting younger.

'God, that's the truth in it,' Mr Traynor agreed, wagging his head in a pretence that this hadn't occurred to him before.

I picked up my change and made my way back to the table where we sat.

'Nothing grand,' Damian said, as if my absence hadn't interrupted what we'd been saying. 'Any little hovel that could be knocked together. There are things . . .' He let the sentence trail away. 'I have the time now.'

I sipped my drink, disguising amusement: all his life Damian had had time. He ran through time, spending it as a spendthrift, wallowing in idleness. Perhaps poets always did, perhaps it was the way they had to live; I didn't know.

'Stuff accumulates,' Damian confided, 'unsaid. Oh, it's just a thought,' he added, and I concluded, with considerable relief, that this was probably the last we'd hear of his morning's whim. After all, there was no sign whatsoever of his being in possession of the necessary funds to build the modest dwelling he spoke of, and personal loans could be resisted.

'Silly old Damian,' Claire murmured when I told her, with the indulgent smile that talk of Damian always drew from her.

*

Then, quite suddenly, everything was different. Perhaps in the same moment – at dinner two days later – Claire and I were aware that our daughter was being charmed all over again by the man she had once picked out as the man she would like to marry. To this day, I can hear their two voices in my dining-room, and Damian laughing while Claire and I were numbed into silence. To this day I can see the bright flush in Joanna's cheeks.

'And are you settled, Joanna?' Damian asked. 'Here?'

'For the time being,' Joanna said.

The prison is two miles outside the town, a conglomeration of stark grey buildings behind high grey walls, which occasionally I have visited during an epidemic. *Ad sum ard labor*, a waggish inmate has carved on a sundial he made for the governor, a tag that is a talking point when visitors are led around. Joanna has worked in prisons in Dublin and in England; she came here because from conversations she has had with me she was aware that rehabilitation – which is her territory – wasn't being much bothered with. It was a challenge that here on the doorstep of the town she was born and grew up in were circumstances that professionally outraged her.

'I remember sharing a railway carriage with a man who'd

just been released from gaol,' Damian said. 'He robbed
garages.'

In Joanna's view a spell in prison was the offer of another
chance for the offender, a time to come to terms with the world
and with oneself. She was an optimist; you had to be, she
insisted.

'Lonely wayside garages,' Damian said. 'A child working the
pumps.'

'Did he say —'

'All he said was that he didn't intend to get caught the next
time.'

Beneath these exchanges there was something else, a tremor
that was shared; a tick answered another tick, fingers touched
although a dinner-table separated them. I pushed my knife and
fork together; and Claire said something that nobody heard and
went to the kitchen.

Joanna is small and dark-haired, and pretty. She has had
admirers, a proposal of marriage from a map-maker, a longish
affair with an ornithologist, but her passionate devotion to her
work has always seemed to make her draw back when there
was pressure that a relationship should be allowed the
assumption of permanence. It was as though she protected her
own dedication, as though she believed she would experience a
disloyalty in herself if she in any way devoted less time and
energy to her work. Recidivists, penitents, old lags, one-time
defaulters, drug pushers, muggers, burglars, rapists: these were
her lovers. She found the good in them, and yet, when telling us
about them, did not demand that we should too. It has never
been her way to lecture, or stridently to insist, and often people
are surprised at the intensity of her involvement, at the steel
beneath so soft a surface. Neither Claire nor I ever say so, but
there is something in our daughter that is remarkable.

Across the dinner table that evening she became demure.
There was obedience in her glance, and respect for every
ordinary word our visitor uttered, as though she would blindly
have acted as he dictated should his next words express a
desire. I followed Claire into the kitchen, carrying plates and

dishes. 'I always wanted to,' Joanna was saying, drawn out by Damian in a way that was not usual in his conversation. 'I never thought of doing anything else.'

We didn't speak, Claire and I, in the kitchen. We didn't even look at one another. It was our fault; we had permitted this stroke of fate to stake its claim. The suitable admirers – the dark-haired map-maker, the ornithologist, and others – were not what a retriever of lost causes, a daily champion of down-and-outs, had ever wanted. In the dining-room the voices chatted on, and in the kitchen we felt invaded by them, Claire and I, she tumbling raspberries into a blue glass bowl, I spooning coffee into the filter. 'I remember hearing you'd been born,' Damian was saying in the dining-room when we returned.

It was I who had told him. I delivered Joanna myself; Claire and I heard her first cry in the same moment. 'A girl,' I said when Damian arrived six months later for one of his visits, and we drank my whiskey on a bitter January night. 'How nice to have a daughter!' he murmured when we gazed down at the cot by Claire's bedside. And he was right: it was nice having a girl as well as a boy, nice being a family. Even then, two different personalities were apparent: our son's easy-going, rarely ruffled, Joanna's confident. At five and six, long-legged and determined, she won the races she ran because insistently she believed she could. Oh no, she wouldn't, she asserted when it was pointed out that she would tire of looking after the unattractive terrier she rescued after tinkers left it behind. And for years, until the creature died in old age, she did look after it.

'It was snowing outside,' Damian reminisced in the dining-room. 'Black Bush was what we drank, Joanna, the night your father and I wet the baby's head.'

His fingernails were rimmed: ash from the cigarettes he was smoking, as he always does, between courses. Once upon a time, years ago, he affected a cigarette-holder. He had sold it, he told Claire when she asked, and we guessed it had been another gift from a woman, sold when the affair was over.

'Raspberries, Damian?' Claire offered.

He smiled his acceptance. He placed his cigarette, still burning, on a side plate, and poured cream on the fruit. I wondered if children had been born to him; I hadn't wondered that before. I imagined, as I often had, his public-house life in London, some places he could not enter because of debts, late-night disagreements turning sour. I had a feeling that his travels to other places – so often mentioned – had always been of brief duration, that London was where he had mostly belonged, in seedy circumstances. I imagined lodgings, rent unpaid, possessions pawned. How often had there been flits in the small hours? Were small dishonesties a poet's right? And yet, I thought as well, he was our friend and almost always had been. He'd cheered our lives.

'Damian's tired of London,' Joanna said. 'He's going to live at Doul again.'

*

In the night, believing me to be asleep, Claire wept. I whispered, trying to console her. We didn't say to one another that shock came into this, that we must allow a little time to calm us. We lay there, remembering that not much longer than twenty-four hours ago Claire had said our friend was the tonic we needed. On all his visits we'd never been dismayed to see him, and he couldn't help being older now, less handsome than he had been, his grubbiness more noticeable. He was, at heart, as he had always been. It was unfair to say he wasn't, just because he had cast a spell on our house. We'd always known about those spells. We'd read between the lines, we hadn't been misled.

Marriage was what we dreaded, although neither of us used the word. It was not because Damian had so often confessed he liked to marry that our melancholy threw up this stark prediction; it was because Joanna was Joanna. We might be wrong, we felt each other thinking; a tawdry love affair might be enough. But we did not believe it and neither of us suggested the consolation of this lesser pain. Nor did we remind one another that Joanna, all her life, had been attracted by the difficult, nor did we share it with one another when in the dark we were more certainly aware that there had been no challenge in her relationship with the map-maker or the ornithologist, or with any of her suitable admirers. Perhaps, that night, we knew our daughter a little better, and perhaps we loved her just a little more. She would succeed where other women had failed: already we could hear her offering this, already we sensed her not believing that the failure could lie anywhere but with those other women. 'I'm going to marry Damian,' the childish silliness brightly echoed, and with it our amusement.

Had he come to us this time with a purpose? Claire asked when she ceased to weep. Did he intend our daughter to earn his living for him, to tend him in the place of his childhood, cosseting his old man's frailties? Had his future lit up suddenly on a London street, the years ahead radiant as a jewel in his imagination? 'I'll tell them,' had our daughter said already, planning to sit us down, to pour out drinks in celebration? She would break the news that was not news, and we'd embrace her, not pointing out that Damian couldn't help destroying his achievements. And she would hurry to him when he next appeared and they would stand together as lovers do. We could not foretell the details after that, and quite suddenly the form the relationship might take in time hardly seemed to matter any more: enough of it was there already. 'Are we being punished?' Claire asked, and I didn't know if we were or not, or why we should be punished, or what our sin was.

We didn't want that night to end. We didn't want to feel, again, the excitement that had crept into our house, that passed us by and was not ours. It was not in Damian's nature to halt an adventure that was already under way, not in his nature to acquire from nowhere the decency that would forbid it to proceed. His bedroom would not be empty when morning came, the small suitcase gone, a note left on his bedside table. 'Remember the others?' Claire whispered in the dark, and I knew whom she meant without having to think – the daughter of the Bishop of Killaloe, the widow from upstate New York, the

Englishwoman in Venice, and other nameless women mentioned by our friend in passing.

Ill-suited, we said, when we learnt that the first of his marriages had fallen apart, and were too busy in those busy days to be more than sorry. We had hardly wondered about the fate of the bishop's daughter, and not at all about the American widow, except to say to one another that it was typical of Damian to make the same mistake twice. And when the Englishwoman left him it was a joke. Old reprobate, we said. Incorrigible.

The first streaks of dawn came flickering in, the birds began. We lay there silent, not trusting ourselves to comment on this past that the present had thrown up. The bishop's daughter – younger than Joanna was now – smiled in her wedding dress, and I felt again the warm touch of her cheek when I kissed it, and heard her reply to my good wishes, her shy voice saying she was happier than she deserved to be. And a face from a photograph we'd once been shown was the oval face of the American, dark hair, dark eyes, lips slightly parted. And the face of the Englishwoman was just a guess, a face contorted in a quarrel, made bitter with cold tears. The shadows of other men's wives, of lovely women, girls charmed, clamoured for attention, breaking from their shadows, taking form. Old reprobate.

'I think I'll go and talk to her.' Claire's voice was hushed in the twilight, but she didn't move, and I knew that already she had changed her mind; talking would make everything worse. Eighty-one, Claire said: he would be eighty-one when Joanna was forty-eight.

I didn't calculate. It didn't matter. I thought we might quarrel, that tiredness might bring something like that on, but we didn't. We didn't round on each other, blaming in order to shed guilt, bickering as we might have once, when upsets engendered edginess. We didn't because ours are the dog days of marriage and there aren't enough left to waste: dangerous ground has long ago been charted and is avoided now. There was no point in saying, either, that the damage we already sensed would become entertainment for other people, as damage had for us.

'I'll make tea,' I said, and descended the stairs softly as I always do at this early hour so as not to wake our daughter. Some time today Damian and I might again call in at Traynor's; I might, in sickening humility, ask for mercy. I heard my own voice doing so, but the sound was false, wrong in all sorts of ways; I knew I wouldn't say a thing. To ensure that our daughter had a roof over her head I would lend whatever was necessary. A bungalow would replace the fallen house at Doul.

The *Irish Times* was half pushed through the letter-box; I slipped it out. I brought the tray back to our bedroom, with gingersnap biscuits on a plate because we like them in the early morning. We read the paper. We didn't say much else.

Later that morning Joanna hurried through cornflakes and a slice of toast. Her car started, reversed, then dashed away. Damian appeared and we sat outside in the September sunshine; Claire made fresh coffee. It was too late to hate him. It was too late to deny that we'd been grateful when our stay-at-home smugness had been enlivened by the tales of his adventures, or to ask him if he knew how life had turned out for the women who had loved him. Instead we conversed inconsequentially.

CLAIRR O'CONNOR

Rosa's Fat Jeans

Since Rosa died I haven't stopped eating. We worked on the twentieth floor for fifteen years, cleaners in this ugly hotel in St Petersburg. Except it was Leningrad for most of that time. We've known each other since we were students. We studied science. Physics to be precise. Naturally, this equipped us to be hotel cleaners. Suspects, this was the best job we could get. Some say it is useless to fight fate but I find it hard to embrace it. Some days when I clear out a room deftly examining it for soap, tights or even chocolate, I cannot understand why Rosa is not with me. The Armenians smirk in our faces, blowing their Camel cigarette smoke in clouds of disdain. She had the measure of them all. Nowadays, we're supposed to be free.

New freedom? Don't make me laugh. As far as I can see, it's more of the same for the few who can grab it. The waiters have grown fat in the last year. These days they do not eat the leftover food from the tables as was their habit, furtively and fast in a corner. They bundle it up and take it home in plastic bags. But that's not the worst of it. They slap down the food on tables at the appointed hour and if a coachload of tourists are delayed because of a demonstration or simply by getting lost, they take the food away and let them forage for themselves. They no longer give service for the glory of Mother Russia.

Anna, the desk woman on the twentieth floor, turns a blind eye to almost everything. Her task is to give the correct keys to guests and collect them again. But her role has long since expanded. She ingratiates herself with the guests by playing the humble little Russian. That way they give her cartons of Marlboro, tights, scented soaps and dollar tips.

She tips off the pimps as to who are the wealthiest guests.

They telephone the guests' rooms to offer services of all kinds. Some say Anna's small flat is full to bursting point with her stockpiled goods. She supplies all the 'girls' on this floor and floor twenty-one with tights and soap. Her English is good but she pretends she doesn't know any. That way she hears more. Also it gratifies the guests when they believe they have taught her a few phrases by the end of their stay. Each guest believing he or she has a unique relationship with downtrodden Anna. Only yesterday, the distraught American in room 2020 came to Anna with a tale of woe. His three pairs of jeans had been stolen while he was at the ballet. It was his last night.

'Goddamn awful!' he said with feeling.

Anna repeated his distress lines. 'God-damn aw-ful!' she sympathised.

Her parody turned his distress to laughter. 'Mary-Ellen,' he called to his wife, 'Anna has broken into the English language.' His wife was red-eyed and tightless, all lifted at the same time as her husband's jeans, but she managed a smile for Anna.

'Chai? Tea?' Anna offered.

'Something stronger, I think.'

'Champanski?'

'Champagne,' he nodded, 'two bottles. It could be worse, honey, we weren't mugged and our wallets are still intact. Let's celebrate our last night. Tomorrow, we'll be in Vienna.'

Anna brought the champagne to room 2020. The American paid her ten dollars. She had bought it herself for three. Seven dollars profit. Not bad for an act of kindness. Illya, her lover, the pimp who controlled the twentieth floor, had removed the jeans and tights while the Americans were at the ballet. They would split the profits later. At least fifty dollars. Anna enjoyed her work.

Rosa had never liked Anna. 'Beware of the party puritans,' she warned when Anna had reported Antonina. She had accepted a ten-rouble tip from a guest who was emptying his wallet of Russian currency before he left for the airport. That was five years ago. Before the new freedom.

'It's demeaning to accept bribes and tips from decadent

Westerners,' Anna had scolded Antonina, 'our workers serve the state. We will not be insulted in this way.' These days Anna's pockets bulge with western currency.

'Never trust a woman who can't hear music with her heart,' Rosa said. 'To Anna, Tchaikovsky was just a homosexual. She cannot see the glory in "Swan Lake" or "Eugene Onegin".'

'Hush!' I cautioned her. We were sweeping out 2043 at the time. It's the room with the rumbling plumbing and its windows don't open. 'She could hear you.' I checked the corridor. Anna was still at her desk, but any criticism of her made me anxious.

Rosa feared no one. 'After they lock you up in prison without pen or paper, what is there to fear?'

When she said that, her gaze level with me, what could I say? I felt humble but also afraid. Rosa's courage was noble but I feared for her because of it. She had been locked up for sixty days in a damp prison. Solitary confinement for a poem called 'Kick the Bear'.

There were no visitors allowed. When they released her, sick and weak, I did not think she would survive the trolley bus ride home. Our flat is on the third floor but those three flights of stairs seemed to take the last of her strength. I fed her cabbage soup. She could not keep it down.

In the end I let her sleep between sips of water. Two weeks went by in such a way. I was fretful at work. To die on one's own is such a dread of my own that I could not rest when I was away from her. When Anna said, 'There is no place for dissidents in this establishment,' pursing her lips in a tight line of satisfaction, I did not argue.

I put my mind to doing Rosa's work as well as my own. Just in case, as we Russians say. Just in case a loophole in the party system would grant her the indulgence of her menial job again.

She had a former lover, someone she had known in her teens, Alexis. From the same district. A blond boy with soft eyes. He had grown into a KGB hard man. 'How can one know the future at sixteen?' Rosa shrugged philosophically when I first heard of the connection. In any event, he turned out to be quite useful. When I tracked him down and told him of Rosa's plight, it was he who got her released from prison. I did not dare tell her of my craven begging on her behalf. Likewise, it was he who restored her to her place on the twentieth floor.

She looked the other way when he made one of his rare appearances in the hotel. 'That pig,' she spluttered, 'he lives off the likes of us but soon the winds of freedom will bring him to his knees. His kind are a dying breed.'

I made a racket with the hoover to drown out her voice.

Rosa never really recovered from the prison sentence. Her breath was short and her colour ghastly. I did my best. I stood in line outside the Lancôme shop and got her some make-up and rouge. But she only wore the stuff to please me. 'Since you wasted a month's salary on such fripperies, I suppose I must oblige.' Her playful tone removed the sting.

She never gave way to self-pity. Maybe that's why she always had visitors. They came with gifts that caused them sacrifices. Nicholas brought six red apples one weekend. Natasha painted them, each apple ready to come off the canvas with its rounded appeal.

'Yours rival Courbet's apples,' Rosa congratulated her. 'But where did they come from?' We were overcome.

'Don't ask,' Nicholas said lightly, 'eat, enjoy.' By then Rosa was beyond eating.

The supervisor on the twentieth floor, Peter, pretended for a long time not to notice that Rosa could not do her work. He was afraid of Alexis, the KGB man, Rosa's secret protector. But as soon as the winds of change blew through Leningrad, transforming it in reverse to St Petersburg, he started to notice things.

'I do not think Comrade Rosa is able for such physically demanding work anymore. What do you think?' he'd smile the question at me. I covered Rosa's schedule as well as my own. Most days she walked beside me but I made her sit as much as possible.

'He's right,' she said one day.

'Who?' I enquired, as we hadn't been talking about anyone. I was scrubbing out the bath in room 2053. Rosa was sitting, staring in front of her.

'Peter, the peeved, our almighty supervisor. I'm not fit for this anymore. You do my job as well as your own. It's not right. They won't let it go on much longer.'

Useless to argue with Rosa. I've always known that.

'I'm fine,' I assured her, 'you must come as long as you want.'

'After this week, I will stay home.' Then she gave a derisory snort, 'There's always my pension! I'm lucky really. I won't be around long enough to have to eke out a living from the state's few kopeks. Not like the other poor bastards.'

And that is how she came to stay home. Propped up in bed with a bank of pillows, she slipped away little by little. At first, the loss of flesh to the face and hands was hardly noticeable. Gradually the neck was crumpled and bagged. Eventually the eyes protruded and the hair thinned. Most days, she dozed her way in and out of sleep while I was at the hotel.

But in the evenings she roused herself to animation and attention while I retold the day's trivia. Most of the news was not good. The 'bar girls' who could be bought for a few dollars, some tights and a pack of Marlboro; the waiters who were working the black market money exchange; Anna who stockpiled from free enterprise. I could not keep it from her. She wanted to hear.

'What price perestroika!' she laughed. 'The irony is, I was one of the true believers. They may have locked me up and broken my health for a third-rate poem but part of my spirit always believed in the Revolution. These days, she's a tart in black tights with a dollar in her hand.'

Summer came and with it her friends, the unpublished writers, the artists who never got an exhibition, the scientist who works as a janitor in a factory. They read to her and fed her gossip. And when she was too tired she'd say, 'My friends, I think you should take a little walk now,' always with a smile, and they knew they were dismissed. 'It's a good day for a walk and since we're not in Moscow, you won't be treading on Stalin's snow.'

'I was there last week,' Leon said. 'The trees were really shedding. My poor mother is choked with her allergies. Someone ought to cut down Stalin's trees. Every summer it's the same.'

On their way out they'd mutter their anxiety each in turn.

'She looks thinner.'

'Does she sleep the nights?'

'I'll bring the car next weekend. We'll have a drive.'

'We're useless to her really. No *blat*. If she could only get to the Black Sea!'

'Pigs might dance before Rosa gets a holiday.'

Blat. Influence. Ways of getting things within the system. But none of us had the connections. We did the best we could but it wasn't enough to save Rosa. I myself became very depressed at this time. I didn't realise it until much later of course. When your days and nights are occupied with survival there is little time for reflection. Hotel work, queueing for food and looking after Rosa in the evenings took all my energy. My frustration with things as they stood and my inability to change them exhausted me.

I left the flat at seven o'clock each morning, taking with me my 'just-in-case bag'. Just in case there was fruit or vegetables available anywhere. I always checked on Rosa before I left. Most days she pretended to be asleep in the mornings. Often her eyelids fluttered but I accepted her pretence. It was her only independence now.

Anna, the desk woman on my floor, invariably greeted me with, 'How's the invalid? Still alive?'

My reply never varied, 'She's well, thank you.' Anna's lover, Peter the pimp, was even more direct: 'How's Rosa? Still taking up space in that cubby-hole of a flat? Between the smell of cabbage soup and the stench of death, you'll be overwhelmed yourself. It will be too late for you then to become one of my little girls.' His gold teeth glinted in my face. They chomped on my nerves like hot pincers.

Alexandra, my partner since Rosa's retirement, laughed skittishly. She's a brazen young thing. Too chatty for my liking but she does her fair share of work, so it's alright. There's talk that she's one of Peter's bar girls at night and maybe that accounts for her sweet-smelling perfume and her three pairs of shoes, but I didn't encourage her confidences.

I pushed my trolley ahead of me and ignored the fact that Peter was walking beside me down a long stretch of corridor.

'Would you like to be moved to floor eighteen?' His tone is threateningly solicitous.

'I'm happy where I am. Thank you,' I say, as neutrally as possible.

Floor eighteen is the drug floor. Soft and hard drugs available twenty-four hours of the day. Marijuana cigarettes sold in Marlboro packets, uppers, downers, heroin, syringes. All pushed by the Armenians and there's never a shortage. How they manage it, I don't quite know. There's a lot of violence on floor eighteen. Drug and drink fights break out regularly and you're as liable to find a blood-soaked syringe or broken bottles in bedrooms as the usual wet towels and tossed beds.

From time to time a corpse is found or a body as close to a corpse as makes no difference. The cleaners on floor eighteen have to pay the Armenians to protect them. One cleaner had her front teeth knocked out simply by knocking on a door to clean a room.

'Everyone has a price, my little Katya. And it's never as high as you might think. You'll want to talk to uncle Peter yet. Just don't leave it too late, darling.'

I was shaking with tension by the time I got to room 2015. I had to sit down to recover. Floor eighteen was hell on earth. I fingered the Toblerone bar in my pocket. The Englishwoman had given it to me that morning before she left for the airport. Up to that point I had never tasted western chocolate. I had no idea what a treat was in store for me. I broke off two pieces of chocolate and put them in my mouth. I crunched the chocolate with relish and became an instant convert.

That night, I cut the remainder of the chocolate into small pieces for Rosa. She loved it as much as I did. Our indulgence took on a party atmosphere.

'We're eating the fruits of the decadent West,' Rosa said. A spasm of coughing convulsed her but she smiled as she lay back on her pillows, a trail of chocolate dribbled to her chin. We picnicked on Toblerone bars after that as often as I could procure them. But neither western chocolate nor my care could save Rosa. She was slipping away week by week.

One day I brought her home a pair of jeans. I had been saving for them for months. I had bought them from Anna, the desk woman. As young women we had always wanted jeans, Rosa and I. Silly the things you crave. As students we had poured over contraband western magazines which had photographs of young women in jeans casually going about their everyday business. Those magazines had engrossed us as much as our science manuals. Now, fifteen years on, I had a pair of jeans, a gift for Rosa.

I helped her into them, only then realising they were several sizes too big. I had been thinking of big Rosa, Rosa before her illness. We had to secure them with a belt. I had forgotten how thin she had become.

'You've bought fat jeans for a scarecrow,' she laughed. 'You mustn't waste them, though. When I go, you must have them.'

She died that night. Since Rosa died I haven't stopped eating. At first, I folded the jeans carefully and put them at the back of my wardrobe. As time went on I took to trying them on. Much too big, they fell from my hips. I thought of taking them in, adjusting them to my size but somehow that didn't seem right. I wanted to have the same jeans as Rosa wore. My answer lay in Toblerones. I took to stealing them from tourists' rooms. One here, another there. They didn't even notice. Most of them bought in bulk before entering our chocolate-starved land. Now I fit into Rosa's jeans. Peter says I'm too fat to be one of his bar girls.

KEITH RIDGWAY

Watling Street Bridge

I stood on the bridge before dawn with the rain hitting my face, and I stared into the river, waiting for something to occur to me. That was why I stood there. It is in such situations that the great moments come. I have read about it. Some conclusion is reached, some decision is made, some revelation settles at the corner of the mind and is slowly lit, like the sun that grows out of the cold ground in the east.

But nothing came. I felt the rain break the banks of my eyebrows and drip from my lashes and run down my cheeks. It worked its way into my ears somehow, so that I had to tilt my head to one side and knock the heel of my hand against my temple. It ran down my chin to my neck, disappearing beneath the layers of my clothes. I could feel the rain on my chest. I could feel the rain inside me. I cannot explain that.

Below, the water swirled darkly, the rain and the street lights making it glisten a little; choppy like a landslide of black rock, running like the blood of a cut.

Nothing happened. Everything stayed the same. The same twisting of the heart, as if blind hands were attempting to wring it dry. I could not tell what it was, what name to give it. Sorrow does not cover it, but despair would be too strong. And there was anger there too: a background but distinct rage, like a razor-sharp knife wielded in the distance – thin lines of sudden red, and a sound with it, a night-time tearing.

I have done nothing wrong. It's not like that. I have committed no sin at least, none to speak of; and certainly I have committed no crime. Not lately. Not that I know of. But I am struggling with hindsight, and regret has placed a hand on me, and a dim shadow has loomed up in front of me, and I am seen by strange eyes and I know not the reason.

Eyes I said. Grotesque and familiar. I know the reason.

There are cars that go by, taxis mostly. I'm sure the drivers think that I'm going to jump. But it's not that. That is not in my nature.

When my lover threw me out, he did so without anger. He was calm and practical. I stood there in the street with things neatly packed, all my belongings piled up and labelled, boxed and retrievable. The items I might need were close to hand. The heavy stuff was distributed cleverly, so that I could lift every package single-handed. It was as if he wanted to emphasise something. That I did not need help.

And he was right to throw me out, and he was wrong. But that comes later. Firstly, there were the good years, and then there were just years, when we knew about the future because it was the same as the present. We had passed from the comfort of believing that we were safe from ourselves, and moved into a bleaker place. We began to look at the ground and kick up dust and stumble half-heartedly over whatever obstacles we could find in the empty spaces that surrounded us. We sought out ways of getting lost. We tried to walk in perfect circles, to come across footsteps that we could recognise as our own. There was nothing in the way of pain that we did not taste for the simple sake of tasting it. We were trying to break the skin that held us – or rather, we were trying to see if it could hold. We played with the sharp strings and the pointed turning of minutes, watching each other constantly, as a gambler watches God and hopes that God is watching. It was not good.

In the late afternoon I came home to find him with another. I had expected it. They lay sleeping, wrapped up in each other in a way that suggested practice. I pulled the covers from the bed and sprayed the soft white foam of a fire extinguisher on their bodies. There was a loudness then, and a blur of white panic like the frantic thrashing of birds thrown down in a storm. They struggled and spluttered, trying constantly to rise, but slipping back against each other until I thought that they would drown. I stopped then.

His friend had to shower before dressing. I watched him standing in the bath, running his hands over the kind of body that I could never have had. He looked at me and cursed under his breath, but he continued, and did not turn away. My lover meanwhile cleaned himself with towels, and put on his dressing-gown, and lit a cigarette, and sat on the edge of the bed, surveying the mess with disdain.

I watched the stranger get dressed. I followed him out of our flat and down the stairs to the street, and I followed him all the way into the city centre and watched as he climbed, nervously, on to a number sixteen bus. Then I went and got drunk, and I did not go home for a week. I stayed with friends and told them nothing. I went to work as usual and did the best I could. He did not ring. He did not look for me. I supposed he did not care.

When eventually I returned, it was with the intention of simply gathering my belongings and moving out permanently. But I was greeted with tears, and with remorse, and with the assurance that the man who had slept in my bed had been a 'necessary failure'. That the 'whole mess' had served only to enable a realisation on the part of my lover that I was the man for him. The only one that mattered. The love of his life.

I should have seen it for what it was. But I did not. I saw only my home, and my lover, and the years that we had notched up together, and I folded and I threw in my hand. I slept that night like a child sleeps, possessed of a security that is not of this world. In my mind I herded my fears into a circle and called it 'the bad patch', and I carried on.

We moved out of this bleak region for a while. We travelled through a different place, where we reckoned ourselves stronger, wiser, closer. We strode. But it did not last. Eventually we became self-conscious, and needed to concentrate to keep our footing. And then our concentration began to slip, and we with it. The silence returned, and the watchfulness.

I felt myself drawn to the clearly structured tedium of work. I stayed late and did more than I was asked to do. To my surprise I began to enjoy it. Tentatively, they began to give me more responsibilities. After some months they promoted me. They even gave me a raise. My lover observed it all with a bemused disinterest. He carried on as he always had. What he did with the extra time which he now had to himself I have no idea. There was nothing to suggest that he saw anybody else. Perhaps he just covered his tracks. Perhaps he simply enjoyed his own company, as I enjoyed mine. We did not socialise. We stopped making love. We stopped touching. Eventually we stopped talking.

I have never understood those straight couples who speak of their children as the means by which their marriages survive. I do not believe them. It is fear that keeps most relationships together, straight or gay. Children might deepen the fear, but that is all. We dread the end of everything.

My lover and I had failed. We were no longer lovers. We were not even friends. We lived together still, and were referred to by others as a couple. But we had failed. And yet we continued. We could not stop. We could not settle it. We could not even mention it. It was as if we were involved in some shameful conspiracy that necessitated our silence on the only thing on which we really agreed. We waited patiently for one of us to make a mistake, to break this tortured, wordless agreement that had us tied to parallel train tracks like two helpless, fluttering, silent movie starlets.

If I could talk to him now.

It was me of course. I was the one who finally did it. I can no longer remember why. Perhaps I did not decide to do it, perhaps it just happened. But I don't think so. I remember only a weight on me, in the middle of winter, like the cold that presses the ground to cracking. I just stood up.

There is a small guesthouse on Gardiner Street that I had passed every day for nearly fifteen years on my way to and from work. I had seen it repainted, seen its name changed at least twice, seen the double glazing go in and the neon sign replaced by something more 'discreet', more fashionable. I had seen the old panelled front door discarded and its place taken by a revolving contraption of tinted glass and bristled edges. And I had seen

that out as well, replaced this time by an imitation of the
original, painted white, with a brand new brass knocker from
Lenehans, £15.99. I've seen them.

It was a bitter night. The darkness had been dense and
complete since five o'clock, and the cold had stretched itself
evenly over the city, forming frost on everything that did not
move. I was making my way home, clutching parking meters
as I skidded slowly along the empty pavements on the lookout
for a taxi. I stopped by that white door, and without really
thinking about it, I rang the bell. I waited to be admitted,
stamping my feet like a soldier.

I do not know what it was that was in my head as I stood
there. I cannot remember what I thought about, if anything. I
have no recollection. It seems to me now that I must have had
some idea of what I was doing. But I remember only the cold,
and the smile of the woman who opened the door, and the
roaring fire inside, and the hot meal, and the bed where I slept
undisturbed until dawn, when I awoke with the clear knowledge that I had stepped, however innocently, however acci-
dentally, out of the lie. I knew that he would be worried. And I
knew that the first thing that would cross his mind would not be
that I had been involved in an accident, or had come to some
harm, but that I had stayed the night with somebody else.

I went to work that day in the same clothes I had worn the
day before. In the evening I went home. He asked me where I
had been. I told him that I'd stayed with a friend. That was all.
The next day I took a small bag with me. A change of clothes,
my toothbrush and razor, and stayed again in the bed and
breakfast with the white door. The next day he did not ask.

So it went on. I would stay out three, sometimes four nights a
week. My lover said nothing. He would look up at me when I
came in, as if startled. Then his gaze would return to the
television, or the newspaper, on his book.

There were moments when I glimpsed the truth of what I was
doing. Moments when I caught his eye, just briefly, in passing,
and I was able to see, as clear as a cut on white skin, the pain
that I was causing. I remember smiling at those moments,

taking that pain and tucking it away somewhere inside myself. I thought I did not love him.

You know what happened. I have already told you. I let him assume that I was having some kind of affair. I let him tell people about it. Slowly our friends gathered around him, protecting him, holding him, staring at me with hard eyes. Some of them tried to talk to me. They made the assumptions anyone would make, and I did not correct them. There was no difference. They tried to tell me what it was that I was doing. I heard the words, but I did not listen. Rain on the roof. The words stayed with me. But it was not until years later that I listened to them.

I felt no fear. I felt a kind of rush, an energy, a pulse that joined my own and drove me on. I could not have stopped. I smiled at everything.

My lover found strength somewhere. He lifted the world and flung it. I came home to find my bags packed, cardboard boxes already lined up in the street, a small van hired and waiting, a friend expecting me with a room cleared and a fridge full of beer. Even then I smiled.

There were the practicalities. I had to find a new place to live. I had to sign the documents to allow the sale of our flat. I had to move, to settle. I rented a place in Phibsborough, near the prison. It was a small cottage, one of a streetful, recently modernised and very expensive. I decided that I would not go out much.

At first there was the novelty of it all. The long hours, rooms of my own. I spent my spare time buying second-hand books and watching television. I bought a video recorder with borrowed money and taped late-night films. I began to watch sports. I had never done that before.

It was a Tuesday night, about two months after my lover had thrown me out. I had seen him only once since then, when we had met in his solicitor's office, like a married couple, to sort out the legal situation. He had barely looked at me. I glanced at him, at the side of his face, pale and drawn and tired. I had realised then how old we had become. Since then, nothing. I had not thought of him. Or I had not realised.

I came in from work and I was, for a moment, surprised that the house was empty. It was as if I had forgotten. I had to stop, to stand in the hall in the silence, and work it out. It took only a moment, but it was as if it was the first time I had thought of it. I realised that it was over. I lived somewhere else now. I would not see him again. I had lost him.

I remember that my eyes opened wide, and my hand went to my mouth and my bag fell to the floor. I remember that I gasped and I stumbled forward and I thought that the sound in my throat meant that I was going to be sick, but it did not. I found my way to the bathroom and leaned over the sink, trying to swallow and trying to close my eyes.

A roar came out of me, starting quietly like a moan, and building up steadily, howling, like a steam kettle, spitting tears against the mirror, twisting the skin of my face and clenching my fists to the smooth enamel of the sink until something somewhere had to burst or tear, until eventually I felt the ripping deep inside me, and I felt the strength and the pulse and the energy go out of me as surely as if the air had left the room, and with the same sucking sound as my mouth now made, the water running down my face like the undertow on a rain-soaked beach when the tide has turned and something on the horizon has moved, and the light is somehow different, like a light that is going out.

It started that night, and it has not stopped.

I tried to see him, but nobody would tell me where he was. I gave them messages for him. I asked for him to call. I invented emergencies, dilemmas, problems with the sale. He would send someone else. After a while he sent no-one, he just ignored me.

I wrote letters and gave them to our mutual friends. In them I said that I needed to talk to him, that I thought a terrible mistake had been made. That I could explain. That I had not had an affair at all. I told him about the bed and breakfast, about the woman, how she would remember me. He should go and see her. I said sorry. I filled pages with the word, like a schoolboy doing lines. There was no reply. Eventually his friends refused to accept any more. They said that he would only accept letters sent to his solicitor's office.

I went there. I took a day off work and sat in a coffee shop across the street. I felt like Humphrey Bogart. He did not appear. I wrote a dozen urgent letters and posted them on the following Monday morning, took the week off work and sat drinking coffee all day. I saw the solicitor come and go. I saw his secretary. She came to the coffee shop for lunch. I saw his clients, men and women who took deep breaths before going through the door. On the Wednesday I thought I saw my lover, but it was not him. He was not my lover.

I thought of breaking into the office. I thought of the tools I might need, of the layout, the location of the files. I tried to remember. Then I thought of buying the secretary lunch, of winning her over, asking her for a small favour. But she would recognise me. She would know what I was doing.

On the Friday I stood in the street. I paced up and down in front of the door and waited for the solicitor to appear. It rained on me. He arrived at midday and he said hello without realising who I was. He would tell me nothing. He said simply that my lover no longer lived in Dublin, and if I had to get in touch with him at all, then I should leave a message and he would pass it on. Where did he live then? The solicitor looked at me as if I was mad. He shook his head. Was he still in the country? He laughed and nodded and turned and pushed the door open with his shoulder.

I tried visiting our old friends. Some of them asked me in. If they left the room I would rummage in drawers and handbags. I would take trips to the bathroom via bedrooms and studies, speed-reading address books, scanning the pages of diaries. I could find nothing. I rang up and tried to get their children to give me the number. All our friends' children were too polite, too well-trained. They told me they'd give their mummies a message.

I began to take trips down the country to the places we had visited together. I tried asking around. I went into post offices and mentioned his name. It was hopeless, and it was not long before I gave it up.

There were problems at work. I could not concentrate. I refused to do overtime of any kind and left promptly each evening at five. In the mornings I slept late and did not arrive until half-nine, or sometimes ten o'clock. My boss took me aside and asked me whether there was a problem that I wanted to talk to him about. For a moment I considered it, but then shook my head and smiled at him. He warned me. He told me that I was not performing. He told me that I was not inexpendable; that although I was good at my job and had given good service, I was not going to be carried. He told me that I must make an effort. He told me that I should tell him if there was a specific problem. He could help me with it. But if there was not, then it was up to me to prove that I was still worth employing.

There is nothing in the language of business that allows an explanation. There is no facility for this. It is outside the range of two suited men in an air-conditioned office overlooking the river. It cannot be expressed in terms of units, of figures, of input, output and margins. I know that he was making an appeal to me on another level. I know that he was reaching out a hand, in his way. But there are different languages in our lives. On one extreme there is the language of the workplace, and on the other there is the language our hearts. There are no shared words.

I could not perform.

It took another six months before they fired me. I tried, for a while, to concentrate, to get things done, to restore some kind of confidence. But I was being closely watched and I could not stand it. In the end it was a missed day that did it. I had stayed up the night before, drinking, writing letters that I could not send, listening over and over again to certain records. I did not fall asleep until dawn and I slept all day. The next morning I arrived at work to find a note on my desk summoning me. I was given a cheque and told that there would be no need for me to work out my notice. By lunchtime I was at home again, slightly confused, hung-over, unemployed.

I cannot remember now how long it took before everything was gone. I don't think it was more than a year. I did all the wrong things. My money was spent on drink. The rent was overdue. I took what benefits I could get, but even with the help they gave me, I could not keep the house. I moved up the road to a bedsit beside the church. From my window I could see into an alleyway where couples went at night.

I did not think of looking for work. A few old friends found me and talked to me. They offered to help. They told me that I was sliding into self-pity, that there was no point to it. I listened to them and nodded. For weeks afterwards I thought my lover would come. I thought that he would hear how bad I was and that he would feel something and that he would come to me. He did not.

I did not wash. I slept and drank, drank and slept. I sold the video recorder and the television. Even then I found it hard to pay the rent. The woman from the Health Board who visited me every month asked me whether I had any family. I thought for a moment that she meant my lover. I almost told her that yes, I did have a family, but he had left me. Then I realised what she meant. I have no family.

The drink got me evicted. I was always drunk, or at least hazy. I had no money. The landlord had been patient, but he could not put up with it any longer. I found myself suddenly homeless and suddenly sober and suddenly scared. I had everything I owned in a dirty suitcase. I kept on thinking that I must have left some things in the bedsit, or in the house, but I had not. Everything was sold.

For two nights I wandered around the city, penniless and frightened. I did not know where I could go. There were no friends left. I collected my dole and looked for a cheap bed and breakfast. I remembered the place on Gardiner Street with the white door, but I could not afford it now. I went to the Health Board and asked the woman what I should do. She sent me to the hostel. The hostel by the bridge.

They told me that there was no drink allowed, and they took me in and gave me a room that overlooked the rushing water, and the rain that dripped from the green-painted iron work of Watling Street Bridge. I remembered it then. I looked out of my window and I remembered.

It had been a summer's day when we were still young, still in our twenties. We had walked from O'Connell Street, down along the river's edge, talking to each other, taking our time, finding things out. It was not long after we had first met. We walked as far as Heuston Station, where the road leaves the riverside and disappears into the suburbs. We had turned then and walked back, first on the quay down which we had come, and then crossing Watling Street Bridge to the other side. We stopped in the middle to look down into the water, the hazy green water that lapped gently at the old stone. We stood side by side, our arms touching, our elbows on the parapet, feeling the breeze on our skin. My lover turned to me and took my head in his hands. He kissed me. At first I was afraid. There were cars on the bridge. There were people walking. But he kissed me again, and I closed my eyes, and slowly I wrapped my arms around him and knew, calmly, like an adult comes to know these things, that there was nothing that could be done, ever, to take him from me.

I do not drink now. My head is clear. I am sober like the iron, like the rain that runs down my face, like the lessening of the darkness that struggles out of the east. There has been no sign.

I have waited for something else to come into my mind. I have expected it. It is not sensible for me to stand here and wait for my lover. I know that there is something about it that is not right. Each night I hope that he will come, and I hope that I will cease to care. But when I think about it, a pain starts inside me and I know that it is the only thing. It is what I am, there is nothing else.

Today, if they let me, I will get some sleep in the hostel and eat their food. While I do that, they keep an eye out for me, in case he comes. I know some of them say they will and then do not, but some of them understand, and they watch, and when I get up they shake their heads.

I know that one day he will come here. I know that he has forgotten, or is trying to forget. But one day something will happen and he will remember, and he will make his way to where I am. He will be old by now, like I am. But he will not die before I've seen him again. He will not.

It is a simple thing that keeps me. It is love.

JENNIFER CORNELL

Hydrophobic

Eddie Cranston asked my sister to marry him three times before she stopped saying no. The first time he'd come with flowers and gone down in front of her on one knee, even though he was a big man and the position was difficult for him. The second time he asked her he put it in writing and then stood on the corner across from our house, so she'd know where to find him when she wanted to look. A postal strike delayed the letter but still he kept standing there three days in the rain – which impressed her enough that she went out to him, told him directly that he was a heathen and there must be no mingling of the heathen and the saved. So he said that he'd do whatever she wanted, anything at all if it made her change her mind. That's when she told him about the Holy Spirit, the need for forgiveness and a cleansing of sin. That should do it, my father had said, turning away from the window and shaking his head. If he's got any sense now he'll give up and go home. But instead Eddie told her he'd think about it, and in the end said Okay, if that's what it takes.

We were eleven days now from the end of February, and I was thinking that the water would be cold. The grass beneath us was brittle with frost, and the ice spread like filigree from the banks around the water, reaching out like fairy fingers towards the belly of the Lough.

How you doin? Eddie asked me. You okay?

I nodded. How you doin? I said.

I'm okay, he said. I'm alright.

I didn't believe him. For a man who couldn't swim he was taking it very well, but I had felt the cool damp of his skin when he took my hand on the way into the church. I knew he was afraid.

It was too early, really, for an outdoor baptism. The only one I'd ever seen had been in the summer, two dozen people in white robes with Bibles standing face front to the Irish Sea, lapped by the water and equidistant like the driftwood pillars of an obsolete pier. We'd spent that day in the Sperrin Mountains, were on our way back along the Antrim coast, headed for Whiteabbey where the hospital was when my sister saw them and made us pull over for a better look. There was a family of swans in the reeds by the water, an elegant female and three grey cygnets; my father and I stood watching them till my sister called us over, crouched down beside me and made me look along her arm. Reminds me of Emily, my father said – my Aunt Emily who had been to Israel, who had gone with her church to the Dead Sea. When the bus had stopped to change a flat tyre practically everyone had stripped to their swimsuits and offered their wounds to the heavy brine before reboarding the bus and going on to En Gedi. Only my aunt had remained on the shore, where she stood with their cameras and other possessions and watched as the rest of the congregation descended until they were nothing but knobs of saffron, ash-grey, and auburn against the even, eggshell green of the Sea. She'd gone in later when they got to the Spa. You can't drown in it, she told me, the water won't let you. One minute you're standing, just touching bottom, and the next something starts to upend you, lifts you up by the balls of your feet and tips you over; you keep coming up whatever you do. And you can only stay in for a little while, or the pull of the minerals saps all your strength. Once you come out you go straight to the showers, and then you can sleep, or buy ice cream, or a lovely tall glass of something cold to drink. There had been some, she said, who'd refused to shower, who, having bathed in the salt tears of Jesus, would not give them back to the Sea. Fools, my aunt had called them, fools to let their faith eat away at their skin.

Two readings had been chosen for the opening service, Deuteronomy 7, the first five verses, and Luke 12: 49–53. We stood and sat down several times in the course of it, then the service was over and the hymn had begun.

Well, Eddie said, I guess that's my cue.

He rose and leaned forward to edge around past us, obstructed by an uneven battlement of knees. My father turned to look after him as he headed up the aisle, but I closed my eyes and imagined his movements, thinking, *He's in the foyer now with the rest of them; there, they've just handed him a robe.* I imagined him undressing behind a curtain in the vestry, the lift first of one leg and then the other, each sock rolled individually and tucked, one each, into separate shoes. I wondered if he took off his shirts like my father, both hands reaching round to tug at the garment and pull from behind with a crackle of static, or if he crossed his arms in front of him the way I did and took hold of the hem, his face distorted by the snag of the buttons or reddened for a moment by the chafing wool. Then the organ pipes swelled and the full force of them reached me, a thousand throaty voices answering every pressed key, the space in which to hear them filling with sound from one end to the other like water fills an ice cube tray.

When the hymn finished we all moved outside. A wind was gathering on the edge of the water; it moved confidently among the assembled, tousling hair and examining gowns, lifting hems and cuffs for inspection before moving on. My sister stood to one side and consulted her Bible; even the wind seemed to know better and give her a wide berth. Here, daughter, my father said softly, go see how he's doing. So I went over to Eddie and took hold of his hand.

How do I look? he said.

Cold, I said. Do you know what you're supposed to do, now? You tell me again, he said.

There is one body and one Spirit, I said, one Lord, one faith, one baptism, one God and Father of us all, who is above all and through all and in all. That's all you need to know, I told him. Please don't be afraid.

There were three to be baptised, two women and Eddie, and as they were church members he'd agreed to go last. The first woman sank back in the water like a slumberer, surrounded by the cushions of air in her clothes. I remembered how my sister had washed a coat once without having emptied its pockets first. Eighty-five quid and a bill of sale, all that was left of some forgotten transaction my mother had made before she died came out in a lump, and we had to submerge it in a bowl of warm water till the layers separated and the creases relaxed. That's what it looked like, that jellyfish way the cloth sank and lifted just below the surface. Then there was another time when they'd let us out early, told us not to ask questions and to head straight for home. The police had been there, and the army, too, but still Jimmy Macken had torn leaves from his textbook and hurled them in celebration straight back at the school. A gust of wind had lifted the pages, pressed them up into the bare limbs and branches of the trees in the schoolyard. The next morning they hung there dripping with rain, and that's what the woman's arms looked like, buoyed up beside her in the cold clasp of her sleeves.

When she resurfaced, the water ran off her in all directions with the soft spit and sigh of a bubble breaking. The deacon caught hold of her wrists as she straightened and gave her a push as her eyes scanned the shore, a little shove to get her started as she struck out towards whomever she'd come with, waving, bright pearls of water sliding off of her skin.

Ah, your poor sister, my father said. We both knew my sister had wanted this for herself. Standing once in the corridor just outside the ward, I'd heard her describing her plans to my mother, the changes she'd make in the way she'd been living, the difference that Christ had already made in her approach to things, good or bad. I'd listened to their voices, rising and falling like gulls in strong wind, until my father returned with three cups of coffee and a glass of orange from the hospital canteen. Whatever brings you strength, my mother had said, whatever you trust enough to believe. But then her church had acquired a transparent tank with internal wiring, waterproof lights, and a set of steps with a handrail leading down, and though she'd considered moving to some other parish, eventually she'd reconciled herself to a second birth indoors. Poor thing, my father said, it's been hard for her, too.

The next woman, taller, lay back in the Lough like a plank of wood. When she righted, the water broke over her arms first, then her face, burbling from her mouth and nostrils, twist-spinning off her hair; she was smiling. The minister helped stand her erect, kept his hand at her elbow as she moved away, until the swing of her arms as she walked through the water pulled his touch free and other arms reached out towards her with towels, welcoming her back to the shore.

Then it was Eddie. I heard the tide hiss and swallow on the sand as he entered, and made up my mind not to take my eyes off him until I was sure he was going to be okay. I'd asked him once why he'd never learned to swim, and he'd answered quite simply, I don't like the water. I know in the absence of riptides and whirlpools the odds of drowning are very slight, but still I'm afraid of being pulled under, of stepping suddenly out of my depth. You must think that's awfully silly, he'd said. Not at all, my father'd said. There's no one I know who isn't afraid.

When I was younger, I'd spent a week on a peace camp with Catholics, one of several cross-community ventures to be held that summer in Ballyclare. The leaders who had organised it had stood each one of us on a four-foot stump the second day, had us fold our arms across our chests, close our eyes and fall backwards stiffly, into the arms of the rest of us below. I remember the sensation of gathering momentum, the surge of my heart and the heaviness behind – and then the clutch of many fingers, my clothes tightening like sheets snapped taut, and the hard heels of hands, buoying me up. A trust fall, they'd called it. There'd been twenty-eight altogether, fourteen of them and the same number of us, and we were almost through it when one of the boys had refused to participate. No one would do anything after that, and the rest of the week went trying to remember just how much each one of us had told the others, wondering what they'd do with the information, wondering if we'd given too much away.

My own ears filled as his went below water. The sound of everything suddenly grew thick, as when I lay in the bath with my head submerged listening to the subterraneous whine of a tap in the kitchen, the soft, hollow whisper of my knee on enamel, or the low, cetaceous echo that answered when I knocked on the floor of the tub with my heel. I held my breath when I saw him go under, felt fire spread from my heart to my lungs to the pit of my stomach, my whole body brimming with a flammable gas, my joints swelled, i could see only udders, old tubes of toothpaste, bakers in white hats filling pastry with cream, and I gasped. When I opened my eyes Eddie's arms were reaching up through the face of the water, and I thought of a picture I'd seen of some famous fountain – Laocoon and his sons encoiled by serpents: their fingers, too, had been sharply angular, just so had the water around them heaved and churned. From the top tier the gods had looked down through the windows of heaven, and wide jets of water had streamed out from their mouths.

Later, back in school, we'd tried it ourselves, the trust falling. There'd been no stump so we'd stood in a circle and taken turns being in the middle and allowing ourselves to fall back against the crowd. But part of the circle was weaker than the rest; it did not surprise me when at last I broke through. It seemed to take ages before I hit asphalt, and as I was falling I imagined them watching, caught off-guard by their error, observing the breeze in the force of my fall.

He came up choking. Even as he left it the water dragged him down. He'd thrashed so much all three were sodden – Eddie, the minister, and the deacon as well. When they reached the shore with Eddie between them, my father was there, and together they lay him out on his back a few yards from the water. Then my sister got down on her knees in the sand beside him, and when she had loosened the clasp at his collar she took his chin in one hand, his nose in the other, covered his mouth with her own and kissed him, kissed him, till his eyes fluttered open and again he breathed.

JANE S. FLYNN

Fleadh

'We're flyin' it, girleen. Sound as a bell. We've a way down. Grab my jumper. I'll round up the lads.'

Joanna sprang from the bar stool and rooted through a tangle of clothes for Christy's sweater. There was a hole unravelling in the elbow, and the scratchy wool smelled of Woodbine cigarettes, smoke, salt-and-vinegar crisps and Guinness. Its orangey-yellow set him off from the crowd of black-jacketed farmers and gangs of young men in bog-green and -brown pullovers. A peaty musk rose from the honeycomb of stitches. She squeezed it into her crocheted bag with her camera and wallet.

There was a fleadh in Kilmurray that weekend, Christy'd said. '*A flaaah.*' She had never heard the word spoken before, only seen it in a magazine. It looked so exotic, with the d and h at the end. There was something romantic in the sound – like what you imagined when you heard 'Fair', or 'Ball'. Christy said they'd get a lift down and suss it out. 'We'll rise a session, and tear out some reels,' he had said. She ticked through her vocabulary of newly acquired words, delighting in the antique phrases like 'coorting' and 'take a spin'. She whispered 'porter' to herself, imitating Christy's 'R' sound by folding her tongue, and making tisking flips with the tip. She wasn't used to the cursing, but even the very dirty words sounded harmless, without the threat or violence they would have suggested in New York. She wasn't quite sure what some of them meant, even.

Joanna had met Christy two days before in a pub. He was playing the flute, and she was with her girlfriend, Candy, sitting right behind the musicians. They had been there for hours. He turned around to her and asked if she had a fag, and she gave him what was left in her pack of duty-free Marlboro and told him to keep them. They got talking after that, and at closing time he had joined them for chips and walked out to their tent at the strand. He and Joanna had talked and smoked and drank cans of Harp for hours, until it started to get bright again.

They slept in the sand dunes in Joanna's sleeping bag. Christy fell off quickly, but she lay awake for a long time listening to birds, and to water lapping and tumbling sea stones. It was paradise, she thought.

They slept until the heat woke them, breakfasted on oranges and cheese sandwiches, and gazed at the sea. A haze on the horizon blurred the distinction between heaven and earth. Christy pulled his socks off, balled them up, and threw them over the cliff, and they heeled down the hill to the grey shingle, leaping stones like kid goats, onto the beach. The sand was rippled and swirled, as if combed by the tide. They hopped gullies, their vulnerable insteps landing on hard mud ridges. At the water's edge they kicked shivering yellow bubbles at each other, and rinsed dried sand from their faces and ears with fresh waves.

Joanna gave him her new pair of socks, and they hit for town to thumb a lift to the Fleadh, Christy holding the flute like a book, walking nearest the traffic, and Joanna inside, along the verge. She pulled stems of meadow grass, stripped spikelets with pinched fingers, and scattered the husky seeds along the ditch. She snapped wild flowers, delicate sprays of creamy froth dusted with saffron. Their perfume was dizzying. 'That's meadowsweet,' Christy said. His sweater was thrown over his shoulders like a cape. Tractors hummed somewhere beyond the stone walls, and haystacks, criss-crossed, dotted the fields.

'Cocks of hay,' Christy called them. 'I'm stone mad about that smell.' Ssh-tone maad, she repeated mentally.

Joanna never expected such a stroke of luck. Only a week into the vacation, to meet real traditional musicians, especially

Christy. Candy told her yesterday she was 'hyper, running in overdrive, out of control.' She was glowing, energized by the excitement of the music and the unfamiliar. She shed her urban defences as neatly as an orange peel, trusting completely in these good-humoured characters. And now this – to be going off with them, getting a ride down to a village, to a fleadh.

She bought another box of fags on the way out, and climbed into the car after the lads, onto Christy's lap. There were instrument cases poking up everywhere. He pulled the door shut with two smoke-stained fingers. Joanna balanced atop his bony knees at first, then eased back onto the slender thighs. Fag ashes blew back on them and her hair tatted in the crosswind. She stole peeps at her white socks on his feet, between hers. It was perfect.

Kilmurray was a one-street village. Christy led them into a pub with a façade of white-and-brown mosaic tiles, saluted the woman behind the bar, and moved to a vacant corner. Joanna called two pints, carried them to the table, and slid in beside him. The session began – a timeless stretch of a summer's day, an afternoon that became evening before they ever thought about it, or felt it pass. Music carried them all along. The lads gathered energy as they played; like dynamos they renewed themselves, feeding off their own output, refuelling on cigarettes, foamy porter, and the company. The bar sent pints down to them, and several trays of drinks were bought by appreciative friendly men in dark caps with pinched visors. The crowd ebbed and flowed around the musicians all day and evening. It became so thronged it was difficult for Joanna to wind herself through the swarm of bodies to the ladies' bathroom in the backyard. 'The Jacks,' Christy called it. There was a pleasant intimacy in squeezing by, rubbing the backs of strangers who didn't stiffen, or snap heads around in reproach, like they did at home. She liked placing her open palm on a shoulder and saying the word 'sorry,' and making an instant-aneous friend. So different from New York, where they freak out and lose it if you even smile at them. On one run, an old man almost fell into her as he came through from the men's room. At first Joanna thought he was blind, stumbling through with his arms stretched out in front, eyes glazed, and he caught her blouse with crusty red hands to balance himself. 'Isn't he a fright,' someone said.

She watched the musicians tune up, fascinated. More joined in and the circle widened. They all knew each other. Christy introduced her to them all. 'Johanna,' he pronounced her name. She sat surrounded by a phalanx of beating, blowing, rubbing, pumping, plucking young men – next to Christy, the leader. He set the pace, started the tunes, gave the note they all tuned up on, called for a halt for song. He was brilliant. Every time he took a swig of porter she followed the reflexes of his throat muscles and Adam's apple, admiring the cords in his neck. She studied him – as he swallowed, licked his fingertips, raced flat pads over the openings in the black wood, straightened his back, rotated a shoulder, turned his head, jackknifed an elbow across his chest, formed a perfect triangle of flute, forearm and biceps, rolled the cylinder fractions of a degree, felt the blow hole with a kiss of almond shaped lips, directed a preliminary air stream across the opening, then closed his eyes, and unloosed from the timber a rhapsodic stream of music.

'A schratter of reels.'

She felt privy to a ritual with its own intimate language and gestures, as if she'd chanced into another world and was taken in hand by a native guide. Never had she been so utterly, unaffectedly, supremely happy – as free and uninhibited as the music that escaped from the flute.

At some point baskets of sandwiches were put on the cluttered table. Empties and dead remains were collected, and overflowing ashtrays dumped. Christy ate the white triangles two at a time, piggyback, in two chomps between tunes. Sometime much later, the publican came out from behind the bar, and people drifted away, and the session broke up. The lads packed up, disassembling instruments, shrouding fiddles in silk, snapping stray hairs from bows, tucking plectrums under strings, and venting and buckling bellows. Christy drew a scarf through the flute with a silver stick. Like magic it unfurled out the top. Methodically he wiped, then uncoupled the pieces, and laid them into their velvet furrows. The smooth wooden box closed with a miniature silver lock that fastened like the snap on a dress – a tiny round head clipped through the hole on an ornate clasp. He placed the case atop his sweater on Joanna's lap. 'Keep a hand on that for me. There's blackguards around everywhere.' His fingernails were wide and flat.

Joanna bought more fags for the morning, and they walked out onto the main road to wait for a lift. There were no lights on in the village, and no cars on the road. 'Arrah, we'll walk out to the Four Crosses and we'll have a better chance,' he said. His voice sounded even richer in the silence. Gravel crunched under their feet. There was no moon. Varying shades of black and grey formed flat silhouettes. A million silver rivets hammered in stunning confusion fastened the navy-blue sky above them. Very far away, car lights swept the sky in arcs, then vanished, like beacons from a lighthouse.

They sat on a dewy stone wall at the cross, smoking fags, and watched the lights appear, then vanish. 'Some shagger will surely be travelling this road soon,' he said.

He spotted it before she did, before there was the sound of an engine. A subtle sheen at the top of the pole, strengthened until it turned light green, and finally grey in the headlamp beams of the Fiesta.

'By Jaysus, it was God that sent you, John Joe.' A man with a bald head and an overbite leaned over from the driver's seat. Christy opened the passenger door, and tilted the front seat forward for her to precede him, placed the flute next to her, and sat in front beside John Joe, sinking deeply into the dry velveteen upholstery. His bronze shoulders dropped behind the seat, and half his salty curls disappeared behind the headrest. Joanna moved into the centre of the rear seat, inclining towards the front while introductions were made. She pressed her palm on the flute case, running her fingertips around the bevelled edges, the hinges, then over the clasps. She drew her fingernails around the perimeter, tracking lightly in the fine incision under the lid, round and round and round. She relaxed completely, lulled by the sibilant flow of talk between Christy and John Joe, about the fleadh, and the rakes of music, and the fine weather, and the hay . . .

A soft finger crept up her leg, feeling its way along the shinbone, its tip burrowing into the interstices. 'What tune is that?' John Joe was asking Christy. She tried not to giggle, to break the spell and ruin their secret. It was lovely. That was the word she'd heard all day. Lovely. 'Loov-lee,' Christy said.

John Joe asked her if she was enjoying her holiday, and she said, 'I am, of course,' just like Christy. And they resumed speaking about pubs and sessions, and then he felt her leg again, like a cat this time, rubbing back and forth from side to side . . . Fookin' great, she thought. She moved her foot forward a bit, closer to the gap between the bucket seats. The clasp tightened on her ankle; she glanced down, blinking to see better in the dark, summoning up off-duty nerve-endings and reflexes, feeling a weird disassociation, as though eyes and brain and psyche were not in sync, and realized that a flaccid hand protruded grotesquely, obscenely from a dark sleeve, not a gold one. And as quick as a flash, the sleeve retracted and there were two fat hands on the steering wheel, and not a word had been lost in the conversation up front.

Joanna shuddered, moved instinctively back into the corner of the seat in controlled panic, trying to remember what you did when this happened, and how long they had been on the road, and how far they were from the village. She sat traumatized for another five or ten minutes, like an animal in shock playing possum until it can escape. When the Fiesta passed the petrol station just outside town, John Joe asked would they like him to drop them off at their door, and Christy started, 'Thanks, that's dacent . . .' and she interrupted boldly, 'No. Stop. We'll get out here.' She clutched the wooden case on her lap. Christy tilted his head sideways, and looked at her as if she were mad. Bewildered, he opened the door. John Joe sat stock still, looking straight ahead, his flabby hands a morbid green under the fluorescent streetlamp. As her foot touched the street she

unloosed a rush of shaken, disjointed phrases about a black
arm and a bloated corpse's hand that grabbed her leg, and that
she thought he was Christy's friend and didn't know what to
do . . .

Christy pulled off his warm jumper, and put it across her
shoulders and tied the sleeves under her neck.

'Yerra – don't mind that cunt, cratur. Everybody knows
about him. He's always sniffin' around sessions for the leavings.
His wife won't even give him a scrape for Christmas. That eejit
would go up on a bantam hen if he got half a chance. You
should have pounded the old bollocks down on the poll with the
fuckin' flute.'

They started out the road to the tent in silence. Joanna sorted
through the day's and night's events, abstracting bits and
pieces, ordering them into sequence, trying to make sense of it
all. She stopped shivering, and began to laugh.

'I was just imagining,' she said, 'a baldy black-jacketed fatty
with big fucking hands, covered with splinters, chasing after a
bantam hen in front of the whole shaggin' town at a fleadh.'

EUGENE STRANNEY

Sudden

From a distance the scene looked picturesque. The white-walled building with shuttered windows and the low-set roof. At one gable end the chimney sent up a straight stream of smoke into the still night. To the right lay a wide gravel-covered patch. Trees and shrubs followed the line of the road, shielding this area from full view. The backdrop was a wide expanse of lake reflecting the moon and stars of a late winter evening. The mirror effect culminated in dark rolling hills which were a patchwork of greens during daylight.

On closer inspection the paintwork peeled and the shutters defied all odds by hanging on to their rusting hinges. The white of the walls was chipped and in places urine-stained. The gravel patch was nothing but a flat area strewn with rough stone bought cheap from a local quarry. The shrubs were overgrown with weeds, allowing untaxed cars and the vehicles of those who should have been elsewhere to hide from prying eyes.

Inside, the neglect continued, but it was comfortable. The locals liked it that way. At the bar McCready sat with his back to the wall and side on, so that he could watch everything and follow the comings and goings. His cap lay cocked on his head and the hair growing in his ears and nostrils gave him a kind of scarecrow look. His pockmarked face was splattered with black tar, evidence of his days spent on the roads at the back of a council lorry.

His companion, O'Rawe, perched on the stool next to him, was attempting unsuccessfully to draw the barman into the baiting of his friend. 'God's curse, McCready,' he growled, 'if there was as much tar on the roads as there is in them holes on yer face, it'd be like driving on a baby's bum.' All three laughed together, content in the fraternity of the drinker.

Over in the corner, settled below the dartboard, two old hands were joined by a nephew of one of them. In between listening to and enjoying the banter at the bar, sheep and cattle prices were exchanged. One of the older ones, his hands clasped around the top of his bent cane stick, spat on the floor and declared to God that he didn't know how young ones could make a living with the sort of prices beasts were fetching today. His friend nodded sagely and agreed, it was no wonder young ones didn't want to work on the land anymore.

In the middle of the wall, directly facing the bar, a coal fire burned. The coals were watched by Shay Morgan, a young man trying vainly to deal with depression. He had not taken his tablets for a few days now and while he had come in earlier in good form, his face was now darkening as his gaze penetrated the fire. He was left undisturbed by the others. This was not done out of ignorance but rather understanding. If he talked, they talked, if he didn't, they knew to leave him alone.

Gathered in the corner to one side of the door, three labouring men, their legs stretched long under the table, relaxed in silence. Quietly amused by the cabaret from the men on the stools, the three nursed tired arms and backs from a long day laying concrete for a silo pit. Occasionally a comment passed about someone's new car but no effort was made to engage in full-blown conversation.

Down the steps and through the door at the end of the bar counter lay the pool room, lit only by a couple of cheap red lights. This attempt at atmosphere would have been laughable anywhere else, but here it seemed to fit. A young man with a belly bursting his shirt buttons practised alone at the solitary table. On the bench along the wall sat his only spectator, cradling a pint. The two found solace in each other's company, here, away from the drinkers. They talked of women, the ones who would and the ones who wouldn't. Neither of them was ever likely to find out one way or the other, but for now they were happy enough to pretend to themselves.

The main source of alcohol seemed to be black with a white

top. The younger ones favoured lager, though. Spirits were
nowhere to be seen apart from in the bottles behind the bar. It
was mid-week and an hour still to closing time, when the odd
brave one might attempt a stiffener. Frost was settling outside.

The force which opened the door was so great, the handle
embedded itself in the soft plaster of the opposite wall. The pump
action shotgun released its first cartridge, sending shreds of
shirt, skin and bone from the shoulder of the barman splatter-
ing into the glass behind him. The gun dropped lower, waist
high, and exploded a second bolt into the base of O'Rawe's
back. The sheer power of the blow projected the big man into
the face of his partner. Momentarily he clung there, locked in an
obscene kiss. The shock wave shot along his spinal cord,
stabbing into his brain, shredding it into cerebral mucus. The
great body slid downwards, no pressure from the knees to
sustain it. Before crumpling on the floor, life had expired.

A second gun, smaller, held in one hand, spat wickedly from
the direction of the right door jamb. The old man with the cane
felt a punch to his neck. The bullet went right through and died
in the wall. His nephew grabbed roughly at his uncle's collar
and down the two went, upending the table. The shotgun
roared again, smashing into the formica top of the table
barricade. The second old man threw himself helplessly on top
of the others. His bladder panicked into releasing its contents.

The three labourers in the corner, to the right of the guns,
were moving. Awkwardly, comically diving below the table.
The handgun discharged its hate into the Formica. A yell of
pain and anguish rose up. Blood poured from a fat thigh and
mixed with concrete dust.

The shotgun blasted again. The hole left in Shay's leg was
almost geometrical in shape. Thumped to the ground by the
force of the passing cartridge, he hugged the floor and tightly
closed his eyes.

In the pool room the spectator had abandoned his pint at the
second shot. In his exit through the back door, he left about an
entire shirt sleeve caught on the latch. Crossing the gravel he
threw himself painfully into gorse bushes. He lay in the

darkness, crying for fear his pounding heart would give him
away. He winced at every gun blast.

The pool player stood immobilised, his white-knuckled hands
grasping cue and corner pocket. A great gush of cold sweat
broke on his forehead. His back was wet. He did not shake, but
inside a great screaming volcano was erupting as bullet and
cartridge flew only feet from him. His eyes fixed on the ancient
curtains he screeched silently, 'Please, God, stop it!'

The sudden silence was almost profound. From somewhere,
maybe more than one place, liquid dripped onto stone floor.
Splintered glass tinkled from the smashed optics.

Shay opened his eyes. It was not fear that had shut them. He
didn't like loud noises, sudden noises. Across the floor, through
the chair legs, he saw the shoes. Black, polished brogues with a
slightly raised heel. He took in the detail of the leather soles, the
small wrinkles in the good quality upper and the way the lace
was double tied. He had had a good pair like that once.

The shoes moved. It shook him out of his delirium. He
watched as first the left and then the right stepped onto the
broken glass and entered deeper, further into the bar.

There was no fear in those shoes. Shay could tell that. The
brogues came nearer to him, stopped at his head. He could see
the shadow of the shotgun fall across his left hand. The brogues
moved on.

Under the red lights the pool player clung tenaciously to the
corner pocket. He had almost released his grip when he heard
the footsteps. Fear paralysed him. In his whole world now there
was only one sound. He was not aware of his own breathing, of
drips, of glass, not even the moans now starting to emanate
from crumpled heaps in the bar. Each falling step, crushing
glass on stone-tiled floor, grated in his ears. The pressure was
building up, it felt like blood vessels were going to burst in his
head.

The steps approached the door of the pool room and stopped.
Shay, still prone on the floor, could see the heels clearly now. He
watched them swivel in the pool of Guinness. The final blast
caused him to shut his eyes tight and jerk. The cartridge

exploded a red light, sending shards of bulb over the table and around the pool player.

Black shoes turned again, Guinness-stained, and disappeared rapidly at the door. Shay heard a car screech off. Silence reigned for a few seconds, then he attempted to rise. Only at that point did he become aware of his injury. He cursed, not out of pain, just annoyed. On top of everything else he had suffered, he had now to endure this.

'Shay, are you alright?'

He looked up to see the man from the pool-room step up into the bar. He almost laughed at the sight of him covered in red bulb glass. He turned to point this out to the others. His eyes hit on O'Rawe and above him, rigid on the stool, McCready stared down at the blood oozing from his own stomach.

BIOGRAPHICAL NOTES

VINCENT BANVILLE was born in Wexford, in 1940. He taught for five years in Nigeria – where his Robert Pitman Award-winning first novel was set – and then in Dublin. Winner of a Hennessy Literary Award, his short stories have been published in Faber and Faber's *First Fictions* series, and in many other Irish and British periodicals. In recent years he has written bestselling detective novels and stories for children.

CLARE BOYLAN was born in Dublin in 1948. She was one of Ireland's leading journalists before turning to fiction. Since then, her short stories have been widely published in Britain, Ireland and the USA. She is the author of three short story collections and four novels.

MIRIAM BURKE was born and brought up in Galway. A PhD in Psychology she has worked as a clinical psychologist for many years. She lives in London, and began writing fiction in 1995.

KEVIN CASEY was born in Kells, County Meath, in 1940. A playwright and critic, he is the author of three highly praised novels.

HARRY CLIFTON was born in Dublin in 1952. His first poems and short stories were published in the *Irish Press* 'New Irish Writing' page, and he won the Patrick Kavanagh Poetry Award in 1981. He has worked and travelled extensively in Europe, Africa and Asia and is presently Writer in Residence at Bordeaux University.

JENNIFER CORNELL was born in the USA of Irish and Italian stock. She came to Belfast in the 1980s to work in a cross-community project, before taking an MA in Peace Studies at the University of Ulster. Her short stories have been widely published and her first collection *All There Is* (Brandon Books), was awarded the Drue Heinz Literature Prize in 1994. She teaches creative writing at Oregon State University.

JOHN F. DEANE was born in Achill Island, County Mayo, in 1943. A highly praised poet, he is the founder of the national poetry society, Poetry Ireland. In recent years, he has turned to fiction and has published two novels and a collection of short stories. 'A Migrant Bird' was a prizewinner in the 1995 Maurice Walsh Short Story Competition.

URSULA DE BRÚN was born in Dublin in 1952. A Philosophy student at University College Dublin, she has had three radio plays and a stage play produced and short stories published in a range of Irish magazines.

JANE S. FLYNN was born in Atlantic City in 1939, to Irish-American parents. A graduate of Temple University, Philadelphia, she moved to Ireland in 1978 and married a traditional singer from County Clare. In 1993 she won the *Image*/Oil of Ulay Short Story Competition, and, more recently, was a prizewinner in the 1995 Maurice Walsh Short Story Competition.

MARIE HANNIGAN was born in London, but has lived in Donegal since the age of two. Her short stories have been published in many Irish periodicals and broadcast on RTE Radio. She is a winner of the William Allingham Short Story Award, and, twice, the Listowel Writer's Week Award.

KATY HAYES was born in Dublin in 1965. She won the RTE Francis MacManus Short Story Award in 1993, and in 1995 her first short story collection, *Forecourt*, was published by Poolbeg. Her first play has also been produced by the Abbey Theatre.

MARTIN HEALY was born in Cloonlurg, County Sligo, in 1957. In 1994 he was named *Sunday Tribune* New Irish Writer of the

Year and was also the winner of the Year of the Family Writers' Award. His short stories have appeared in a number of Irish and British periodicals.

MARGARET LISTON was born in Ballyragget, County Kilkenny in 1951. 'Bread, I Said' is her first published story.

PHILIP MacCANN was born in England in 1966, but came to Ireland at an early age. A graduate of Trinity College Dublin, his short story collection, *The Miracle Shed*, (Faber and Faber) received much praise on publication in 1994.

JOHN MacKENNA is a native of Castledermot, County Clare. His first stories won him a Hennessy Literary Award in 1983. He then won C. Day Lewis Fiction Awards in both 1989 and 1990, and in 1992, the *Irish Times* First Fiction Award for his short story collection *The Fallen* (Blackstaff). Since then, he has published a novel, *Clare*, and a new short story collection, *A Year of our Lives* (Picador, 1995).

MOLLY McCLOSKEY was born in Philadelphia in 1964. She studied English literature at St Joseph's University, Philadelphia, and moved to County Sligo in 1989. She won the George A. Birmingham Short Story Award in 1991 and in 1994, and the RTE/Francis MacManus Award in 1995.

DAVID MURPHY was born in Cork in 1953. After graduating from University College Cork in Celtic languages and European History, he spent two years travelling, but has been a teacher in County Dublin since 1977. His stories have been published in many literary magazines and he was the winner of the Maurice Walsh Short Story Competition in 1995.

CLAIRR O'CONNOR is a Graduate of University College Cork and now teaches in County Kildare. Her poetry has appeared in a number of magazines and anthologies, her plays have been produced by both RTE and BBC, and she has published two novels, most recently *Belonging* (Attic Press).

JULIA O'FAOLAIN was born in Dublin. After graduating from

University College Dublin, she continued her education in Rome and Paris. One of Ireland's leading writers, she has published two short story collections and six novels.

KEITH RIDGWAY was born in Dublin. He has had poetry and short stories published in many Irish publications.

FRANK RONAN was born in New Ross, County Wexford in 1963. A winner of the 1989 *Irish Times*/Aer Lingus Irish Literature Prize, has published four novels and a collection of short stories.

EUGENE STRANNEY was born in Northern Ireland in 1954. He has travelled and worked extensively in Europe, the Middle East, India, Afghanistan and the Far East. At present a bookkeeper in Co Down, *Sudden* is his first published short story.

WILLIAM TREVOR was born in Mitchelstown, County Cork, in 1928. He is one of Ireland's most distinguished living writers. His novels and short stories have gained him wide acclaim and have won many awards, including the Hawthornden Prize, the Allied Irish Banks Prize and the Whitbread Prize.

Unpublished and recently-published short stories are invited for consideration for future volumes of Phoenix Best Irish Short Stories. Details of where and when recently-published stories appeared must be provided. MSS will not be returned unless a stamped, addressed envelope is enclosed. Writers outside the Republic of Ireland are reminded that, in the absence of Irish stamps, return postage must be covered by International Reply Coupons: 2 Coupons for packages up to 100g, 3 Coupons for packages 101g to 250g. All MSS should be addressed to David Marcus, PO Box 4937, Rathmines, Dublin 6. Ireland.